THE CONSEQUENCE CLAUSE

RJ FLYNN

SILENT PRESS

Published by Silent K Press, Ltd.

Copyright © 2022 RJ Flynn
All rights reserved

Developmental Editor: Theodora Bryant
Cover Design by Raffy Hoylar

First Edition

This book is a work of fiction. Apart from well-known actual locales and some actual events that figure into the narrative, names, characters, places, and incidents are either products of the author's imagination or are used fictitiously. Any resemblance to actual events, locales, or persons living or dead, is entirely coincidental. This book or any portion thereof may not be reproduced or used in any manner whatsoever without the express written permission of the publisher except for the use of brief quotations in a book review.

Printed in the United States of America.
ISBN-13: 978-1-7334530-1-1

"There is only one basic human right, the right to do as you damn well please. And with it comes the only basic human duty, the duty to take the consequences."
—*P.J. O'Rourke*

ONE

The camera zoomed in on the blonde standing twenty yards away. She'd been camped out in the shade of a fifteen-foot-tall saguaro cactus for the last two hours, inching slowly around with the shadow as it chased the sun. The air was thick with dust that tasted like it smelled, earthy and pungent with sage. Standard-issue black khakis adorned the woman's lower body, the close fit accentuating strong legs and a curvy backside. Her top was covered in a gray cotton tee-shirt, the short sleeves snug around gently sculpted biceps, compliments of her self-imposed training regimen.

In contrast to her physical on-camera perfection, an unflattering stain of sweat ran the length of her spine. And when she shifted her stance to brace a palm over the weapon holstered against her hip, there was a dark crescent visible beneath her armpit. The standard-issue cotton fabric tee was both friend and foe in the unrelenting Arizona "dry" heat.

The woman was engaged in conversation with two men. One man, a scrawny fellow wearing a white polo, shorts, and hiking boots, held a long wooden picket against his shoulder. A cardboard sign affixed to the top read: Keep Them Out. At something he said, the woman's head tilted back slightly when she laughed. The musical sound of her voice carried across the hot, dusty air to reach the cameraman's ears.

The third party among them stood to the woman's left. The sweat-stained ballcap atop his head identified him as a supporter of the Open Borders Let Them In cause. When the picket-holder extended his hand out, the man with the ballcap accepted the gesture of peaceful accord and joined in on the conversation with the blonde.

While this picture of calm dominated the camera's eye in the foreground, the scene in the background and off to his left and right told a drastically different story. The cameraman zoomed his lens out, broadening the view.

To the left, surrounded by cholla, barrel, and prickly pear cacti, all of which decorated the landscape with their beautifully wicked and wickedly beautiful presence, sat a raised wooden platform. There were three people on the small stage.

The first could have been the Hulk's younger brother, sans the green, of course. He was tall and had wide shoulders that tapered down to lean, narrow hips. Even from this distance, the ripples in his abs were visible beneath his snug-fitting shirt. He stood with his feet braced apart, arms crossed at his chest and thick neck straight as a ruler. His lips pressed into a thin line, drawing attention to the severity of his square jaw. Assumptions would have to be made about any warmth or lack thereof in his eyes, as they were hidden behind reflective aviator glasses. Everything about the guy screamed "Come-near-this-stage-and-you'll-regret-it!"

The second person on the platform, a woman, stood slightly to the man's right and directly behind another woman positioned near the front of the stage. Of the two women, the one in the background was noticeably younger. She was far more attractive than the other, too, except for the angry-looking scar racing down the side of one cheek, extending to the corner of her mouth. The end result was something one might have seen in a Tim Burton animated film.

The third person, the woman up front preparing to speak, wore a mint-green jumpsuit with a wide brown belt around her not-so-flat waistline. She had salt-and-pepper gray hair—more salt than pepper—twisted into a thick braid reaching halfway down her back. Some of the long, wiry strands had escaped the cinch, and they lifted in wild disarray about her face and head as the dry air around her stirred. A leather cord hung from her neck, an overly large silver bauble attached to the end doing little to detract from the waddle of thick flesh beneath her chin.

A person operating a camera could be a subject's best friend or worst enemy, hiding all the flaws, the truths, the details. But this cameraman, this reporter, believed in transparency, full disclosure, and *never* aired anything but the facts, no matter how awful or good they proved to be. That was his way.

The woman with the megaphone was United States Senator Harriet Clarkson. She lifted the device to her lips and fisted her other hand high over her head. "My people!" she yelled into the megaphone, her words barely breaching the cacophony around her. "Every moment is an opportunity to fight for the rights of our friends outside our borders! Today," she added, her voice deep and raspy, like someone who'd smoked a pack a day her whole life. She pointed a thick finger belligerently at the sky. "Today is the monumental and unprecedented grand finale to a hard-won fight! This week our President signed the Open Borders Act, which my wife, Representative Anita Grant, and I sponsored and fought to get approved for all!"

As a roar of cheers went up, carrying on for several long minutes, Senator Clarkson grasped her wife's hand and raised their joined fingers high in the air. The man who was there to look intimidating, and doing a fine job of it, lowered his arms and shifted sideways so he was standing directly behind the couple. Representative Grant's lips spread into a smile, but the resulting fiendish look, aided by the scar, was something children's nightmares were made of.

As Senator Clarkson began to speak again, the drone of an indistinct chant slowly gained in volume, the words quickly forming into a phrase.

The cameraman lifted his head to search for the source. Locating it, he panned the lens toward a group of protesters holding ground some distance away from the mosh pit of supporters praising Clarkson and Grant.

"Keep them out! Keep them out!" An undulating wave of signs bobbed up and down as hundreds of voices cried out in opposition to the Open Borders Act and Clarkson's pompous victory speech.

And still farther to the cameraman's right, beyond both sides of protesters supporting or opposing the day's event, stood a twenty-foot-tall, rusted steel fence rising majestically high into the air. At one section low to the ground there was a large, jagged hole, the edges folded back on itself. The cameraman likened it to a vagina—a huge, gaping metal one—opened wide to give birth. Bodies spewed through the hole one, two, and three at a time. Those emerging scrambled away, quickly assembling behind a swath of others who'd preceded them. A cloud of dust followed their passing as the newborns marched across the baked earth to a destination somewhere off-camera.

Senator Clarkson, still glorying in the adulation of her supporters and desperately trying to be louder than her opponents, spread her arms wide. Representative Grant had returned to her post a few feet behind Clarkson, and the Hulk look-alike was no longer on the platform at all. Like Moses parting the Red Sea, only in this case it was the Sonoran Desert being metaphorically parted, Clarkson welcomed all those entering the country.

She called out to them, "Come! Share in the abundance of freedoms and opportunities your new homeland offers."

Given the circumstances, the events of the day had been

THE CONSEQUENCE CLAUSE

well organized and free of the violence and destruction so typical at protests where Clarkson, especially, and her cult of followers were involved. The calm today was, in part, due to the efforts of the blonde still conversing with the two hashtag leaders. The cameraman returned his focus to her, zooming in close enough so only she and the two men beside her were in his picture frame. She lifted the bill of the field cap off her brow and swiped the heel of one palm across her damp forehead before settling the cap back in place.

This wasn't the first time the woman had been present at an event where the cameraman was on scene. On numerous occasions, he'd witnessed her use of charm and talent to de-escalate some of the worst situations. It's what made her so exceptional at her job and as an individual. Away from here, in her personal life, he knew she was a wife and that she volunteered at a field hospital near her home in Virginia. He knew she left scraps of food out for the countless number of stray animals which had lost their owners to the riots ravaging the nation.

Riots. Unrest. Civil war. These terms had become nearly interchangeable.

But here, today, the blonde was an Agent, a peacekeeper between two opposing factions. There she stood with the leaders of both, sharing a friendly chat, ensuring respect and civility reigned between them during the day's controversial event. That was her way.

Her name was Melissa.

The two hashtag leaders turned slightly away from her, caught up in their own conversation. Melissa craned her neck around to look toward the camera. Lifting a hand in a small wave, she shrugged one shoulder and winked. The cameraman gave her a thumbs up, acknowledging her success at helping the hashtags come to middle ground, yet again.

As the temperature in the desert peaked at a scorching degree, the crowd of hashtags, those who'd come to fight against or support the Open Borders Act—commonly known as the OBA—slowly began to disperse. The video captured from today's events was streaming live across the country, but it was time to wrap things up. The cameraman had begun a slow zoom out, his intent to end the segment with a panoramic view of the scene at the border, when movement to Melissa's left caught his attention.

Someone other than her and the two hashtag leaders suddenly appeared in the cameraman's viewfinder. The size and shape of the figure easily identified him as a man. He was a big guy, a few inches taller than most nearby. His upper body was hidden beneath an overly large brown hoodie and his head was covered, so only his nose and chin were visible from the cameraman's angle. The woman hadn't noticed his approach, her attention focused on the two hashtag leaders. The cameraman watched for a second with unsuspecting curiosity.

As if in slow motion, the hooded man's arm lifted out straight, elbow locked, a pistol clutched in his palm. When the barrel of the gun touched against the side of Melissa's head, her body tensed. She turned partway around, away from the pressure and toward the camera, her eyes rounding with surprise and her mouth opening slightly.

In that split second, while she watched the cameraman shove away from his tripod and lunge toward her, the confused expression on her face gave way to a look of shock, immediately followed by one of terror.

Her wide eyes locked on the cameraman's as he scrambled forward, struggling to gain purchase on the dry, cracked earth beneath his feet. His arms flung wide for balance, brushing against the fuzzy barbs of a nearby cholla cactus, but he failed to notice the sting of pain as he reached out in a desperate effort to close the distance between himself and Melissa. She cried out, once, before the sharp crack of gunfire sounded. The repercussion of it made her eyes go even wider a microsecond before the first of two bullets tore into her brain and out through her forehead.

Before her lifeless body hit the ground, the shooter disappeared, swallowed up by the sea of hashtags and the swath of people entering the land once known as the United States of America.

TWO

"Okay, folks. Who else would like to share?" asked the man standing near the pulpit at the front of the church.

There were eight people in attendance today, all of whom sat scattered around the two rows of pews at the front of the musty room.

Devlin Johnson had sat in the same spot every week for the past four years: Second pew, inside left, nearest to the worn, carpeted aisle. After the moderator had commandeered the old church for their use, the group had attempted to gather in other more private rooms around the building. But the Sunday school classroom had felt too small, too close, while a conference room boasting a long folding table had seemed too large and impersonal. The congregation hall, with its fifteen rows of wooden pews situated on either side of the center aisle, seemed a better fit for everyone's personal space needs.

The group had always been a small one, never boasting more than a dozen or so damaged souls. For this reason, only the first two rows on both sides of the aisle had been freed of the tarps and layers of dust covering them. The other three-quarters of the room remained hidden beneath canvas. Stacks of boxes and miscellaneous furniture cluttered the walkway on the far side of the cavernous space as well as the stage beyond the podium standing as sentinel over the dilapidated hall. The only areas free of dust and debris were the two rows up front. It was all they'd needed.

THE CONSEQUENCE CLAUSE

Nothing, however, took away the persistent musty odor synonymous with old, abandoned buildings. After a while, everyone seemed to have gotten used to the smell. In some ways, for Devlin at least, it had become a welcome odor. It wasn't so much the smell of mildew that he appreciated as it was the place and why he was there.

Each week, inside these walls, he'd set free the terrors that chased him in his nightmares. Like living things, those dark dreams would slither back in, take over his subconscious and do their best to deprive him of peace, until he returned here and unburdened his mind yet again. It's what kept him coming back to the church, the place where he sought the healing offered. He doubted he'd ever fully return to what he remembered as being normal again, but he had at least progressed to a point where his demons merely lurked and no longer consumed, as they once had.

Devlin rubbed his hands together in a brisk motion before cupping them against his mouth, blowing warmth into his fingers. The church's original occupants, Presbyterians, according to what remained of the lettering affixed to the stone exterior, had been forced to close its doors to all parishioners some time back, maybe six or seven years ago, along with every other church across the country.

Fortunately, for those in attendance today, the electricity and gas hadn't been turned off. This meant there was heat running through the building, but the high-ceilinged sanctuary pocketed most of it in the rafters. The objects adding much of the physical and symbolic warmth to the space were two large, stained-glass windows, one to the left and the other to the right of the stage. Sunlight beaming in through the images of angels cast shimmers of blue, green, yellow, and red on those in attendance. It was indeed a miracle the windows had survived all that had happened over the last decade. In fact, the entire building had fared relatively well. Devlin had seen many other similarly abandoned houses of worship, relics of a different time, destroyed to their foundations.

Each attendee today sat where they wanted, some positioned sideways in a pew with a leg pulled up onto the bench, an arm slung over the back, while others sat stiff and upright, moving barely enough to look at whoever was speaking. One man, Conrad—no last name, just Conrad as he'd introduced himself—stood at the far end of the second row, down from Devlin, his ass perched against the front pew. He had his arms crossed over his chest and was facing toward the back of the room. He was the only one present who'd been attending meetings almost as long as Devlin had, joining a few months after him. Over time, they'd become friends of a sort, meeting up on occasion for a morning run or popping over to a nearby pub for a quick drink after group. But that happened rarely.

Conrad was a private man, sharing little about himself with Devlin or with the group. It was as if the demons he possessed kept him always at arm's length, regardless of how close anyone tried to get to him. He was huge, too—as in he worked out a lot. And he stood at a height of at least six foot three, taller than Devlin by a couple inches. His brown hair was typically kept at a length that could be described as moppy; he was constantly sweeping it back off his forehead and away from his face. And, regardless of the season, he always wore long sleeves. Covering what? Devlin didn't know. Scars, perhaps? War injuries? He'd only guessed at it, never feeling comfortable enough to ask. Like the rules of the group, share if you want, don't pressure anyone to share if they didn't offer.

Conrad was ex-military. Over the years there'd been several like him who'd attended meetings, there for a while and then gone, usually leaving without any advance warning or farewell. Today, besides Conrad, there was only one other man in attendance who'd served the country. He went by Ken, but Devlin suspected that wasn't his real name. He'd been a Navy SEAL, so maybe that was why he wanted anonymity.

Most group members, including Devlin, stopped trying to get close to Ken soon after he'd first shown up. They'd quickly realized that he was short-tempered and spoke with zero compassion to the plights of others there trying to get their lives back on track. Yet unexplainably, he returned week after week, being his normal, brooding, unapproachable self. To each his own, Devlin thought.

Conrad wasn't too far different from Ken in the brooding department, but he was at least slightly more approachable and occasionally offered kind words to others.

From their time in these meetings, Devlin knew Conrad had been a sharpshooter in the military. It was because of this occupation he'd landed in this room seeking to silence his demons, just like Devlin and the others had been doing. What didn't fit Conrad's badass military persona were the chunky, black-framed glasses perched on his face. They screamed geek, which Devlin had eventually learned was an accurate stereotype.

Conrad looked up and met Devlin's stare, as if he knew he'd been contemplating him and his past. The man stood, leaving his perch, shifting around the end of the row before taking three steps toward the center of the room. Everyone stilled, the only sound a soft mechanical whirring as the heater fan kicked on somewhere far away in the building. Conrad had something to say.

"Sometimes, I did . . . ." he began haltingly. Both his hands were clenched into tight fists against his thighs. Realizing this, he lifted them to his waist before gripping one wrist with his other hand. In short, choppy movements, he began rocking the captured forearm back and forth, as if he were massaging his wrist bones. His Adam's apple bobbed when he swallowed hard. "Sometimes I had to do terrible things. As part of my job," he said, his voice a rich tenor that sounded strong yet unsure at the same time.

Conrad didn't often share his past, the main reason most people attended these types of meetings—for the help others offered. In all the years they'd been in group together, Devlin had mostly only ever heard him refer to his demons in general terms. Rarely did he give any of the gritty details like most people shared. His job had been a difficult one, and from the few bits he had revealed to Devlin, it might even have been considered horrific. He'd lost his humanity.

And to top things off, his wife had left him right at a time when he'd finally decided to exit the military and escape the insanity that was his job. He hadn't told Devlin much about her or why she'd gone. But from the way Conrad acted in the few times he did mention her, her leaving had taken him by surprise.

He looked out over everyone's heads, not meeting the sympathetic gazes of the curious watchers, Devlin's included. "There was one assignment where I was directed to . . . ." He faltered, his eyes glazing over as if he was seeing the scene play out in his mind all over again.

Devlin knew that feeling too well. Only his was made worse because not only did he relive his terror in his nightmares, but he also had the video footage of it to watch on repeat. At least Conrad's memories could shift, alter slightly, maybe enough to dull the reality of it.

Conrad's spine shot ramrod straight, and he snapped his palms flat against his thighs, his shoulders squaring back to a military stance. "I was a killer," he blurted, saying words everyone had already assumed, even if he'd never stated it so clearly before.

THE CONSEQUENCE CLAUSE

Upon his admission, there were no shocked gasps, nobody surged to their feet to run from the room, away from the terrible, awful being his confession announced him to be. After a few silent seconds, his gaze lowered, touching on each person, his brows furrowing and his head tilting slightly. He shifted his feet, the ingrained posture of his former career relaxing with each beat of his heart. He'd clearly expected reactions of shock, fear, disgust, or worse, directed his way. But nothing remotely close to that followed, at least not until Ken chimed in.

In a voice laced with derision, Ken said, "You think you're the only one with a monopoly on killing? Most people like us have kills on our conscience. It was your job. You knew what you were signing on for." He shook his head and scoffed. "More people have bigger issues than you, done worse things. Get over yourself."

Conrad's eyes rounded in surprise, but he quickly masked his feelings. Glaring hard at Ken, with hands clenched once again into fists, he opened his mouth to respond but before he could, Steve, the moderator, intervened.

"Okay, guys," he said stepping forward and positioning himself so that he blocked Conrad's view of Ken. "Let's keep things positive here. Supportive. Let's not berate those who share. If you have problems to address, ones that brought you here today, then by all rights, we welcome you to step up front and share." This he said while looking directly at Ken. "Hmm?" he added, forcing the man to acknowledge him.

"If I wanted to talk, I'd have done so," Ken bit out. "I was simply saying that his shit"—he dipped his head back, pointing at Conrad with his chin—"shit we had to do, we agreed to, somewhere along the way during our military days." He unsheathed a large knife from his belt. "It's what we've had to do to survive ever since that's fucked up," he mumbled.

Ducking his head, he began scraping the pointed tip of his blade to the underside of his nails, the bulging bicep of the arm operating the knife flexing with the movement. Rather than leave the premises and the group that irritated him and offered him little benefit, he did at least stop talking.

The guy was unstable and needed serious help, in Devlin's opinion. He was such an ass but based on what he'd said today, there were dark things from his past, too, giving him reason to be the way he was. Devlin didn't wish any ill to befall the man, but he did wish he'd stop attending this group and find another, one more compatible to him. Ken was a loose cannon and Devlin didn't trust him.

"We get it, Conrad," Patty, a soft-spoken redhead said, her voice laced with the compassion one should expect in a group setting like this. "You did what you had to do, not because you liked it, but because it was a skill you had and one the government capitalized on."

Heads bobbed, some strongly, others subtly. Either way, all relayed support and understanding. Nobody liked the idea the military used sharpshooters to pick off targets, but the truth was there were some damn bad people in the world and the only way to halt their evil was to take them out. Conrad, and Ken, happened to be ones who'd excelled at the art. But even now, years later, both, but specifically Conrad, seemed incapable of accepting the empathy offered by others.

Conrad shook his head sharply. "I was given targets, and I did it. Even when it didn't seem right, I did it anyway." The agony of his regret was becoming more visible with each passing second.

Ken groaned but didn't speak.

Devlin glared at him, almost daring him to say something. He wasn't one to start a fight, but right then he championed the idea of punching the guy in the face. But his rational brain reminded him that Ken had military skills only a select few humans could achieve, not to mention the notable size difference between them.

Turning his attention again to Conrad, Devlin curved a hand over the back of the pew in front of him and scooted to the edge of his seat. "What would have happened if you'd have refused?" He knew the answer already but believed Conrad speaking the words aloud might help ease some of his burden, even if only a tiny bit.

Pain flickered in Conrad's eyes. "It doesn't matter what would have happened to me," he bit out. "I should have accepted those consequences before—"

"Before what?" Devlin interrupted. "Your directives came from your commander. Hell, chances were, they came from as high up as the Commander-in-Chief."

Murmurs of agreement were heard, but Conrad's agonized gaze never left Devlin's empathetic one.

"Even if you didn't feel it was right at the time . . . ." Devlin softened his tone, so he didn't come off sounding like a hardhearted asshole. "It wouldn't have been directed if someone higher up hadn't had intel indicating it was the only way to eliminate a threat."

Conrad sighed loudly and lowered his eyes. He nudged his glasses up with a finger at the bridge of his nose before scraping the same hand across the top of his head. The muscles at his jaw flexed visibly. "Shit," he hissed. "Never mind."

The raw emotion in his voice sounded like acid had been poured down his throat. He marched back to the second pew and slumped onto the bench, his chest rising and falling heavily, his expression tight with his inner turmoil. Few, if any, knew the full extent of the things Conrad had been made to do during his time in the military. Whatever it had been, the resulting damage went deep.

Post-traumatic stress disorder. It's what everyone in the room had been diagnosed with, the cause of trauma different for each.

For Devlin, watching a person's brains get blown out of the front of her skull would apparently cause such a thing. The night terrors, the anxiety, the event playing on repeat in his mind every time he peered through the viewfinder of a camera were common side effects, or so he'd been told. Those effects had been so strong at the beginning he'd shut down and did the thing he shouldn't have done to silence the dark visions. He drank away nearly an entire year of his life. Of course, that hadn't been a sustainable lifestyle for him, as he had a news network to run.

Fortunately for him and his followers, he'd turned most decision-making authority for *The People's News* over to his manager, Mario Gonzales. Mario had kept him afloat while he lost himself to the darkness. Devlin had eventually made it through the worst of the PTSD side effects, but he'd still not fully returned to the helm at the network. It was easier to let Mario keep doing the excellent work he did while Devlin focused on his search for a killer.

Conrad continued to keep his trauma locked away inside his head. And though it was obviously real, it perplexed Devlin because he knew he'd been stationed right here in the country for most of his career. And he'd been released from active duty a decade ago when the government had shrunk the military to a size barely large enough to fill Fenway Park. Unfortunately, they'd done so amid the civil unrest that had already spread to every corner of the nation. But Conrad hadn't been called back into duty then, as the people believed would happen to all former military, to help protect the people from the people. But the government hadn't intervened.

THE CONSEQUENCE CLAUSE

The President at the time had ignored the devastation taking place right outside the doors of the White House. While the unrest grew worse, both Congress and the country's leader had carried on as if their actions had nothing to do with the violence running rampant like a rabid beast across the land. Every day that passed, things declined for the people, and still, they'd not called back the military. What did they do, instead? They'd acted like nothing was different in their world. They'd even pushed through the Open Borders Act, allowing hundreds of thousands of people into the country to join the chaos.

Silence blossomed in the room again, the soft clicking sound of someone biting their nails the most prominent noise.

Devlin pulled to his feet and walked to the front of the room, sensing several sets of eyes directed on him. He hated talking about his stuff, but he knew it helped. And maybe it would help Conrad right now, in this moment. The man needed to find a way to forgive himself for things he'd had no control over, things that had happened long ago. *Said the pot to the kettle.*

"As you're all aware, I've been away from work for a while now." Swiping a hand across his jaw, he rubbed the light stubble there, easing the tension that typically occurred during times when he talked about himself. "A few years back, I watched—" His throat tightened, as if a vise had clenched over it. He drew in a long breath before forcing words out in one drawn out sentence. "I watched a person get assassinated right in front of me and from all I've been able to find out about the matter, which is next to nothing, it was a freak and random killing." He shrugged away the words, but his head moved side to side, as if the body and mind were separate entities, one accepting, the other holding to the disbelief of it all.

After a couple minutes of encouraging words from around the room, Devlin prepared to say what he'd really stepped up here to announce. He hoped it'd help those present, especially Conrad, to understand the strides he was making in this journey of self-recovery. He didn't have it in him at this point to hold out hope for Ken.

"I've decided to return to work. Well, that is, I'm going to get back out in the field of reporting."

A few clapped their hands, and some offered congratulations. This caused more embarrassment than comfort for Devlin, so he quickly interrupted the praise. "Even more surprising is that I'm going to work for the government."

Smiles instantly turned upside down and the sounds of sharp, indrawn breaths escaped into the chilly room.

During those years when politicians had reduced the Constitution to little more than a comic strip, the country was being torn apart. Us versus Them. Liberals versus Conservatives. Whites versus Non-Whites. Everyone versus Men. Yet the government had responded by turning its back on the nation. Those in high positions had been, and continued to be, on a perpetual power high right along with the mainstream media, which had become the politicians' right-hand agents. The government was a place where nobody wanted to be.

It was an avalanche of issues, attitudes, and demands that had started as tiny grumbles, creating a fissure in the fabric of the nation. Pieces of that fabric were torn away, the tattered chunks falling into the abyss, collecting debris with it in its descent down. As the country fought for survival, chunks of the crumbling detritus above kept piling on, growing larger with every new claim of fraud, racism, discrimination, prejudice, and more. This massive ball of decimated fabric crashed down, large, and out of control upon the people, with nothing or no one capable of stopping it. Not when the government sanctioned the devastation.

That was, not until the people in the wake of its destruction rose and became the wall in which the avalanche collided. That wall was a group known as We The People, or the WTP, and its leader was Josh Stevens. He was the man who now sat at the helm of the federal government, managing Congress and the President. And, it was this new government, under Josh's management, which Devlin had agreed to work.

It had been a much-needed revolution that had happened, but the day of the revolt had merely been the first step in a far grander plan. Josh had spent years devising a way to return the power of government back to the people. But his plan demanded massive change, something so big, so different, it could inspire hope and confidence among those living in what had once been considered one of the world's greatest nations. However, to implement this plan without the WTP and Josh both being overthrown, he'd needed to make it legal and binding. And to do that required bipartisan support.

It took many long days and nights discussing the idea with members of the House and Senate, and even the President, before he'd managed to get enough votes of agreement— barely, but still enough—to get an amendment passed establishing the leader of We The People as the Government Overseer. In this role, Josh could ride herd over all of Congress and the President in ways they never expected.

Devlin had always wondered why the majority had agreed to the WTP's plan. He eventually concluded that those who'd approved it had been searching for a scapegoat in which to blame for the shit show they'd orchestrated. The mess they'd made had been a result of their decisions, ones that had and still were strangling the Republic near to death, all for what they'd called "progress." Whatever their reasons, making the WTP's plan the law gave Josh a degree of authority that many would say was mightier than that of both Congress and the President.

Devlin bit the inside of his cheek, reluctant to tell his group peers the rest of what he had to share. "As I said, I'm going to work for the government." He paused before dropping the bombshell. "I'll be working with Tara Carlson of the Consequence Compliance Oversight Committee, the CCOC."

Upon hearing these words, multiple sets of eyes went wide and most of Devlin's peers gasped.

He knew it wasn't *what* the committee did that drew the looks of concern from those in the room. Most believed the Consequence Clause, one of the first changes enacted by Josh following the revolution, had been the perfect solution to all the unreasonable and ridiculous decisions made into law or causes backed by politicians. The CC was designed to add an element of balance to what Congress and the President decided for the people. The first issue to get the Clause assigned? The Open Borders Act—the OBA.

No, it wasn't what the Oversight Committee did, it was *who* sat at the helm: Ms. Tara Carlson.

"Come on, now," Devlin said with a small laugh. "She's not as bad as we've all been made to believe. I met with her, talked to her face-to-face. She's . . . interesting."

At Josh's encouragement, Ms. Carlson had reached out to Devlin. He'd met with her for the first time yesterday.

It had been unseasonably cold and blustery outside for a November day in Washington DC. When the door to the diner they'd picked as their meeting place swung open, a blast of wicked, frigid air followed the person he knew right away as Ms. Carlson into the room. She'd resembled a snowwoman of red, covered as she'd been in a knee-length red wool coat, and red boots with a trim of faux fur around the tops. A thick, knitted, white scarf circled her neck and half her face. There'd been a similarly styled wool hat covering her hair, pulled low on her forehead. Between the scarf and the hat, her face had been fully hidden, except for her eyes.

He'd watched with curious fascination as she disassembled her outerwear in the entryway, unraveling and peeling off the layers, until the form underneath was revealed. She was above average height and slim. Her upper body had been covered in a forest green, ribbed sweater, long-sleeved with a modest v-neckline. Dark slacks adorned long legs, ending at her boot-covered feet.

She'd slid her fingers through shiny, black, shoulder-length hair, fluffing and reorganizing the disarray created by the hat. As she did, she'd scanned the room until her gaze settled on Devlin. The corners of her mouth had turned up in a warm smile of recognition as she began her walk toward him, plucking her fingers from white gloves on the approach. An invisible cloud of icy air still clinging to her person swirled around Devlin as she'd stopped beside the booth where he sat.

"Hi. You're Devlin?" she'd drawled, her voice rich and provocative, and distinctly Southern. "I'm Tara Carlson. Sorry I'm late. It's a bitch out there."

She'd asked, answered, apologized, complained, and sat, all before Devlin had the chance to stand and greet her.

"I liked her right away." Devlin appealed again to his frowning audience after relaying details of his meeting with Tara, explaining what she wanted from him as a reporter. "I think she's a good one, working for We The People. She specifically asked I do nothing more than report in my style, no bullshit, no editing, no lying. Air the truth."

"Why you?" It was Conrad who spoke first, his green eyes sharp, intense, and fixed hard on Devlin.

Devlin shrugged and lifted his hands palm up. "She said the MSM was putting its own spin on her Consequence Engagements. Instead of telling viewers the crimes committed and subsequent consequences, according to whichever Consequence Clause was being applied, they've been 'forgetting,'" he air quoted, "to tell the actual crime. Instead, they're making it sound like the CC is bad and the criminals are being punished unjustly."

Conrad nodded, in apparent acceptance of Devlin's answer, while eyeing him warily. "Chances are it's someone in government directing what the MSM is doing. One is the puppet, the other the puppeteer."

"Yes, and that's exactly why Ms. Carlson wants me. She knows I'll tell the whole story, good or bad, regardless of who's being called out or why."

When Devlin set out to start his news network and make it different from all the others, he specifically wanted to be better. Ethical. Staying on the right side of ethical when greed and government made it easy to take advantage required conscious thought. It really wasn't all that difficult, but even so, nearly all his counterparts in the media business struggled with the concept.

His gaze jumped from one attendee to the next, watching as their wariness faded, though not all were easy to persuade. For all but Ken, whose lips curled in an expression of disgust, he could tell he'd sparked some interest.

"I'll have a segment run daily, specifically about Consequence Engagements. It's the only way to show the people our new government is following through on holding Congress and everyone in the country accountable by way of Consequence Clauses. Hopefully, it'll curb people's bad choices and behaviors." He paused a moment before asking, "Will you watch? Give it a chance to make a difference?"

The attendees looked around at each other questioningly. It was as if they needed the others' agreement to one of their own stepping into what had become known as the lion's den—the government. Most offered hesitant agreements to give it a chance, to give him a chance.

And then their meeting time had come to an end.

Devlin hadn't yet left center stage when Conrad marched across the front of the room as if he had something more to say. But he didn't stop walking. He strode past Devlin, turned up the center aisle and marched toward the exit, casting a glare at Ken before leaving without saying goodbye to anyone. Devlin frowned. He really wished the man would find peace, and soon.

"One more thing," he called out before the room emptied. "My hope is that the work Ms. Carlson is doing will bring justice for a woman whose life was brutally ended. If I'm lucky enough, that justice will unfold through the lens of my camera, live for the world to see, the same as her murder was." His voice had grown sharp, edgy, the anger brewing as he relayed his hopes.

"You'll never find what you're looking for," Ken said presumptively or knowingly, Devlin wasn't sure.

He remained at the front of the room, contemplating the doors where Conrad had disappeared through. Devlin still wasn't the person he'd been before that day at the border; however, he was at least better than he was a year ago. Conrad's moment would come soon, he hoped. It had to. It was no life at all, being lost in the agony of painful memories.

THREE

Three days later, Devlin stood along the roadside out of the path of a bulldozer as the machinery grumbled slowly around a sharp curve. The heavy equipment's oblong tracks scraped across the asphalt as it went, leaving a trail of divots in the warm surface. A red Porsche with dark, tinted windows suddenly careened up behind the dozer. The sports car's RPMs soared as the driver geared down and darted into the wrong side of the narrow lane, skirting past the machinery. But instead of maneuvering back onto the correct side of the road to avoid hitting Devlin, the driver hit the gas and came straight at him like a bullet.

Devlin barely had time to register the demon car now coming at him. With a split second to spare, he leaped onto the curb at the same moment the driver zipped by. As the car screamed away, Devlin committed the license plate numbers and letters to memory. He wasn't sure what he'd do with the information he would drum up in a search, but if he was still as mad later as he was right then, he'd get his new partner to help dole out some consequences to the idiot driver.

"Asshole!" he shouted at the red car before it disappeared around the next curve ahead. His legs were shaky as he established his footing on the slant of a small embankment covered with low-lying shrubbery.

The bulldozer continued to amble slowly past. The

operator lifted his palm, shrugged his shoulders, and shot him a questioning thumb up. Though rattled, Devlin had sustained no injuries, so he simply scowled and replied with a similar hand gesture.

There was a backhoe idling along the shoulder across the street from Devlin, too, the operator tucked safely inside the cab. The dozer eased to a stop beside it at the edge of a paved driveway along Lago Vista Drive.

Directly in front of the bulldozer was a fancy iron gate, closed tight to ward off unwanted visitors. The gate was anchored on both ends to a solid, eight-foot-high stone wall running along the boundary lines of the property. This was the home of one of Hollywood's most popular television talk show hosts, whom Devlin admittedly never watched. He rarely watched television, as most of his spare time, up until recently, had been spent scouring old news footage in search of a murderer. This new job was his chance to start over, but even so, he knew deep down he'd never fully let his search die. He'd simply have less time to focus on it, for now.

The rumble of both diesel engines idling were presently the only sounds interrupting the peaceful quiet of the Beverly Hills neighborhood. The day was comfortably warm, a welcomed change from the freezing temperatures out east. A tall tree behind him offered some respite from the bright California sun overhead.

Retrieving a black tripod from the confines of his backpack, he expanded the legs and propped it on the road's flat surface. Securing a large and expensive camera on top of the stand, he fiddled with the angle before aiming the lens at the gate and the dozer. A shiver of excitement mixed with a tingle of apprehension moved beneath his skin as the engine of the bulldozer roared to life before slowly crawling forward.

Besides the behind-the-scenes tasks he managed at the

news station, this was Devlin's first official job out in the field in an exceptionally long time. Although, he hadn't expected to arrive first at the scene. Ms. Carlson was late—again—like she'd been the day they'd met at the diner. There was irony in the fact that the head of the Consequence Compliance Oversight Committee's record for being late was two-for-two. Not a good attribute for someone whose job it was to enforce accountability in others. The lack of her presence only added to his nervousness. And that surprised him, considering he'd spent nearly twenty of his thirty-nine years of life behind a camera, with the exception of these last few years. It had him feeling like a rookie all over again.

He bent down and peered through the viewer lens in silent readiness for the action about to commence. A loud, aching screech sounded as the dozer's blade scraped upward across the iron to a height level with its center. A thrust of the throttle resulted in the scream of twisting metal as the gate wrenched free from its moorings. Chunks of stone clattered to the ground as iron separated from both ends of the wall where it had been embedded.

Click click click. The camera shutter whizzed faster than the eye could see, capturing what appeared to be little more than a construction crew at work, presumably at the homeowner's request.

It was anything but that.

Diesel exhaust wafted past Devlin's nose and he turned away to cough. A high-pitched shriek sounded above the other noise, instantly drawing his attention. He peered into the camera again and directed the lens toward the lush green yard beyond the newly mangled gate when a tall, slender brunette entered the scene in his viewfinder. Devlin watched through the lens as she raced across the wide expanse of the perfectly landscaped yard. It was clear the racket happening on her property had pulled her from her bed, as she was still in her pajamas—a barely-there two-piece pink silk thing. There was nary a jiggle on her toned white legs, exposed as they were from the crotch down of her skimpy shorts. She jarred to a halt, anger and shock etched on her face. Her chest heaved, allowing Devlin a view of professionally sculpted breasts—the best discretionary money could buy—only half hidden beneath the thin silk of her nightie.

"Stop! What are you doing?" Amy Silvers cried out, hands pushed forward as if she could somehow magically hold back the three-ton monster encroaching onto her property.

Devlin moved quickly, retrieving a different camera from his bag. He flipped open the lens cap and turned the dial to record as the steel gate tore completely free from the stone wall with an unearthly clatter. The dozer driver shifted the engine into idle, altering the roar into a rumbling purr.

A white, compact electric car appeared at the same curve the Porsche had blazed around earlier. The driver parked in front of Devlin's rental a hundred feet away, and the sole occupant exited the vehicle.

Dressed in black slacks, a short-sleeved yellow blouse, and shiny, very unsensible high-heeled shoes that somehow accentuated her already tall, thin stature, Tara Carlson marched up the sloping asphalt roadway toward the gate, or what was left of the gate. She lifted a hand to the operator of the bulldozer, silently communicating her request for him to remain at a halt. Her heels clacked delicately as she strode past Devlin.

"Mornin', Devlin. Glad to see you here," she offered in her richly Southern voice. Her demeanor was as cool as a fresh glass of lemonade, the opposite of Devlin's adrenaline-laced feeling of excitement. She gave him a quick flash of straight, bright teeth before carefully maneuvering around the mangled edges of iron and rubble.

"Ms. Carlson," Devlin returned with a nod before warning, "She doesn't appear to be happy."

Tara rolled her eyes and sighed in resignation. "They always seem so surprised."

She progressed up the sloping drive and came to a halt in front of the irate homeowner. Tara was breathing heavily after the short walk, which surprised Devlin. Considering her line of work, it seemed there'd be times where she'd need to fight or run, depending on the situation and the person she was confronting. By the looks of it now, if anyone chased her, she'd be toast after the first thirty strides, heels notwithstanding. As he got to know her better, he might suggest she consider taking up jogging.

"Get the hell off my property!" Amy screamed.

Tara ignored the demand as she swiped a hand across her forehead. Devlin zoomed in the camera lens enough to see the sweat beading on her brow. When a sense of déjà vu struck him, he jerked the camera away from his face. For a moment he was in another place, saw another face when he'd zoomed in, seconds before—

Son of a bitch! Pressing one hand over his eyes, he forced the memory back. Watching someone's skull get blown apart, combined with the ability to have done absolutely nothing to stop it—or worse, having the ability but not acting fast enough—had a way of messing with a person's mind, even a seasoned reporter like Devlin, who'd spent years in the field witnessing civil unrest spread like wildfire across the country. Even he, who'd watched neighbors and families tear each other apart, wasn't immune to the point-blank aftermath of the killing of the woman at the border.

After a few deep breaths, something the trauma counselor he'd visited for a short while had coached him on, he pulled it together. He needed to get past this; and knew the only way that would happen was to run at it head on. Which is why he'd agreed to take this job.

Abandoning the still camera perched atop the tripod, he trotted across the road, video camera clutched tight in his fingers. Near the portion of the wall where the gate had been embedded, he leaned against the jagged edges of stone and mortar for support before lifting the camera to eye level.

Tara pressed both hands on her hips and squared her shoulders, while heaving a few steadying breaths. "Miss Silvers," she began in an official-sounding voice that thickened her Southern drawl ever so slightly. "As I'm sure you're aware, you are responsible for the removal of any structure that functions as a fence surrounding your property." She glanced over her shoulder and swung one arm toward the crumpled gate lying haphazardly in front of the beast that tore it from its perch.

"This is preposterous! You can't destroy my property like this!" Amy spat, fists clenched tight at her sides. The look in her eyes was as wild as the uncombed morning nest of chestnut brown hair atop her head.

"Welllll," Tara began, stretching out the single syllable, "ma'am, yes, we can." She pulled from the back pocket of her dark slacks a blue-covered booklet. Flipping it open, she read loud enough so Devlin had no trouble catching the words. "According to the Consequence Clause associated with the Open Borders Act, *all walls functioning as borders"*—she air-quoted with one hand—*"shall be removed by the owner of the property or entity to whom the title is owned. If the owner does not remove said walls in a timely manner . . . ."* She paused, adding as an aside, "Three years is beyond what's considered timely." Then, returning her attention to the little book, she continued. *"The Government will act upon its authority to comply with the laws of the land at the owner's expense."*

Seconds ticked by on the digital display of Devlin's camera

as Amy huffed with outrage. "I don't care what your book says," she snapped, her face twisting into a sneer. Thrusting an elegantly manicured finger at the book still propped open in Tara's hand, she yelled, "You can't do this to me!"

"Well, ma'am"—Tara drawled, as if Amy hadn't acted like she was a queen ruling over the country. Reaching into her other pocket Tara retrieved a cell phone. With her thumb, she swiped across the screen a couple times. Her lips pursed slightly, and then her teeth bit gently over one corner of her lower lip—"per the Consequence Clause on the OBA," she again reminded the irate woman as to the reason for the day's visit, "which, let me point out, according to the Voter Information Log you are confirmed as having voted in favor of,"—she tilted her head and cocked one eyebrow, as if daring Amy to deny her words—"you've had ample time and opportunity to remove these boundaries yourself."

She swung an arm out and back slightly behind her again, as if Amy needed the reminder to which boundary was in question. "You've been sent non-compliance notices and letters of intent informing you that today was D-day. Destruction day, that is."

Tara brought the phone closer to her face, pecked at the screen with one finger of the hand still clutching the book.

"Actually, you got one, two, three, four notices referencing today's date. It appears to me," she added with a flip of her head to move strands of long, black hair off her shoulder, "that you *chose* not to comply of your own accord, which puts the burden on us, We The People."

Amy's mouth gaped, her eyes narrowed to slits, and her face flushed a fiery red. Her fists clenched so tight at her sides the skin across her knuckles turned white. "Do you know who I am?" she bit out. "I could ruin you and expose this . . . this violation of my rights, this forced intrusion upon my property with one show. I also have friends in government and in the media!"

Tara pivoted halfway around, locating Devlin where he stood hidden behind the camera. When she pointed at him, he peeked up and gave a small wave.

"I certainly hope that wasn't a threat, ma'am, because you see, I've done this a time or two and have come prepared." She turned halfway back toward Amy. "Do you recognize that man over there?" Devlin waved again. "He's been away from the scene for a while, but lucky for me and for his viewers, he's now working almost exclusively with me, for exactly this reason." She smiled warmly at Devlin. "That's Devlin Johnson from *The People's News*. Have you heard of *his* show? I'm sure you're aware it's become supremely popular. Maybe even more so than yours, I think," she taunted.

The People's News had indeed grown immensely popular. Devlin started the channel after becoming disenchanted with his job in the mainstream media. His philosophy on how news should be reported contradicted the MSM's—*all* the networks. He believed news should be told without bias and without opinion added in. A reporter should tell the whole truth of a story, and not pieces of it which best fit the context in which the network was told it should fit. Sadly, that context had stealthily shifted into nothing more than a political platform, isolating the pieces of a story designed to promote the ideology of the political party lining each network's pockets. They didn't always outright lie, but their manipulation of the material they presented was equally as bad, if not worse than a lie. Devlin wanted better for the people.

So caught up in her fury, his current subject hadn't seen him hovering at the edge of her property. There was, not surprisingly, an absence of other media present, which might have made him stand out a bit more had there been a mosh pit of cameras and reporters, he supposed. But Tara had explained to him during his initial interview that the lack of any other media's presence was attributed to the fact that she intentionally didn't advertise her scheduled Consequence Engagements, though that hadn't always been the case.

Immediately following the revolution, the WTP announced as part of their mission that the government would become impressively transparent in all aspects of operations. Most especially with those actions coming from Congress and the President's office. Consequence Engagements like the one today were deemed the best and easiest way to relay this promise to the people.

Televising Consequence Engagements—CEs—it had been presumed, would allow the people to witness the impacts from decisions made at all levels of government. CEs were issued when violations occurred. Everyone, including those previously deemed untouchable—politicians and the wealthy—all the way down to the simplest of residents across the nation, were now susceptible to real outcomes when laws were violated, thus eradicating discrimination under the law.

That was the new way. We The People's way.

But the media frenzy which had occurred at Tara's compliance confrontations early on had become so outrageous, the CCOC were, on several occasions, prevented from completing their assigned tasks. As a result, Tara had been forced to change processes to avoid such impediments. She'd switched to sharing written details of her Consequence Engagements with news channels for them to air or run as a banner feed, whichever way they preferred to relay the story. Unfortunately, the manner they chose did not bring about the hoped-for outcomes of the intent behind Consequence Clauses. This, Tara had learned, was due to the MSM stripping her communication as prepared and altering the context to fit their agendas. In most cases, they simply chose not to publish anything submitted by Tara's office.

This was why Josh wanted Tara to meet Devlin, which is how he ended up where he was today.

Through the camera, he watched Amy's back stiffen and her hand lift to hide her face from him. "My lawyer will hear about this!"

"That's fine, ma'am. Waste your money as you choose." Tara looked past the widely-known celebrity to the three-story, stucco façade monstrosity of a home—a mansion by most folks' standards. "If you make it as far as a judge, it'll be tossed out within minutes, I can assure you, since you're unquestionably in non-compliance of the CC."

The Clauses all but eliminated the need for any lawyer engagement, in most cases, anyway. Consequence Clauses were the final decision.

Tara turned and flagged the attention of the machinery operators standing by patiently. Sweeping a hand in an encouraging circle above her head, she urged them to continue with their work.

Per the Consequence Clause specific to today's situation, all properties, privately or publicly owned, including government properties, were not allowed to fully surround land or structures with any form of barrier; there were very few exceptions to this rule, wild animal preserves being about the only properties permitted to be fully fenced. All others were allowed a maximum of fencing around three-quarters of their property, so long as the entire boundary was not enclosed completely. Backyards could be fully fenced to allow for children's play or pets to safely wander; however, there were certain specifications as to height and materials used that needed to be followed.

The Open Borders Act had been passed prior to the

revolution, and it was still the biggest, most impactful decision ever approved by the government. Once the Consequence Clause concept had been established, Josh directed Congress to create a set of consequences for laws broken as they related to opening the borders. Everyone quickly realized this was no easy task and as it turned out it would become evergreen work, meaning new Clauses were being attached to the OBA all the time.

Though highly contested by many members of Congress, We The People's decree ruled. Josh and several others had liked the concept of Clauses so much, they'd decided to extend beyond the OBA. The country's leaders were directed to create CCs for *all* Congressional and presidential decisions as well as federal laws, new and old. A very time-consuming and daunting process indeed, one which Tara had claimed she'd been consumed with, as a result, over the last few years. But it had been deemed worth the effort, if it slowed bad decisions made by the people and by the government.

"We'll see about that!" Amy shrieked as Tara sauntered away, her hips swaying like a supermodel walking a runway. The sound of her heels clicking across the pavement was lost in the rumble of diesel engines revving.

"And stop calling me ma'am!" Amy shouted.

When Tara reached Devlin, she turned back to the distressed and highly disheveled celebrity. Cupping her hands around her mouth she called out in a loud voice, "Oh, and . . . ma'am?" When Amy's gaze shot daggers back at her, Tara added, "I'll send you the bill."

Devlin's camera whirred, capturing the string of expletives, the stomping of feet, strands of hair coming loose from her bun, flying wildly about under the California sun. And finally, the *coup de gras*: Both Amy's arms extended out, her elbows locking, as she barreled her middle fingers at Tara, at the bulldozer driver, and finally at Devlin and his camera.

Coincidentally, or possibly not, as this was happening, the sound of a helicopter's blades filled the air. All eyes turned up to find a mainstream media network's chopper coming into view and hovering—a neighbor must have reported the incident—capturing one of Hollywood's finest in all her glory.

Devlin knew exactly how the evening news would relay this scene. They'd lead with the bulldozer, Devlin, and Tara. Then they'd show a tearful Amy who would claim vandalism, destruction of property, and claim Tara threatened her. No mention would be made of the numerous notices sent from the CCOC's office. The scene the reporters couldn't have missed upon their arrival, showing an outraged Amy's vulgar actions directed at We The People's spokesperson, would never hit the airwaves. At least not on any of the mainstream media networks.

Devlin knew he wouldn't remain unscathed in the bashing, either. They'd search for something on him. He guessed they'd dredge up the footage he'd aired about the border killing and his insinuation that it was too easily done to not be a professional hit. Instead of airing his pleas to the public for help identifying a killer, they'd edit it to make him look like a madman. They'd claim he was there that day supporting the "Keep Them Out" cause. But those who knew him and knew his reporting style would see the lies for what they were. The cult of followers who supported the likes of Senator Clarkson and the President and their causes, those people would believe whatever the MSM told them.

What aired tonight on *The People's News* would share the real story of consequences for choices people made. Fortunately for everyone in this country, We The People—the new government—did not discriminate, regardless of status, wealth, or political affiliation, no matter how rich, important, or powerful they may be.

FOUR

"I've seen the footage," Tara said without looking up, her hands tucked inside the pockets of her coat as they strode along the busy sidewalk.

They were back in Washington DC, after returning from California two days earlier. The arctic front from a week ago, the one that had lowered temperatures into the thirties had moved out. Today the sun was up, the air crisp, and the only reminder of the wintry blast were the piles of snow lining sidewalks.

It was midafternoon, the streets and walkways a bog of bicycles, scooters, bumpers, and shoulders. Vendors had set up shop along building fronts, their spaces demarcated by swaths of fabric draped over wires or baskets filled with colorful wares from places all around the world. The conglomeration of goods being hawked was a mixture of dozens of cultures converging into one. All this combined made foot travel throughout the city a maze-like endeavor, a much slower, more tedious process than in years past.

Devlin didn't need to ask which footage Tara referred to. By the sullen tone of her voice, he knew. "I suppose I should thank you, then." His body posture mimicked hers as he kept pace, occasionally slipping behind her to avoid oncoming pedestrians. When she gave him a questioning glance, he added, "Since I know it never appeared on any of the big news networks, it means you were one of my viewers."

At the intersection across from their destination, Devlin drew up short, allowing the mob of pedestrians behind him to swirl past, like water rushing over a large boulder.

"Shit," he exclaimed, instantly changing direction to a bank of machines that resembled old ATMs, yet another relic of times past. "What's the date?" There was a hint of panic evident in his voice.

Tara, who had surprisingly worn sensible shoes today, ones that were flat with rubber soles to aid in maneuvering over any ice remaining on the shoveled sidewalks, balked but shifted direction with him.

"It's the twenty-eighth. Wait," she said with a crooked grin. "Are you seriously implying you haven't voted yet?"

"I'm not implying anything," he countered matter-of-factly as he strode up to an empty voter kiosk at the end of the row. The three other systems to his left were occupied. Tara braced a shoulder against the device Devlin was about to use, her head moving slowly side to side, an amused expression on her face.

"Wouldn't that be a tragedy. Me having to come for you, to charge you and send you to the FRP for failure to comply. Tsk tsk," she chided teasingly.

Devlin scowled at her. The Free-Range Prison was not something he ever wanted to experience. On the heels of defunding law enforcement, the government passed the Humanity Act, which not only abolished capital punishment, but it also closed all prisons and jails across the country and established Nevada as a Free-Range Prison. The State had the most federal land within the Lower 48, which was why the FRP found a home there.

Alaska had significantly more available land, but much of it was deemed too extreme and too remote, plus, it would have been cumbersome to transport convicts up there. Many members of Congress felt the location would have continued

THE CONSEQUENCE CLAUSE

the inhumane existence for prisoners if they were forced to move into such extreme winter conditions. It was also considered to be unnecessarily far away from the prisoners' families.

And so, after clearing the State of all fences, gates, or walls and forcing residents to leave their homes in Nevada, the government relocated all those incarcerated in the country to the new FRP. There the prisoners would be able to move about the State as a "free" society, so long as they remained within the boundaries of the State, until they completed their sentence or succumbed to death, natural or otherwise.

Because the government took the extreme stance that it had on discrimination of any kind, knowing in the end there'd be a hashtag group out there demanding they include something or someone they hadn't, meant jail was jail. This extended to all those relocated to the FRP and anyone facing incarceration for crimes committed. Regardless of the crime, the FRP was where lawbreakers went if sentenced with jail time, no matter how petty or extreme the offense, including failure to vote.

"First of all, it's not as if I haven't been busy," Devlin lied.

He'd had plenty of spare time on his hands these last two months of the voting window. Most of it, however, had been filled with scouring old news footage, still searching for a face, something, anything to connect the dots leading to who and why the woman at the border had been targeted that day. A long time back, he'd stopped referring to her as Melissa, instead calling her the woman at the border, or the blonde who'd been murdered. Doing so allowed him to distance himself from the helplessness that nearly consumed him in the early days. This way, he'd been able to continue his pursuit for answers day in and day out without feeling like his insides were being shredded.

But the fib he'd told Tara now was a wasted effort. Every street corner across the country had a kiosk. All of which were accessible twenty-four hours of the day, specifically for the purpose of contradicting his own argument of having no time to vote. It didn't matter if he were busy, there'd always be a moment, every year somewhere between the first of October, the opening of the voting window, to the last day of November, the closing date, in which he could have found time to vote. He'd simply forgotten about it. And then, he'd gotten caught up in his recent resurrection from the non-living and it completely slipped his mind.

"And secondly," he continued, pointing out a serious flaw in Tara's threat, stating a fact that was all the protection from consequences he needed. "I'm not high profile enough to warrant *your* services. You'd send one of your flunkies. Besides, the window's still open. That's all that matters." He couldn't help his cocky grin, because he was right, and they both knew it.

He typed in his name and held his forearm over a square glass area on the kiosk. When the device prompted him, he looked up at a green light appearing at the back of the machine. The eye scan took seconds, then Please Wait appeared on the main display. A blue light flashed over his arm, scanning the Unilateral Socially Fundamental Control Device, USFCD for short, embedded on the top side of his forearm, approximately two inches above the wrist. This linked his age, address, political affiliation, and so much more to the Voter Information Log, which was then tied to the main Control Database.

In less than one minute, Devlin's identity was confirmed, and his ballot was presented. He scrolled through the list of languages, one that grew with each passing year as more people from other places flowed steadily into the country. Finding "English," he selected it.

THE CONSEQUENCE CLAUSE

This year's Annual Ballot was, not surprisingly, one of the longest Devlin had seen since all the changes in the new government had been implemented, specifically with the addition of Consequence Clauses. During non-general election years, as this one was, the Annual Ballot, the AB as people called it, was simply a law-approval ballot. Since the inception of annual voting, he'd only had one other of the non-general election variety. Last year had been a general election year, with the outgoing President having only served one four-year term before Anita Grant—the one married to Senator Harriet Clarkson—had won and become President.

The WTP had taken over management of the government, however, the process and term limits for presidential and Congressional elections remained the same as before. The WTP's plan wasn't to undo systems built into the government; its goal was to simply point out the biases of those in Congress and make the members work in ways that were honest, true, and ethical. A remarkably challenging feat, as it turned out.

There were at least sixty items Devlin needed to submit his opinion on, either for or against. During what had become known as the Double-Ds, the Destructive Decades, when the Constitution was painfully and viciously torn to pieces, one of the many rights stripped away from the people had been the right of States in the Union to govern their own boundaries. Hence the reason the United States was no longer such and was now simply referred to as the States. This meant for Devlin that he didn't have any State related laws to vote on, as all laws were now federal, enforceable by an associated Consequence Clause. And there were still many more laws Congress needed to catch up on.

The items on the AB today were a combination of new legal decisions issued by Congress as well as existing laws, all requiring Devlin's yay/in favor or nay/against vote. Bringing all laws to the voters would take years of lengthy ballots, like this one. Fortunately, he'd already read through his AB and knew which way he was leaning, on most items anyway.

"Why didn't you do this when we were in California, at the airport, where we sat doing nothing for nearly two hours?" Tara groaned.

"I wasn't in the mood then," he admitted.

It was true, he hadn't been in the mood. After their encounter with Amy Silvers, they'd begun their journey south to San Diego when their next scheduled CE had been aborted. The change in plans was due to the roadblock they'd come upon several miles outside Los Angeles. Agents, dozens of them, were there to ward off travelers headed south. Apparently, the Mexicans had migrated across the border, intent upon extending their boundaries. They'd filed the necessary paperwork indicating the area they wanted to claim, so their movement wasn't considered aggressive in any way. The Agents were situated on the road merely to inform travelers of what they'd find ahead, should they wish to continue.

Somewhere within the three-thousand-page document that made up the Open Borders Act, the right of foreigners to claim boundaries had been added. The language stated that by not permitting this would have created a hardship for those seeking to live in an environment similar to where they'd come from, their homelands. To not allow this was deemed discriminatory.

Therefore, so long as the proper process of boundary claiming as outlined in the OBA was followed, they were within their legal right to do so. Having seen occurrences like this in other areas around the country, it hadn't been all that shocking for Devlin or Tara to run into the issue in California. But they'd decided to let the dust settle on the claiming and return to address the target of their CE later.

"As you'll recall," Devlin reminded his partner, "our entire schedule was disrupted. I wasn't in the right frame of mind to make decisions that could affect the rest of my life, should my name come up in a random selection during a consequence enforcement."

Tara pushed the sleeve of her coat back and glanced at her watch. "Okay, fine. I guess that's fair. But I'm starving, so can you at least hurry up."

He rolled his eyes at her but didn't otherwise acknowledge her lack of sensitivity to this serious task, considering that voting was the number one most important, and required, task an individual living in the States had to do. He spent the next ten minutes plugging in his responses. "Almost done. Only two left."

With a resigned sigh, Tara pulled her phone from her pocket and granted him silence and time to ponder the last questions on the screen, the ones he'd struggled the most with in his decision-making.

There'd been three voting seasons since the inception of ABs. The first year had included so many major laws, it had taken him a full day to read them all and submit his responses. The Humanity Act and the Open Borders Act, two of the most profound Acts passed by Congress, ones that significantly impacted people all around the country, had been on that first ballot. Beyond that he couldn't remember which year he'd had to vote for or against what, but he recalled having to choose his stance on laws related to gun control, abortion, espionage, civil rights, legal age limits, and more. Every law would eventually make it to the AB. The government believed it was important to make the people choose a side on all matters. As responses were recorded and tracked through the Voter Information Log, it also provided the CCOC the information they needed in situations involving Consequence Engagements.

Devlin read his last item. "Honestly, if abstention was permitted, I think I'd skip this vote." Not voting, however, wasn't allowed. Every person aged fourteen or greater residing in the country, citizen or otherwise, was required to vote, to pick a side on a law, to make a choice, one way or the other.

The Humanity Act was a good example of why he didn't like to vote. Was it fair to allow criminals, vicious ones in some cases, to wander free among others within the FRP who'd committed non-violent crimes? The best one could hope for was to hole up in an abandoned home or casino or cave maybe and hide until their time was up. Either that or fight for survival. Humane treatment, and non-discriminatory treatment, meant even those inside the FRP got to move about as they wanted. But to Devlin it also meant only the fittest would survive. He supposed it was the better outcome, considering the initial demand had been to simply release all the prisoners, because they deserved to be given second chances.

He read his last question again.

Do you support or oppose the Degenderizing Act, which removes all reference to sexual gender or identified sex on all forms, applications, and documents for any purpose? This Act determines that no special privileges will be given to any person based on gender or sex, biologically made, or identifying preference chosen, in any and all instances, including but not limited to entrance into organizations with gender preferences, all environments, business loan applications, employment, pay status, cases of sexual discrimination, and all other situations where one gender or sex might benefit over another?

Devlin raked his fingers through his hair again, not caring that with all the ruffling, it had to be quite a disaster by now. "Do you support this? I mean, you're a woman. How is this going to help or harm you?"

THE CONSEQUENCE CLAUSE

Tara frowned before swiping through her phone, searching for, and locating what she was after. "Next week I have a meeting to go over the list of businesses, programs, and who knows what else, where this new rule will apply. In a way, it's a great idea. I mean, there's always been a fight for women's equal rights, like forever." At Devlin's nod of acknowledgment, she added, "This grants the right for women to be treated exactly like men in *all* ways, as so many women demanded. But." She held up one finger. "Now no woman can ask for special privilege of any kind based on their being female, or any other identified gender. No man can either, of course. You and me, Dev." She punched his arm lightly. "We're equals in everything we do. Hell, even our bathrooms are equally accessible now." She closed her eyes and shivered. "Gross. I don't see how that's an advantage, but, whatever."

"Well, then," he said, resigned to his decision. "Here's to equality, I suppose. I have a feeling this is going to backfire sooner rather than later." He selected his response and punched the submit ballot icon. A notification chimed on his phone, the receipt for his ballot acceptance. The information would be uploaded into the VIL and accessed, if needed, for any Consequence Clause infractions, should he do something that resulted in one being implemented against him or should his name pop up in a random selection during someone else's consequence. "And done. Let's go eat!"

"Finally," she groaned. "Next year, could you not do this at the last minute? And could you not do it when I'm with you? Especially when I'm hungry?"

It hadn't taken Devlin long to learn that Tara did not do well if she missed a meal. And the woman could pile away the food, though her figure didn't suffer for it. He wondered about her comment on next year's voting, and if they'd still be working together then. With all the Consequence Engagements being aired the way they were, crimes should eventually slow down, at least he assumed they would. When that happened, would Tara want or need to continue their working relationship?

They strolled along their original path, crossing the street to head over to the pizza joint down the way. Bustling through the throng of pedestrians made the journey a slow one, as the population in the city had nearly tripled since the passing of the OBA. People from all over the world, dressed in all manner of fashion from their homelands surrounded them. The various odors of bodies, soaps, and perfumes collided with the rich scents of spices and grease from curbside food stands situated every few feet along the sidewalk.

When they neared the restaurant Devlin had originally suggested when Tara first mentioned she needed to eat, he wasn't surprised to see a small line had formed out the door. It had always been a popular place, made so by the expertise of the chef who was also the owner.

After several minutes, they'd managed to inch their way nearly to the front of the line while more guests filed in behind them. He and Tara spoke of insignificant things until he saw the hostess approach. He offered her a smile, recognizing her from the last time he'd visited the place last year. With menus and silverware in hand, she slowed next to the person in front of Devlin and Tara, but then peered toward the back of the line. Lowering her gaze, she proceeded quickly past, stopping farther back beside an attractive young couple engaged in an animated conversation in a language Devlin couldn't identify.

"If you'll come with me," he heard the hostess say to the pair. "I'll get you seated." She offered Devlin a tight, uncomfortable smile when she hurried by him and Tara.

Tara's indrawn breath had him turning to face her.

THE CONSEQUENCE CLAUSE

"What the hell?" Devlin blurted, causing the hostess's steps to falter. "This person was here first." He pointed to the individual standing in front of him and Tara. "And we were here before them." He indicated the couple beside the waitress who were eyeing him warily. "You literally walked right by us." This time his hand gestures indicated the person first in line and then him and Tara.

The poor hostess leaned in close to Devlin. Lowering her voice, she said, "I understand, and I am sorry. But," she pointed behind him to a sign taped to the window near the door.

In large, bold, black letters printed on white paper it read: We honor First Rights Rules.

The hostess's gaze shifted to the first person in line and then to the back of the line before returning to Devlin and Tara. "It looks like you'll be next," she offered with a forced smile.

As if he'd been slapped across the face, Devlin drew back, his eyes darting from the sign to the hostess to Tara, and then back to the sign. "Are you kidding me?"

He looked questioningly around him, in that way one might after slipping and falling on ice and hoping nobody witnessed the embarrassing act.

"When did this happen?" he demanded angrily.

When the distressed hostess shied away from him, Tara touched his arm. "Devlin—" she began, but he shrugged her off.

"No, Ms. Carlson. This is unacceptable. It's shit like this that nearly pushed us into a civil war. There are laws that ban racism. For fuck's sake, I just voted on something that eliminates the one thing that since the beginning of time makes us different as humans," he exclaimed, referring to the new degenderizing and de-sexing law. "How can *this* still be allowed?" he said, pointing at the sign. His chest was heaving up and down and he knew his face had gone red.

"Devlin," Tara tried again, "it *isn't* allowed. Give me a minute to ask some questions," she urged, before requesting to speak to the manager.

First Rights Rules had popped up out West, along the coast somewhere, during the time when the hashtags had begun ravaging the land. Because white people were deemed the reason for all the country's problems, the call to give preferential treatment to anyone other than white folks went out. Initially, it prevailed mostly in the private sector, starting in Seattle as Devlin recollected, then slowly spread from there. But, like a poison injected into a vein, the racist practice of First Rights slithered its way into all areas of life, private and public.

What it meant was if there was a situation where a person of color, any color except white, assembled in a line together, regardless of the venue or circumstance, the non-white would be moved to the front for first access to whatever it may be. The rule had barely reached the level of the public sector, like medical facilities and hospitals, when war nearly erupted, right before the revolution. With casualties piling in, doctors were forced to cast aside First Rights Rules—the Hippocratic Oath prevailing over the demands of the hashtags.

Devlin's anger continued to heat his blood, but he granted Tara her request to consider the situation. He huffed and gave her a sharp nod, but he damned well wasn't going to let this go. Reaching for his video camera, he clicked it on, determined to use this as a teaching moment for the rest of the holdouts in the country who continued racist behaviors like the one here.

After a couple of anxious minutes, his patience reached its limit and he stepped inside the establishment, Tara directly behind him. Patrons glanced his way, their chewing halted or their forks hovering midway between plate and mouth. He met each person's accusatory stare, silently daring any of them to say one word to him. The kitchen was along the far wall. Bright heating lamps lined the aluminum counter where dishes of prepared food were placed for the servers to collect. Two cooks were behind the counter. The smell of pizza dough and cheese made Devlin's mouth water and his stomach growl in angry protest, which pissed him off even more than he already was.

When one of the cooks looked up, Devlin lifted his hand and beckoned Carl, the owner, with a sharp gesture.

As he approached, Devlin said, "Carl. What the hell is going on here?"

He'd not spent any time together with Carl outside the confines of the restaurant, but Devlin had enjoyed many lunchtimes there conversing with the man. He liked him. He was good and kind. What was happening now with the sign wasn't the Carl he knew at all.

Carl was wringing his hands in the apron tied about his waist. The smile he offered was stiff and didn't reach his eyes. "Devlin, uh," he said hesitantly.

He looked back, his gaze drifting over the customers seated in the room beyond. The previous stares they'd received had turned dark, hostile even—the way Devlin had remembered from back in the old days, before the revolution, when the hashtag cults had begun to destroy the country. Devlin's anger flared even brighter. He'd thought, no, he'd been *certain* progress had been made in the last few years, what with the influx of people entering the country from all areas of the world. There'd been little to no issues from or sign of the primary hashtag group which started the downfall of American society, the one most prevalent during the eight-year run with the President at the time.

Tara didn't know Devlin well, considering they'd only spent a handful of days together by then, but she was astute enough to recognize the ensuing engagement with Carl was unlikely to be civil. In a move that he barely had time to register, she angled her body in front of him and greeted Carl before Devlin lost his temper.

"Are you the manager?" she asked in her official voice, notably different from her unofficial one.

Carl nodded. "I'm the owner, ma'am."

"My companion and I became aware of your First Rights Rule sign. I have some questions for you about it." With exaggerated calm, Tara retrieved her little blue book from her pocket. Her neck elongated as she lifted her chin in such a way it appeared she was looking down on Carl, which she wasn't.

Carl stroked a hand over his jaw, his mouth drawing open as if to ease tension there. Then, before anyone could say anything more, he clutched Devlin's upper arm and steered him back toward the building's entrance. The bell overhead jingled when he pushed the door open, and the trio stepped outside.

Devlin jerked his arm free and rounded on Carl, but Tara quickly intervened. "Sir. Are you aware the First Rights Rule was deemed illegal with the passage of the OBA?" she asked, while flipping past pages near the front of her booklet.

Carl began twisting his fingers in his apron like he was determined to tear the fabric apart. Something was off, Devlin sensed it in his gut. This single-minded attitude was not the Carl he knew. He was seriously worried and not belligerently holding claim to any racist attitudes.

"Carl?" Devlin forced back his frustration. "What happened? This isn't you." He pointed at the sign. "Is someone making you do this?"

Carl had three children with his wife. He knew the loyal and kind business owner would do anything to protect and provide for his family. But, if his assumptions were correct, and it was the hashtag hate group he was thinking of that had a hand in this, he knew they'd push to get what they wanted at any cost.

"Devlin," Carl said, speaking more to him than Tara, before realizing it and addressing her, too. "Ms. Carlson."

So, he did know who she was. Tara wasn't a celebrity by any means, but the mainstream media had bashed her on enough occasions, it only made sense she'd be recognizable. Especially when she flashed the little blue book, her iconic symbol of authority.

"I didn't want to do this." Carl's head shook in fast, jerky movements. "But the guy said if I didn't put it up, they'd destroy the place and my family. They would come after everything that's important to me." He pressed his lips into a tight line, then his tongue poked out to lick across them. Clearing his throat, he swallowed hard, casting a furtive glance at the offensive window sign.

"Is it the hashtag group?" Devlin didn't have to specify which one.

Again, the quick, negative headshake. Beads of sweat formed on Carl's upper lip, even though the air outside was chilly. "No!" His brows shot up high on his forehead. "This came from somewhere else. A man dressed in a fancy suit, with a long coat. You know, the kind them up there wear." He pointed with his chin.

"You mean someone from Capitol Hill?" Tara asked.

"Yes, ma'am. He was white and tall. Taller than me. And he wore dark glasses and a ballcap." His head lowered, as if he were ashamed of his lack of ability to better identify the man who'd brought this injustice on him and his business. "But he was big and tall," he added again, as if that were enough to identify one person out of hundreds of people who walked the halls of Capitol Hill. He pointed at the row of businesses on the opposite side of the street, his finger moving from one to another. "Look," he said resolutely. "I'm not the only one, either. It's like the Biblical Passover. A sign on the door keeps you safe?" His voice lifted in question.

"Or destroys you if you don't comply," Tara mumbled, looking across the street.

Four establishments on one side of the long, heavily trafficked city block had windows and doors boarded up. Two buildings, side by side, had the brick façade scorched black.

"They refused." Carl stared at the results of those owners' refusal, the memory of watching the flames destroy everything within was clear in the worried expression marring his face.

Devlin couldn't hide his shock and outrage even if he'd wanted to. "Son of a bitch!"

Carl nodded. "I agree, but so many others are doing it, because . . . ." He leaned slightly closer as if to keep prying ears nearby from hearing. "We all think the guy coming around here is doing so at the bidding of someone higher up." His hands lifted in a gesture of defeat.

Devlin swiped his palm over his face. "This is absurd." A patron exiting the restaurant paused in surprise when he nearly bumped into Carl. The small, elderly man and the woman at his side glanced at Devlin and Tara, before scowling at Carl and hastily walking away, noses high in the air.

Lost in his own angry thoughts, Devlin hadn't been paying attention to Tara, who was digging furiously through her book. That she was doing it caused him no concern. It was the way she was so intent, almost desperate to find something specific that had him worried.

"Ms. Carlson? What is it?"

After more frantic page turns, Tara pressed the book closed. With both palms holding it tight, she held it butted up against her chin, the action giving the appearance of her praying.

"The law is the law," she whispered.

THE CONSEQUENCE CLAUSE

Devlin's heart sank. "Ms. Carlson, you can't." His head began to shake, denying everything she hadn't said yet.

"Can't what?" Carl asked, oblivious to the direction Devlin suspected Tara was headed.

Her lips pressed into a tight line and deep grooves appeared between her brows. "I have no choice. The law specifically states First Rights would end and any such occurrence of it found anywhere was punishable through Consequence Clause enforcement. I'm sorry," she said with a note of sadness tingeing her voice. She'd turned to address Carl when she apologized, but Devlin suspected it was meant equally as much for him.

He clutched his fingers around her wrist, squeezing gently, pleadingly. "You can't. This isn't right. He was coerced. Threatened even. Doesn't that action counter his?"

"What do you mean? What's happening?" Carl's voice shook. He clearly sensed an unknown impending threat.

"Carl. I have no choice but to enforce the Consequence Clause associated with this violation." She pointed at the First Rights sign on the door to Carl's restaurant. "The sentence is—"

"You can't be serious!" Devlin pulled Tara around by the shoulders to face him, then went a little farther by making her take a couple steps away from Carl, who was growing more anxious by the second. "Clearly, he's being threatened to do this. Why would he have to face any consequences? Whoever is doing this to him, and the others, should be dealt with. Not them," he added, sweeping his arms wide, indicating the businesses nearby.

"The law is the law, Devlin. You know better than most that it's because of shit like this we nearly went to war. Since the OBA, the WTP has cracked down on *all* lawbreakers. There are no wishy-washy decisions when it comes to sentencing and consequences. Things are spelled out right here." She lifted the blue book. "Look, I agree that whoever threatened Carl and all the rest should be punished. And trust me, there are even more severe consequences for that sort of behavior." She peered over Devlin's shoulder before adding in a much lower voice. "Especially if it's coming from someone in a position of power." Her shoulders sagged and she frowned. "But it was his responsibility to *not break the law*," she said, emphasizing the one thing that people, all people, had the ability and the responsibility to do. "He had a choice, regardless of it being a difficult one to make."

Her words shot through Devlin. Conrad had said the same thing about what he'd been directed to do. Terrible things to which Devlin had expressed his understanding to, supporting his inability to choose to walk away. It had been his job. He couldn't have chosen any different. Carl being threatened made choosing impossible, too. Didn't it?

"Hell, I don't know, he should have at least called someone to report it," Tara whispered.

Carl, who'd up to this point remained mostly silent but visibly nervous, interrupted them in a hushed voice. "Who was I supposed to call? The police? Law enforcement we don't have anymore? I did notify the Agent Department," he admitted, defending his actions. "But nobody's followed up yet. What was I to do?"

Devlin had to look away when he saw the threat of tears in Carl's eyes. Tara turned away, presenting both men with her back. Devlin stepped in front of her, forcing her to look up.

"The CC is clear when it comes to acts of racism in any form. It even specifically mentions First Rights." Her voice crept higher as she tried to justify the outcome, one she knew she was supposed to deliver, but Devlin could tell her conscience cried foul against it.

"I understand your position. I do." He hoped the sound of his voice came across as calm and placating.

"I have to charge him, Dev."

She blinked fast, a deep worry furrowing her brow again. "It's my job. Whether I agree with it or not."

"How about we don't ignore it, but let's instead postpone the consequence until we, we . . . ." He stroked his fingers back and forth over his jaw as he searched for something Tara might agree to. "You follow up with the Agent Department. If you can confirm Carl attempted to seek help, then that should exonerate him. Or at a minimum, reduce the consequence due him." Tara's eyes danced side to side with his as she considered the suggestion. He pressed further. "I'll ask around with the other business owners. Maybe there's a camera somewhere that caught the image of the guy making the threats. If we can find who he works for, then the bigger crime is what *he's* doing and who's having him do it."

The tug of war going on inside Tara's head was visibly painful to watch. Finally, she tilted her head back, closed her eyes, and expelled a huge sigh.

She turned to Carl. "I'm not promising there won't be a consequence, but I'll postpone it while we do more investigating." Her hand raked over the top of her head and stopped there. "For god's sake, take the sign down. If you get challenged again, call us or something." Before Tara could dig out a business card from a slot inside the case of her cell phone, Devlin had retrieved his own card.

"Here. Call me if the guy comes back around. Catching him in the act is our best hope."

"Yes, sir," he eagerly agreed, still glancing about nervously, as though expecting repercussions from getting caught talking to Devlin. An invisible shroud of weariness settled over the restaurant owner. He suddenly looked exhausted, from fear of the consequences to come or from the pressure he'd been under from an as-yet unidentified person making threats, Devlin didn't know.

"What they're doing goes beyond ignorance," Carl said. "Maybe it is the same hashtag group from a long time ago that is influencing someone up there. I thought they'd been shut down when it became illegal to blame white folks for all the problems in the country. Could be they were simply laying low for a time. If this keeps up, I'll lose my business, like I almost did before." He shook his head, remembering those challenging times when racist organizations destroyed the livelihoods of people, especially owners of smaller businesses, by ushering in segregation—it couldn't be called anything but that.

"I do not agree with it, ma'am," he said to Tara. "I understand your position, but government bullies combined with no law enforcement around to help puts me and everyone around here in a tough position."

Tara attempted a reassuring smile, but it fell short. "Let's see if we can figure out a way to mitigate this. A legal way."

Government bullies, hashtags, the media. Devlin shook his head as a darkness settled in his core. It was so reminiscent of a different time. Or what seemed like a different time. It appeared as if there'd only been a mask hiding the truth of the way things still were. It had all been about manipulation and control. And, apparently, not even a revolution and a new, hopeful way of government could stop it.

The OBA, something that literally opened the doors, and it was hoped, minds of every variety of people in existence—not even that could change it, it seemed. Was the country destined to head down the hard road the people had fought so valiantly to escape? He prayed not. He glanced down at his watch. It was almost two and he had a meeting back up at the Capitol to get to. So much for lunch.

"I've got to get going." He turned to Tara. "How long did you say we'll be gone on this next trip?" On the earlier hike down from Capitol Hill, which was where Tara had found Devlin contemplating his options at a vending machine, she'd shared with him the reason she'd wanted him to get lunch with her—lunch that didn't happen after all, damn it. The vending choices he'd looked through earlier flashed in his memory as his stomach growled in angry protest.

Tara had a lengthy list of upcoming CEs between here and Oregon. She'd be traveling for the next several months and wanted Devlin to join her on as many trips as he could manage. After showing him the list of engagements scheduled over the next month, he was intrigued. The plan was to leave in a week's time, which meant he'd need to quickly follow through on his promise to Carl to inquire about cameras that may have captured an image of the person who'd threatened him and the other business owners nearby. He also needed to pack, and update Josh on what happened today.

As manager over Congress and the President, Josh would want to be informed of the potential threat of unrest or a resurgence of government bullying coming from members of Congress. Any action that hurt the people of this country was a direct assault against We The People, and Devlin knew Josh would not tolerate such a thing. Never again.

FIVE

Devlin slowed as he walked across the brick courtyard on the East Front side of the Capitol. No matter how many times he'd been here before, he couldn't help but be in awe of the magnificence of the building. The majestic structure had weathered more than two centuries of growth and strife, inside and out. He paused at the bottom of the stone steps leading up to the bronze Columbus Doors tucked behind sixteen Corinthian marble columns. It was indeed a privilege to be able to stand before such history.

He shook his head in silent introspection. The Founding Fathers had to be rolling in their graves at what had become of the Constitution over the last decade. The well-devised blueprint of checks and balances designed to keep the people safe from and overreaching government failed as political parties stripped away individual liberties amendment by amendment.

Shifting the backpack slung over his shoulder, he climbed the steps, a trek he'd made countless times in the past, before the OBA. The luggage he carried, filled with his tripod, cameras, and other miscellaneous work accoutrements was a familiar burden he'd missed during his hiatus from work.

At the arched entry, he pushed open the heavy door leading into the rotunda. Crossing the threshold, a fluorescent blue laser light flashed over his arm as he passed the USFCD scanner. An instant later, his phone chimed; the indicator that his scan record had been successfully captured and uploaded to the Control Database.

Like the Voter Information Log, which documented a person's voter registration data and responses submitted on Annual Ballots, the Control Database managed everything else about a person's life. It tracked one's pay, their use of discretionary funds, health records, the frequency of their visits to charging stations, gyms, medical facilities, restaurants, bars, and every other establishment in the country.

When the USFCD had first been mandated, the response had been more wariness than enthusiasm. But it didn't matter what the people thought. Every individual residing in the country had to get the chip. Without it, they couldn't travel, receive their paycheck, enter an establishment of any type besides their own place of residence, purchase anything, or qualify for government entitlements. Without the USFCD, one couldn't even vote, a punishable crime. Devlin hadn't come across anyone yet who'd found a way to opt out of getting the chip and have any sort of normal life.

He drew to a stop in the entryway and informed the armed Agent on duty who he was and his purpose there. The Agent spoke into a microphone clipped to his shoulder and a moment later, after listening to someone through the earbud visible against his ear, he nodded at Devlin.

"You've been verified." Before Devlin could turn and walk away, the Agent added, "I remember you." He was an older—older than Devlin—guy whose attempt at a smile oozed pity. When Devlin didn't engage in a trip down memory lane with him, the man lifted a hand and pointed a finger toward a door off to his left. "You know the way?"

Devlin dipped his head in a quick nod, not even trying to force his lips into a smile. "Thanks. I'm sorry, I, uh," he hesitated, "I don't recall you." His gaze shifted to a name tag stitched onto the man's jacket. REARDON. It didn't ring a bell. "It's okay. I was there. That day," he said in choppy sentences. "We worked together. She was one of the good ones." His head bobbed several times.

Knowing the man meant well and understanding now that he'd worked with the woman from the border, he didn't completely brush aside the offering of kind words. He merely gave Reardon a half smile and mumbled a quick thanks before heading off toward a door along the side wall of the circular room.

The rotunda was, in Devlin's opinion, the most magnificent structure in existence in the country. During his years traversing the land and chasing stories, he'd had the privilege to witness many grand sights and landmarks. But the rotunda had always been one of his favorites.

He tilted his head back as far as it would go. In the canopy, one hundred eighty feet up, was the *Apotheosis of Washington*, the mural painted inside the cap of the dome. From the ground, the painting's details were impressively discernible, thanks to the artist's talent and the fact that the images of the people there had been crafted as large as fifteen feet tall. In the center of the mural was a white banner with the Latin words: *E Pluribus Unum*.

Out of many, One.

The country's motto. It was a statement meant to depict the determination to form a single nation from a collection of States. As the nation grew, the motto held true, adopting each State into the fold, into the motto, as those beyond the original thirteen were established.

But the nation, the one that consisted of many, had been attacked from several angles, including from within. Though it was still technically a nation of one, it had been, and continued to be, torn apart by politics, the media, and hashtags.

Which ranked the worst? Nobody was certain anymore.

The build-up to the downfall was, at first, unremarkable: A protest against the migration of an oil pipe through reservation land. The shooting of a criminal by a police officer and vice versa. Religion, regardless of which. People wanting to take from others their guns, their homes, their rights—God-given or country-given. And more power-hungry, greedy demands kept on coming, forming a crevice so wide between people and Party lines, the nation of one had crumbled.

Devlin exited the rotunda, wandering down a long hallway leading to an area where he knew to find Josh and located his office, the wall plaque beside the door noting his title as Government Overseer.

He knocked, then entered when he heard a deep voice boom, "Come in!"

Josh was seated behind a grand mahogany desk. He pushed to his feet and came around the furniture to meet Devlin in the center of the room.

"Devlin! You are a sight for sore eyes. I was mighty pleased when you said you wanted to stop by." His voice held all the authority of a seasoned high school government teacher who'd once taught kids in a rough area of Los Angeles, his occupation before We The People formed and pre-revolution. "Come in, come in." Josh pointed at a chair for Devlin before settling back into his faux-leather seat.

Grinning ear to ear, he thumped a palm on top of the stack of papers in front of him. "Damn, it's good to see you back here." He lifted both hands in the air in reference to the Capitol building, and not specifically his office.

"Josh," Devlin greeted his friend in return. "I appreciate you seeing me on such short notice. I mean, I'm sure you've got more pressing matters than to visit a washed-up reporter, friend or not."

Devlin genuinely liked Josh. He was a good man. A true revolutionary. Someone who'd left behind a life, a home, a job, everything, to fight for his homeland. Untrained, but passionate about protecting the freedoms found in this country, Josh had walked the walk when he said something drastic needed to happen before the people running the government destroyed the very land in which they were meant to serve and protect.

He snorted. "You are not washed up, my friend. You're the best out there, even if you did take time off. We all understood. What you witnessed was terrible. You needed the break to process it. I get it." He frowned tightly, his eyes narrowing as memories of the past flitted through his brain.

Devlin and Josh went way back; almost to the beginnings of We The People. The group had started out on social media as a seemingly quiet and unproductive hashtag protesting people's rights being stripped away. But the success of the group exceeded everyone's expectations, especially Josh's. Little did those in power know, the WTP was a slumbering volcano that would eventually erupt in the most remarkable of ways.

Upon learning that none of the WTP's rallies were being aired on the mainstream news stations, like so many of the other hashtag organizations and their events back then, Devlin had grown curious. How long had it been now? Nearly eight years already? After reaching out to Josh, requesting a face-to-face interview, Devlin had learned his request had been the first from any news agency. And because of that fated meeting, he'd been invited to follow the WTP and report on their progress east toward the nation's capital. Josh had wanted from Devlin nothing more than to do what he'd built his career doing, the thing that had earned him accolades: Show the truth, tell the stories—good or bad—as they traversed the country. Josh wanted the opposite of what mainstream media and the government had decided the people should see. He wanted to share the truth.

The day the sleeping volcano known as the WTP erupted, where hundreds of thousands of revolutionaries—aka the lava—flowed around and through everything that was the country's government, Devlin, unfortunately, hadn't been there reporting for all the world to see. He'd watched it on the news, and to this day, it still made him shake his head in wonder at how pretentious and arrogant the nation's leaders had been. They'd genuinely believed everyone across the land would obediently help destroy the very fabric on which the nation had been built. The event that had finally awakened that volcano had been when the government found the way to force all residents to get the Unilateral Socially Fundamental Control Device—the USFCD. It was then that Josh and his followers knew the country had reached its breaking point and they needed to act immediately.

"But you're here, and by the looks of things"—Josh glanced at the backpack leaning against Devlin's leg—"you took Tara Carlson up on her offer?" There was a hopeful question in his voice, but as it was Josh who'd set him up with Tara, the question was a rhetorical one. She'd certainly already shared the details of their meeting with her boss.

Devlin answered Josh's question with ones of his own, continuing as if even the mention of getting back behind a camera didn't cause a twinge of anxiety. "Yeah, but why me? Of all the people out there, including Mario, why have her seek me out specifically?"

Finally beginning to relax, he leaned back in his chair.

Josh pressed both elbows on his desk and steepled his hands, tapping his chin with his forefingers. "Because only you will show these Consequence Engagements exactly as they unfold. I saw the clip you aired on Amy Silvers," he said, confirming Devlin's assumption that Josh already knew he'd agreed to return to work. "Thanks to that, we've gotten at least six confirmations of wall and other boundary removals from holdouts in our very own Congress." He huffed a derisive sound and shook his head.

The days of Congresspeople not having to abide by their own decrees was supposed to have ended with Josh's arrival. But even after four years in his position at the top, he'd learned the bitter truth about how many still believed they didn't have to abide by the same rules they made the rest of the country follow.

"Speaking of which," Devlin began, using this as a cue to address the reason for his visit, "Ms. Carlson and I attempted to have lunch today, around the corner. I think you've got a problem brewing somewhere here on the Hill."

Josh's eyes widened, and he drew back, pulling his chin close to his neck. "What sort of problem?" he asked, instantly donning a professional mask.

That's when Devlin noticed the tired look in his eyes, and the lengthening crow's feet fanning out toward his temples. He hadn't seen Josh for over two years; however, they'd spoken on the phone regularly during that span.

Devlin briefly explained the situation with Carl and the suggestion of someone working on these grounds being behind the threats.

Josh blew out a heavy, discouraged sigh. "It astounds me, the nerve of people in the highest echelons of government. This is exactly one of the reasons why we created the Consequence Clause and why we formed the CCOC."

One of the first acts of the WTP after they'd assumed management over the government was to announce the opening of a new program and department: The Consequence Compliance Oversight Committee. Like Homeland Security, its title perfectly described the intent of its function.

"We really hoped it would bring an immediate halt to bad behaviors and law breakers, like what you experienced firsthand in California."

"And yet," Devlin finished for him, "that clearly hasn't been the case."

"No, apparently it has not." Josh flicked aside some of the papers on the desk before him, then reconsidered his action and pulled them back, returning them to the tidy stack they were before. "The media still won't allow the truth to get out there. We've always known this to be true. But still." He braced an elbow on the desk and pinched the bridge of his nose. "They claim it's to protect the people, but really it's our politicians who don't want their shit to be aired, and, as we know all too well, it is they who control the MSM." Here, he scoffed, not trying to hold back his irritation with both entities. "Like the people of this country weren't pushed nearly into a war they all but sponsored, while the folks down that hallway right there"—he pointed—"sat in their protected little bubbles watching their constituents tear each other apart, like wolves on fresh meat. The media turned a blind eye then, refusing to air stories about anything that refuted the hashtags and their political antics, and they're still doing it today. It needs to stop."

He heaved an exasperated sigh. "I'll keep a close eye out around here. See if you can get anything more from businesses around your friend Carl's place. We can look at the Control Database if we need to. See if anything unusual shows up, like who scanned in where, check for a pattern. But without a name, we'll have to target business access data, not individuals. Capitol Hill is a bit like a small town, most everyone knows everyone. We should be able to find something." He glanced at his watch, then stood, pulling his blazer off the back of his chair, and lifting the stack of papers from his desk. "I gotta say, I'm hoping you like being back at work so much you'll want to come back here. Like old times."

Devlin quirked a brow at him as he too rose to his feet. Collecting his backpack, he followed Josh out of the office. "I'll confess, I'd been considering a return to work, even before you sent Tara to me with her offer. I know it's time."

"Some of what you're going to see out there won't be easy," Josh warned, casting Devlin a side-eyed glance as they strode down a long hallway. "It's obvious you're doing well these days. Promise me, if you feel it's too much, you'll step back. We'll figure something else out. Be sure to keep going to your group meetings, too. At least until you get a sense of how this new job will affect you."

Devlin nodded, his thoughts instantly turning to Conrad. Until this last group meeting, he'd felt the man was doing well, healing, dealing with his trauma. But it was obvious that he was regressing. It seemed impossible, but Devlin's own issues may have paled in comparison. He'd once heard a saying about no matter how bad one person's trauma was, there's always someone out there experiencing something worse. This resonated with him, and made him feel suddenly stronger, and certainly more compassionate for the likes of Conrad. If he were a better man, he'd even give one more shot at cracking the extremely thick walls built up around Ken. But even as he thought this, a little voice inside his head told him the guy was too far gone and would never accept help from him or anyone else. Yet, Devlin struggled with the idea of not trying one more time. He made a silent promise to reach out to both Conrad and Ken at the next group, to what end he didn't know. But it couldn't hurt.

"If you're interested, I'm headed over to the House Chamber now," Josh said. "I called a special meeting. Everyone will be there. How'd you like to pop in and see how things are going? Get your feet wet again if you will."

There were no pressing matters in Devlin's life that prevented him from jumping into a job on a whim. He had no family nearby. No pets waiting on him. And he had no love interests, either. All he had was his tiny apartment in Virginia, sized right so he wasn't forced to share it with anyone.

Working with Ms. Carlson gave him the opportunity to be productive again, in ways different from the past few years. It caused a little rush of excitement to wriggle up his spine. And here, with Josh, the chance to be part of the decisions coming out of Congress? Well, that was just a bonus.

He agreed and fell into step beside Josh. "Sure. Why not. I've got nothing but time. Bring me up to speed on what's changed among our Congress folk."

SIX

The House of Representatives Chamber was much the same as it had been when Devlin last saw it. Desks and chairs fanned around the room in a large rainbow of rectangular shapes. And among these were a hive of politicians standing, sitting, or milling about while waiting for the day's events to begin. Josh talked on, updating him on who the newcomers were, who'd left, and topics currently being discussed in Congress. One name mentioned, one that no matter the context in which it was said, had Devlin's lips curling in disgust: Senator Harriet Clarkson.

Even with all the changes made since the WTP took over, Clarkson was one who thought her job was to fight for anything that would be devastating to the country and its people. She epitomized old school, Party-line politics, and hadn't, at least not that Devlin had seen even with the intervening WTP, curbed her attempts at dismantling what little remained of the Constitution.

It was Clarkson who'd proposed and pushed to get the OBA passed, an event that would always be a dark reminder for Devlin. Clarkson's wife, President Grant, had also promoted the cause, but his level of resentment toward her wasn't the same as it was for Clarkson. Grant seemed more a follower and not an instigator of the OBA. He didn't care much for her by nature of her association with Clarkson, but he believed she deserved the opportunity to fail or succeed on her own account and was willing to give her the benefit of the doubt.

He listened to Josh, nodding, and making occasional sounds of acknowledgment as his friend rattled off a list of names of those who'd either term-limited out of their seat in Congress or who'd aged out. Senators could serve a maximum of three terms while representatives capped out at ten. And the age of sixty-two had been determined a respectable and healthy retirement age, so anyone having attained that magical number of years were dismissed right along with those who'd reached or surpassed the newly adopted term limits. Both these criteria were but a few changes implemented the first day Josh and the WTP had been given the Congress-approved power to do so. Needless to say, upon his arrival at his new post, more than half of Congress had been officially retired, making room for new and inspiring personalities to take their places. It was unfortunate that Senator Clarkson hadn't yet reached either expiration date. It wouldn't be too soon for Devlin or the country when that day finally arrived.

Devlin followed Josh through the open doors and down the center aisle. But where Josh angled off toward the podium, Devlin veered toward the cluster of reporters situated near the side of the main stage. Mario was there, looking surprised and then instantly worried when he saw Devlin. He popped to his feet, lifting a hand to draw his attention, which wasn't necessary, considering his manager was sitting in the front row of folding chairs situated in the reporters' pit.

"Boss. Is everything okay?" he asked, concern etched in his expression. Considering Devlin had only ever made an appearance at an assignment a small number of times that could be counted on one hand over the last few years, the worried expression he bore was warranted.

He nodded reassuringly. "It's fine. I'm popping in to see how things are going. I think it's about time, don't you?"

Mario's lips parted, as if he were about to speak, but then a large grin spread across his face. Relief, hope, and a genuine look of happiness danced in his eyes. There was no hint of jealousy or concern about his own job in his demeanor, as there shouldn't be. Regardless of Devlin's mental state and ability to do his job, he'd always need Mario.

"All right, folks. Here's the deal," Josh announced, rapping the gavel against the podium until all the voices in the room quieted. There were armed WTP guards along the walls, not hundreds like he knew there'd been during the takeover, but still a few were stationed about the room, there to protect Josh. "It's time, once again, to reevaluate some of what you all have approved and the impact it's having on this country, including, but not limited to, the OBA."

Like an unruly class of teenagers, grumbles of frustration, confusion, and disagreement commenced before Josh shushed them. This was the way of things now. His role was much like a school principal, there to make the children listen and behave. Their childish reaction to the announcement was a bit ridiculous because Josh's suggestion wasn't a new concept. At least once a year, he had them do a reevaluation such as this. They simply didn't like the time it took to do the review, nor did they like realizing the true nature of the outcomes of causes they'd made into law.

"Oh, and I'm hearing some alarming stories about what folks might be doing to get meat. Since this body of people supported a hashtag's push to remove animal proteins from the food pyramid, it sounds like we may have a situation like Prohibition happening. Only it's not alcohol you took away from the people. Since you all helped strip pivotal historical events from the records and stopped allowing history to be taught in school," he scratched his head, his expression turning pained and perplexed at the same time, "it looks like we're going to have to relearn all those lessons we garnered from the Prohibition days."

People could, of course, still get meat but the cost was prohibitive for most, and they'd have to spend their discretionary money to get it. Because non-meat products were part of the free commodities offered to all, most of the population transitioned away from consuming the real stuff. The government didn't give individuals a lot of discretionary funds, so people were very picky about what they'd spend it on. Real meat was one of those things many chose to forgo, but that didn't mean they still didn't want it, and were obviously willing to go to extremes to get it.

And then, as if he were shifting to yet another concern brewing in the once civilized country turned Land of Anything Goes, Josh added, "I've heard reports of some unknown foreign organization operating like a Capone-style gang. They're running trafficking rings which, frighteningly enough, might be related to the people's search for meat." His bewildered gaze swept across the room full of now silent Congresspeople. "So, before you champion any more causes, I think you need to go and see what's really happening out there and how your people are surviving the decisions you've helped make into law."

"Wait a minute!" exclaimed someone Devlin didn't recognize seated near the back of the room, off toward the left of the center aisle. "I for one meet regularly with city leaders. I have visited every Tiny Home Village in Kentucky," he said boastfully. "And I've not heard anything about people . . . ." He swallowed hard and looked as if he'd bitten into a lemon. "Eating human flesh, which I think is what you're implying."

The Tiny Home Villages he referred to, or the THV as it was more commonly called, was by far the fastest-growing government program of late, the CCOC holding a strong second place. With the influx of people entering the country, combined with Congress's decision to end homelessness at the same time, the THV program had flourished.

"I'm paying attention to my people. You can't lump all of us into one bucket here." Kentucky glanced around, seeking acknowledgment for his good deeds and support from his cohorts.

"Calm down. Calm down," Josh said loudly into the microphone. "I think it's great that some of you really get down into the weeds and experience what you've created. Problem is, not all of you do it. I'm aware you newer folks tend to get out there and take part in your communities and listen to the people's concerns. It's you older folks, the ones who can't help but linger in the past, who don't get it," he emphasized, spacing out the last few words.

Heads lowered as if to hide from scrutiny. Others, like the Senator from New Jersey, sat proudly straight, his black-and-white-checkered *ghutra* with the black circle *egal* standing out like a chimney on a roof in the room of drab blue, gray, and black suits.

"Before we veer back toward another civil divide, and revert to caveman-like behaviors," he added as an aside, "you need to spend time with all your folks out there, the ones you've opened the borders to and the original citizens. Many of you supported the efforts behind the OBA. Well, now you need to get out there and experience what life is really like outside your comfort zones."

As Josh paused to allow the crowd to stew on what he'd said, Devlin's gaze wandered over the room. When he located Senator Clarkson off to his far right, the nerve at his jaw twinged involuntarily. The sight of her stirred his anger, darkened his mood. A mood that had been surprisingly bright up to that point. Clarkson made eye contact with him, her lips curling into a snarl. She didn't try to hide her disdain for Devlin, nor did he hide his for her.

Although not him specifically now, not since that day at the border, his network, with the help of Mario, continued to be a thorn in her side. Since before the border opening, airing her activities for the world to see had been one of Devlin's primary goals. He honestly believed much of what she did verged on illegal, if not treasonous, and the public had the right to know. Again, he was willing to hold out judgment against her wife, but surely President Grant had to be aware of the things Clarkson was doing to harm the country. Didn't she?

He leaned in close to Mario and spoke to him without breaking eye contact with Clarkson, making it obvious he was talking about her. "I want all your focus on Clarkson and her activities over these next few weeks or even months, if necessary. Talk to everyone you can. I'm certain she's still up to no good. We must expose her racism, sexism, and any other 'isms' she has. Air every event she's at. The only reason she gets re-elected is because the MSM is too afraid of her to show any of her bullshit. Well, that and she's now married to the POTS."

Devlin had lurked behind the scenes for a time now and wasn't as abreast of current events as he'd once been. Fortunately, Mario had been great at updating him on Clarkson's antics. Her latest project centered around her idea that men, including those identifying as such, should not be permitted to run for President of the States. She'd been actively hosting rallies and inciting her followers into sometimes violent demonstrations to promote her cause. Yet, there was irony and hypocrisy in her campaign, considering the recent decision to degenderize America. It left Devlin shaking his head in wonder.

Josh's voice pulled Devlin's focus away from his bitter thoughts. "Here's the plan we've put together." He shrugged off his outer jacket, draping it over the desk behind him, with plans to settle in for a time. "We're going to do something a bit different for this year's reevaluation process. We're going to break for the next month, and every person in this room is going back to his or her State, and you are going to live with host families."

The room erupted. People lurched to their feet, fingers pointing in accusation. Red, angry faces conflicted with ghostly white, terrified ones. Yet, there were other in the crowd who smiled and nodded in favor of the assignment.

Josh allowed the room to roar until the steam that fueled the eruption began to ebb, settling into grumbles, murmurs, and even a few unprofessional curses.

"This is preposterous," a platinum-haired, pearl necklace-wearing woman said from the front row. "You expect us to go and live with . . . with strangers?" she scoffed, her hands gesturing with her words. "What about our security? Are you arranging any of that for us? I mean, we won't know anything about these people you're telling us to live with?"

A deep-throated chuckle from Josh sounded through the room's speakers. "Well, because We The People have considered this idea very thoroughly, we can and do expect you to go to live with 'strangers,'" he emphasized, "as you put it. Strangers who are your brothers and sisters in this land. Strangers who you, and I'm fully aware that you, Representative Hensley, voted to pass the OBA, were adamant foreigners should be welcomed into this country, because they had the right to be here. So yes, we do expect you to exist with your people and experience day-to-day life as they do. Then, we'll reconvene, and you can share if you still believe the OBA is good for the country."

THE CONSEQUENCE CLAUSE

Representative Hensley's hand floated nervously around her throat. There was a quiver in her voice when she asked, "But what about our safety? What about these gangs you mentioned? You said you don't know which group is running them. Can I take my husband with me? What about a security detail?"

This caused Josh to laugh outright. "No, Ms. Hensley. You all expect everyone out there to exist with no security and no law enforcement. And you know as well as I do, you're equal in all ways now to your husband; the subject is, after all, on the current Annual Ballot. So why would you need him along? The people don't have the luxury of ways to protect themselves. So why should you? Allowing a spouse to provide protection violates the Equality Laws, so that seems unfair, and quite honestly, unethical on your part to even ask," he admonished.

"The Constitution you here have whittled away at over the years in your attempts to erase the foundational guide for this country clearly states that 'We the People of the United States'—well, we've already lost the United part—'in Order to form a more perfect Union, establish Justice'—which is what We The People are here trying to do—and 'insure Domestic Tranquility.' Domestic Tranquility." He repeated the phrase, savoring it like he would a delicious flavor on his tongue. "You are going to go and ensure domestic tranquility in your States." As he spoke, his hand flowed back and forth in the air, like a dancer's might, fluid, tranquil. At the end of his speech, he nodded with his conviction.

"And how will this process work?" Mario called out before Devlin could. The media were permitted to be present at all Congressional sessions but with limits on how often they could interrupt with questions. An occasional one here or there was given a pass, but if they tried to rain down a slew of them at once, Josh had no problem tossing them out one by one, or even sometimes as a pack. It all depended on how irritated he was at the behavior.

Today, he answered. Possibly because there'd been silence from the media groups up to that point, or because it was Devlin's team asking the question, he couldn't be sure.

"It's like Bingo, folks. We'll randomly select four names from the Voter Information Log for each of you. Over the course of the next month, let's say from December first through the thirty-first, you'll go spend six days with your selected family. You'll live with them. Sleep in their house. Dine with them. Work with them. You'll listen to their wants and needs, then come back and share your experiences. Consider it like a long, overnight field trip."

A tall, handsomely dressed, middle-aged woman stood. "Excuse me. I'm from Michigan. Don't you think this is a dangerous plan, considering . . . ?" She looked nervously around her, until her eyes settled on the man wearing the *egal*. "As you're well aware, there are some areas in the country like in Michigan, for example, where the laws have shifted to those of the people who occupy them and where they came from."

"Is that a question?" Josh asked, but he didn't wait for an answer. "As part of the OBA, you all permitted immigrants to settle where they chose and, in some communities, they've established their own principles and laws. Which again this Congress approved. In your case, I'm certain you refer to Sharia law which rules over a large section of your State. Is that right?" The woman nodded, imperceptibly. "I could take a quick look at the VIL and remind you if you voted for all the contingencies permitted under the OBA. But I'm sure you don't need me to do that."

He paused until finally the woman sank slowly down into her seat, like her legs could suddenly no longer support her.

THE CONSEQUENCE CLAUSE

"But the Mexicans have claimed a large part of Arizona. I'd potentially be a target for them to use as leverage against the Uni—" The portly, white-haired fellow, boasting a dark tan from his life spent in the sunny climes of Arizona faltered. "Against the States, no matter where I ended up. You can't send me and my co-Congresspeople there to live with the likes of them. Or the likes of people who might be cannibals, if this information you shared proves true," he said with a visible shudder.

"'The likes of them'?" Josh's mouth hung open in dismay. "Careful there, John. Your words might easily be construed as racist or discriminatory. Or both." He narrowed his eyes and pointed at him. "Regardless of boundaries claimed by our neighbors to the south, Arizona is still part of this country. The Mexicans were welcomed here through the OBA. Those who've come across are our countryfolk now. Just as the cannibals might be, if their hashtag group succeeds in convincing enough of you to legalize it, like you've done so many other questionable initiatives. Look at it this way: You'll get to see firsthand what's happening in their worlds and learn their culture. I'm assuming you haven't traveled throughout your State recently?" He waited for an acknowledgment, but upon receiving neither a nod nor head shake, he continued. "Through the Bingo process, you might not even get a family selected from the areas you seem concerned about. But if you do, you can talk to them, hear their wants and needs. Our job is to ensure domestic tranquility, remember?"

"You're sentencing us to the possibility of harm, or captivity, or death even!" the Arizonan exclaimed.

Josh gasped. "You presume to call your countryfolk murderers?" His eyes rounded, and he pressed his hand to his chest dramatically. "The people in your State are families, that you, sir, eagerly welcomed into this country. Let me check my notes here and see where you landed on that side of the OBA decision." He riffled through the papers he'd brought from his office, however, Devlin suspected he knew exactly who had approved the OBA. Before he could finalize his search and state the obvious, the Representative sat down. He shook his head like someone who'd been clobbered and had to let the stars pass from behind his eyes.

"Now, let's begin," Josh announced and resumed the Bingo process. "We have already randomly generated selections for each of you." Which meant, if he'd read them prior to today, he knew if the Arizonan's host families lived in the areas of the State of most concern to the Representative. What he didn't know, Devlin was certain, was if any of those people were members of the latest hashtag group stealing people and serving them up a la carte.

"I'll read them off, but the addresses, names, and contact info will be sent to you through the USFCD dashboard. We'll start with Alabama. Bob Oglethorpe." Josh peered up over a pair of brown-framed reading glasses he'd perched on his nose. From the audience, a wary hand rose in the air. Bob was one from the old crowd; late-fifties, clean-cut, salt-and-pepper hair, and a bright smile. "You'll visit the families of Jeremy Thompson in Fairhope, Martha Johnson in Selma, Raul Dominguez in Brewton, and Harry Greene over in Enterprise. You'll spend six days and nights with the families and drive to your next stop on the seventh and repeat." He set down the document he was reading from and turned to address the media. "Do you all want to stay for this, or should I forward you the list? It might be a while that we're here."

Devlin would have liked to stay, but he had another pressing engagement to get to and informed Josh of his need to leave. Ms. Carlson had texted him about a situation that had popped into her inbox a bit ago. She wanted to meet right away and brief him on the subject.

"No problem, Devlin. Mario," Josh said to each of them with a nod. "I'll look forward to your report on today's events. And welcome back, Devlin. Anyone else?" he inquired of the other media present. There were skeptical looks cast about the small group of reporters, but eventually all the media disbanded and left the room to the sound of Josh's voice calling out the next name on the list. It would be a long night, indeed.

SEVEN

They were walking near the outskirts of the maze of Tiny Home Village Number 973 at North Kingsville, Ohio. It was a small town situated along the top part of the State, its northern boundary the shoreline of Lake Erie. Fifty-seven miles across the water was Ontario, Canada. Devlin stopped to stare out over the vast expanse of water when a gust of wind came at him. He buried his hands into the depths of his coat pockets, turned his head and pulled his shoulders up to his ears. Icy particles lifted off the partly frozen lake and raced through the air, pummeling his back.

He groaned. "How on earth do people tolerate living here?" White-capped waves rocked the lake beyond the twenty feet or so of ice along the shore's edge. The wind picked up again, like a living thing, roiling the water and lifting tiny shards of ice in its grip before flinging it high up into the air and slamming it outward. Devlin swung around again, pulling Tara with him.

"This CE couldn't have waited for a warmer time of year?" he called out over the gale as they hurried away from the shoreline, seeking shelter behind a wall constructed as a barrier protecting THV Number 973 from winter's wrath.

"Sorry," Tara yelled over an impressively loud gust. "It's too serious to let sit, I'm afraid."

The deeper they strode into the village, the wind at their heels became less fierce.

THE CONSEQUENCE CLAUSE

Tiny Home Villages were designed, typically, in one of two ways: spiral-like, circling round and round like a pinwheel, or square-like, the outer rows forming the edges of a box, each layered box placed inside the next. They were all tidy lines, systematic rows of homes making up each ring or square. The homes on the outer-most edges were designed to house a single person or two people. Each level moving inward was designed a bit larger, depending on the number of children in a family.

Tara and Devlin continued their march through the lanes between the homes, moving closer to the center. Their targets consisted of a family with three children.

Devlin pushed the hood of his coat from his head, feeling distanced enough from the inclement weather to do so. "You said this was a divorce situation. I don't understand why, one, it couldn't wait until a warmer day." He gave her a side-eyed glance, his mouth quirking up slightly. "And two, since when do we, you, the government that is, get involved in church activities?"

Tara stopped in the middle of the road in front of three Tiny Homes painted similarly, each the color of the sun. The color of one's Tiny Home was the only feature owners were permitted to alter, making it different from another. Any reference to a person having more than their neighbor, be it money, privilege, or clothing was not allowed, per the rules of the Tiny Home Village Program. If someone desired a porch railing added to their home, it was only granted if everyone in the village agreed to have the same type of railing installed. Shoes and clothing were to be purchased from the same retailer; styles could vary but the overall total dollar amount could not. Per the Equality Laws, everything about everyone in each village had to be the same. Except the paint color of a home. Relatives of families residing in villages together tended to paint their places in matching colors to denote their kin.

Two people approached from up the road, both wearing long, bulky winter coats. Right away, Devlin knew they weren't residents.

"Ms. Carlson." The shorter of the two reached out a hand first to Tara and then to Devlin. "Mr. Johnson."

Devlin shook the proffered hand and then repeated the gesture with the other stranger.

"I'm Donna Reyes, an Agent for this area, and this here"—she angled an arm out, palm up toward the taller man beside her—"this is Thomas Nguyen, the preacher for the Resurrection Church."

"That's the *virtual* church, mind you." The preacher leaned toward Tara, emphasizing the type of church he ran. "I don't want you thinking we're violating rules of the Church Closure Act, or anything like that. Just wanted you to know." He returned to his previous position, feet planted shoulder-width apart and one palm flat atop the other at his waist.

"Thank you for clarifying that. I think we've got enough to deal with here without having to worry about consequences for other violations."

Tara had told Devlin that after churches had first been shut down there'd been many church leaders who'd ignored the directive, refusing to close their doors to in-person services. When those law breakers had been caught, per the conditions outlined in the associated Consequence Clause, they'd been sentenced to prison. Soon after the message got out, most of the holdouts fell into compliance.

"Thanks for coming out on such short notice." The Agent smiled stiffly and squared her shoulders, readying for what was ahead. "You're going to want to get your camera ready," she added, directing her attention to Devlin.

The fine hairs on the back of his neck prickled, as if a cold finger of dread had drifted over his skin. Most people tried to hide from the camera; few told him to get it ready for whatever it was they were about to witness.

"I've not had to deal with a situation like this since the law changed." The petite woman's hands lifted before her, moving in a slow yet uncertain way, as if in defeat and complete confusion at the same time.

Tara's face was an expressionless mask, but as Devlin watched through the camera lens, he caught the subtle act of her biting the inside of her cheek. She nodded. "I'll need to speak with the family. Where is the wife now?" Both the Agent and the preacher pointed to the yellow home in the middle of the three. "And the husband?"

"He's in that one." The Agent directed them to the farthest left home. "The other boy, well . . . ." She paused, lightly rubbing her gloved fingers across her lips. "The other one is at the medical facility." Turning to Devlin, seeing his camera was up and the little red light flashing, she nodded firmly before leading the way to the home where the husband was said to be. Tara, the preacher, and Devlin all followed, Devlin trailing at the back.

"Let me take it from here." Tara pushed to the front of the line and rapped her knuckles against the door. It wasn't a loud knock, but almost immediately following the door opening, the doors of the two identical homes to her right flung wide, too. In the farthest yellow abode, a man and a woman, late forties possibly, stepped tentatively out onto their little porch. The woman had a pale blue quilt dotted with tiny red roses wrapped tight about her shoulders. Long socks covered her lower legs, and her feet were stuffed inside fuzzy gray slippers.

"I can't take it anymore!" she exclaimed in a thick brogue, either Irish or Scottish, Devlin wasn't sure. "It's not right. The way they treat each other. The fighting. The screams." She shuddered, turning her head to the side, burying her face against the chest of the man next to her.

"It's because they're arseholes." This came from the occupant of the middle Tiny Home. Her accent was heavy, too, like the older couple's. The girl had long, honey-colored hair, pulled into a bouncy ponytail against the back of her head. It swished to and fro as she looked at her neighbors on either side of her. Flip flops adorned her feet, but she seemed impervious to the frigid air turning her toes a bright pink. Her eyes trained on Devlin's camera. "I've had me enough of their cheatin' ways."

The young man standing in the doorway directly in front of Tara thrust his tee-shirt-covered chest out and shouldered past her and onto the porch. This was, as had been identified by the Agent moments ago, the husband and presumably the cheater, according to the blonde bristling on the next porch over.

"It's not cheatin' if the woman is our wife." The young man had curly hair that reached his shoulders; it was a similar shade of blonde as the girl's, only his was a bit unkempt, stringy, and greasy. His face flushed red, further highlighting the heavy case of acne dotting the landscape of his cheeks and forehead.

"Your wife?" the girl hollered back, her arm shooting up and a finger pointing in the direction of a purple-colored Tiny Home across the lane. "She's nothing but a whore." Her smooth, round cheeks burned a bright pink.

When the girl lunged off her porch, her intention to come at the young man apparent, the Agent intercepted her by latching her hand around one thin upper arm. "That's enough! We're here to get to the bottom of this."

"My son." The older man at the third home spoke softly. "How is he? Will he survive? Will he . . . ?" He hesitated, casting a pained glance at the woman by his side. "Will he be n-normal?" he stuttered.

Before whoever had the answer to this question could respond, Tara cleared her throat. "Excuse me. Are you Sean Murphy?"

The acne-faced boy's head whipped around, bright green eyes flaring wide. His head bobbed once.

"And you?" She turned to face the still-restrained girl. "Are you Clara Murphy?"

"Not for much longer!" she shrieked. "I'm goin' ta change my name, so I don't have to be associated with the likes of them."

A quiet sob sounded from the older woman in the background.

"Clara. Enough! You're upsettin' your mother with your talk." The older man had his arm wrapped about the woman's shoulder. He gave her a squeeze and she whimpered pitifully.

"Mr. and Mrs. Murphy," the Agent said to the older couple. "Please refrain from commenting so Ms. Carlson can get the information she needs."

"No, Dad. Let her change her name. She's a disgrace to it anyway." Puffs of white air blew from Sean's nostrils as he rounded on Clara. "She tried to kill Tommy. Nearly hacked off his pecker, she did. And then, when I came runnin' in, she started to come at me. But I stopped her," he added boastfully, shoving his thin chest out again.

Finally, having heard enough of the explanation unfolding that only resulted in more questions than answers, Tara held up a firm hand. "Stop! All of you."

Sean instantly deflated, his shoulders falling forward. The girl stopped pulling against the Agent's restraining hand. The couple now identified as Clara and Sean's parents clamped their mouths shut, too. The older woman's lips were turning purple, her teeth beginning to chatter.

"It's cold out here. Can we step inside?" Tara looked at the Agent and then at Sean.

Sean huffed out a gush of air, as if he'd been punched in the gut. "She's not allowed in my house. Murderous bitch, she is."

"We'll use this one." The Agent stepped up to the doorway of the middle home. "This is where the incident took place."

Sean rolled his eyes but stepped the necessary ten paces it took to get to Clara's doorway. Tara followed.

The preacher paused on the first step. "Mr. and Mrs. Murphy, please go back inside. We'll let you know when we're finished here." As the older couple disappeared inside their home, Devlin entered the middle home and closed the door.

The Tiny Home, a standard-sized model for one to two people, was approximately twenty feet long, eight feet wide, and thirteen feet high. Adding six bodies to the small space went beyond cozy. The Agent and preacher stood to the right, in front of a couch draped with a blanket. Sean was between them. Tara and the girl, Clara, were across from them in front of a television and a chair, the only other pieces of furniture in the room.

Devlin leaned his back to the door, camera directed out. Due to the narrow dimensions of the room, he had no need to pan out to capture all members of his audience.

Adding to the cramped quarters was the amount of disarray, for a better choice of description. Clothes littered the floor as did several dishes—dirty, the lot of them. There were bins overflowing with packaged food items, easily recognizable as the standard, monthly allotment of government commodities all Tiny Home tenants received, or any States' residents who asked for them.

"Mrs. Murphy," Tara began.

"It's Clara. I don't think I want to be Mrs. Murphy anymore." Clara crossed her thin arms together over her chest and her lower lip pushed out into a pout. She flounced down into the cozy corner chair cluttered with at least a dozen stuffed animals. Pulling her legs up to her chin, she wrapped her arms around her shins and pressed her forehead on top of her bony knees.

"Okay, then. Can someone explain what happened?" Tara directed her attention to the Agent and preacher.

The Agent licked her visibly dry and chapped lips. "Clara here accused her husband of engaging in intimate acts with another woman. A neighbor across the street. There was an altercation." She bent down and flung back the end of the blanket covering the couch. Devlin leaned slightly, enough to see past the Agent. A dark stain covered nearly one entire cushion of the three-cushioned couch. It was indistinguishable in color against the chocolate shade of the fabric. But upon closer inspection, he noticed the smear of something that resembled blood on the floor by the Agent's boot. There were also some reddish-brown drops of a substance on the wall behind the couch.

"An altercation, my arse!" Sean took a step forward, anger and something else flitting behind his eyes. "She nearly gutted my brother while trying to cut his parts from him."

Tara's brows shifted upward. "You're her brother," she stated, confirming the relationship. At Sean's nod, she then added, "And you're her husband." Her nose scrunched and she cocked her head slightly, casting a curious glance at the preacher standing beside Sean.

"They're both my husband." The muffled words came from the corner. "We're officially married. It's documented with the church."

Devlin drew in a sharp breath of air through his nostrils. Five sets of eyes shifted his way. He peeked around the camera, understanding dawning as to the reason for the preacher's presence.

"And that church would be the Resurrection Church. Correct?" Devlin asked.

Mr. Nguyen nodded. "Virtual."

Clara's green eyes, so like her brother-slash-husband's, darted about the room with curiosity, as if struggling to follow the line of conversation. Her face pinched and she waved one hand as if shooing away a silly idea. "But it wouldn't have mattered which church. According to the laws, if we have a church to approve the marriage, it's all official."

A warm look passed between Sean and Clara. The hormonal excitement blazing in their gazes made Devlin's skin crawl.

By now, Tara had the little blue book in her hand. Devlin noticed right away that it wasn't the same copy of the book she'd had in California. This one was brand new, the binding perfectly clean, no indication of worn edges anywhere. Consequence Clauses were being assigned to laws, new and old, every day, making it so Tara's book of consequences needed to be updated regularly.

Adding CCs to all laws was a daunting task for Congress to tackle, the process very time-consuming. Basically, those in favor of a law or issue were off the hook, while those who opposed the issue were given the assignment to formulate a CC that would balance the scales of justice. Congress had been busy for the past few years, with no slowing down in sight. As such, there would undoubtedly be more versions of Tara's little blue book printed in the future.

Tara switched to her official-sounding voice. "The matter at hand is not the validity of your wedded state. Agent Reyes and Mr. Nguyen have already verified the church's willingness to perform same-family ceremonies. And as it happens, they also support polygamy and bigamy. Therefore, no laws were violated by your having taken both your brothers as a spouse."

"Ms. Carlson?" Devlin interrupted. "Could you provide some context on how and why marriage among siblings is considered acceptable and legal? As this is a relatively new change to the laws, I'd like to help my viewers gain a full understanding on the matter."

Without further prompting, as this was exactly why she'd wanted Devlin's help during CEs, she turned square to the camera. In a voice lacking any emotion, she stated, as if by rote, "Once States could no longer govern themselves, the decision was made to turn all business related to marriages—licensing and ceremonies—over to the churches. They are now the official authorities over all unions."

She glanced over her shoulder at Sean and Clara. They weren't paying attention to Tara at all. Instead, they were whispering to each other, sweet words, words a brother should not be saying to a sister.

Tara turned back forward. "Polygamists were the first to fight for legal marital rights when the laws changed, but then, on their heels came many more groups claiming they, too, should have rights to marry whoever, or whatever," she added with a small shrug, "they so choose."

Once the polygamists won their fight, another group began demanding rights for familial unions, stealing the motto from the two groups ahead of them who'd fought their battles and won. Love is love, was the claim. Denying them and not the others was argued to be discriminatory. And that was something leaders in government took a firm stance against. But legalizing familial unions challenged even the most liberal-minded members of Congress. So, to remove the potential stain of such a thing affecting the government, they'd found a majority among them to vote in favor of relinquishing all matters relating to marriage back to the church.

"Recently," Tara explained, "laws changed reducing the voting age to fourteen. As such, that is now the official age of legal consent as well. This means, all the young Murphys here needed to do was find a church willing to bind them in matrimony." Tara's calm broke slightly. Lines appeared on her forehead and near the corners of her eyes. Her lips parted, but for the count of three seconds, she said nothing.

"And our church has married us," Sean boasted as he snuggled his sister-slash-wife.

"How old are you both?" Devlin inquired for the sake of sharing with his viewers. He zoomed in so only the couple were in his viewfinder.

Sean's chin shifted higher. "I'm seventeen and she's fourteen. Tommy is sixteen." Then with an air of haughty entitlement, he added, "We're all of legal age to vote. It only makes sense we're legal to marry, too." He ran his long, skinny fingers along one of Clara's legs.

Devlin's gut turned. He'd heard there'd been groups championing a younger legal age for kids to marry. But fourteen? Their brains weren't even fully developed until their early twenties. But rather than face negative press and risk losing a voter base, many in Congress had caved. And now, not only could children fourteen and older enter the bonds of matrimony, they'd also been granted the right to vote on decisions that would affect the country in ways their underdeveloped minds couldn't fully comprehend.

"She lives here with Tommy and over there with me. We trade off nights." The young man, a boy really, explained dreamily about the living arrangements he and his brother shared with their sister-slash-wife. Clara, who still bore the fresh-faced look of innocence, likely barely having reached puberty, was now a wife. Not only a wife, but one claimed by boys who she should have trusted to protect her from the ways of the world. Instead, because a hashtag group pushed and pushed for "equal rights," and because they'd been sponsored by the media and supported by politicians too afraid of losing a vote, the child-wife was now considered an adult in every way.

But Sean wasn't finished with his explanation. Like a boy in a locker room, his instinct to peacock about his accomplishments as well as his brother's came about. "We could hardly wait for her birthday so we could—"

"As I was saying," Tara interrupted in a loud voice that made the children snuggled up together on the chair flinch.

Devlin, who'd been staring open-mouthed at the ridiculousness of the situation playing out live through the lens of his camera, jumped, too. He snapped his jaw shut.

"As I said, the validity of the marriage—marriages," Tara corrected, "are not in question here." She pointed at the bloodstained couch. "What I need to know is what happened to cause that."

The Agent shifted on her feet, stepping away from a smear of blood near the toe of her boot.

"Yesterday, Clara here, returned to her home to find her brother—"

"Husband," Clara corrected.

The Agent's frustrated gaze jumped to Clara. "Husband . . . and brother," she conceded, but not willing to disregard the sibling relationship the two shared. "Tommy was on this couch with another woman." Her head jerked once, pointing without words. "She's a widow. Lives across the way. She lost her husband in a nasty skirmish with a neighbor before the revolution. She has kids, but they're grown and out on their own. Anyway, she invited the boys to, uh, her bed."

The Agent stumbled over the last words, because clearly, discussing such matters in front of children didn't sit well, no matter how legal or not it might be.

"But Tommy and me, we were raised with some morals," Sean chimed in boastfully. "We said we couldn't do that unless we were married. She agreed, so we asked the preacher here to do the honors." He grinned at the preacher, like he was his best pal.

Mr. Nguyen dipped his head solemnly in acceptance of the boy's gratitude.

Clara lurched up from her seat, shoving Sean's hand from where it had been resting on her thigh. "But I don't want them to be married to anyone but me." She stomped her bare foot, ponytail bobbing with the petulant action, her fists clenched tight at her sides. "And so, I did what I did." Her eyes darted to the couch. "It wasn't Tommy I meant to go after, but *her*." Her lips curled into a sneer. "She jumped off him when I came in and raced out of here before I could get to her. The chicken bitch she was didn't even stop to grab her clothes." She braced her hands against her hips.

Tara drew a long, deep breath in through her nose before forcing it out audibly past her lips, her exasperation apparent. With head bowed, she scrunched her eyes closed and began tapping the edge of her little blue book against her forehead. "So, the wedded status of all parties can be confirmed. Yes?"

Mr. Nguyen pursed his lips and nodded. "Yes. They're all official. I've already had their status updated in the Control Database."

Tara turned to Clara. "How did Tommy get injured then if you meant to go after the other woman? His wife," she reminded the girl.

Clara's mouth pushed into a tight pout, and she crossed her arms over her chest again. She glared as hard as she could at

Tara. "He had the nerve to tell me to wait my turn! Or, or—" she stuttered, "that I should go next door and be with Sean while he waited to consummate their marriage!" She screamed, actually screamed as she rounded on Sean.

Her tiny fists began pummeling his chest, but the Agent intervened, gripping her around the biceps and pulling her to stand near the couch.

"Tommy told me she grabbed a knife from the drawer." Sean pointed to a three-foot-long counter past where he was standing, the area of the home that was the kitchen. A drawer beside a small sink, next to a miniature-sized refrigerator, stood open. "He said, before he knew what she was up to, she came at him, like a banshee wailing, is how he described it."

He shuddered at the thought of a banshee's scream, or the knowledge of the damage done to his brother, Devlin wasn't certain.

"Before he could get up, she threw herself at him, stabbing him. Hit him low in the parts." Instinct had Sean covering his crotch with one hand, his posture tightening as if feeling his brother's pain.

"I didn't mean to." Clara's eyes were suddenly wide, frenzied, as if realizing, finally, she did something wrong. "I was mad."

Devlin genuinely felt sorry for the girl. She was a child playing at being an adult and dealing with grown-up things. The preacher had done nothing illegal just as Sean, Tommy, and the older woman—old enough to have grown children already gone from her home—hadn't.

Tara was flipping through pages of her small book. She paused, her eyes moving across the words before her. Finally, straightening her spine and elongating her neck, she looked up.

"Mrs. Murphy," she began, her voice strong, assured. The only hint of emotion Devlin saw were the tendons in her neck straining as she gritted her back teeth. "Per the Consequence Clause in situations like this, assault with a deadly weapon against a spouse . . . ." She trailed off with a sigh. "When the government relinquished their power in decision-making related to marriages, including their willingness to lower the legal age limit, the CC they created was made especially harsh because they believed if people really wanted the union bad enough, they should respect it more. If you'd not been married to Tommy, this would have been a much simpler case, a neighborly argument, possibly. But the consequences are harsh against those who adopt into the concept of marriage." She swallowed hard, her throat convulsing up, then down. "Under these circumstances, the penalty for your crime is set at five years in prison. That would be Nevada's Free-Range Prison. Until—"

Before Tara could state the timeframe in which the sentence would be carried out, Clara's knees buckled, and Sean was on his feet at her side.

"No! Let her divorce him. That way they don't have to be together. He'll forgive her. I know it." Sean pleaded his brother's case on Clara's behalf.

Clara sat on the floor, her small chest heaving, the flush that had been on her face moments ago when she'd stared adoringly at her husband-slash-brother had disappeared. She was close to hyperventilating.

Mr. Nguyen took a step forward, inserting himself into the situation after having been mostly quiet. He shook his head. "I've spoken to Tommy. He doesn't want a divorce. He said he'll be right here waiting for her."

Clara's wide, bright green eyes shot up at this. "H-he's going to hurt me if I come back here. He said he'd kill me. I heard him when they were taking him away." From her perch on the floor, she turned to Tara. "Make him agree to a divorce.

I'll move over to Sean's. Tommy can stay here. We won't have to—"

"To divorce, all parties involved in this union must agree to the termination. Since the boys are married to the neighbor lady, she'd have to give her approval, too, as would Tommy. And he said he doesn't want it. When you come back from the FRP, you'll have to reunite with him. He didn't mean his threat. It was likely said in the heat of the moment."

The preacher did at least sound somewhat sympathetic to the girl's plight. But the law was the law and unless all parties agreed to the divorce, he had no power to end the marriage contract.

When the true impact of what Tara and the preacher had said breached some level of processing in Clara's young brain, she could barely say her next words. "I'm just a little girl. How do I survive in prison by myself?"

Tara shook her head. "You'll have five years to figure it out, I'm afraid. You're a legal adult, after all." Turning her attention to the Agent, she commanded, "Affix the ankle bracelet, then arrange for her transport to Nevada. I'll send over the report, so they know her sentence."

As Sean held tight to the little girl crumpled on the floor, Clara's eyes rolled back in her head as she went limp into a faint.

Devlin let the image on screen fade to black.

EIGHT

"Where'd you disappear to last week?" Tara asked as she stepped through the door Devlin held open for her.

They were at one of those old-fashioned type of diners, a rarity these days amid the endangered population of mom-and-pop businesses. The owner of this one had to be very wealthy, enough to afford the twenty-nine-dollar per hour minimum wage and continuously rising taxes on all businesses. Sadly, it was only a matter of time before the cost to run the small operation became greater than the profits and it succumbed to a fate like many others.

"Take a seat wherever you want," an elderly woman called out from a nearby table where she was pouring coffee for a patron. She looked like Alice from those old Brady Bunch episodes Devlin had seen on cable TV as a kid; tidy hair, white apron, and shoes designed for comfort.

He did as he was bid and ushered Tara to a booth near the back of the establishment. On one side was a window, across from them the end of a long, laminated counter where four other patrons sat spaced apart in solitude. High above the counter, anchored to the wall was a television turned to a news station—not Devlin's—the volume set low. A banner running across the bottom of the screen streamed other news happening.

Upon their entry, the low hum of conversations stemming from the other diners ceased as everyone turned to see who'd entered their domain. In the span of time it took him and Tara to settle into their seats, the only voice in the room was the news anchor's. Seconds later, they were no longer a novelty, and the room crept back into a warm and comfortable buzz. The smell of coffee and breakfast foods cooking reminded him of times his grandfather had taken him to a diner like this one up in the mountains when he was a young boy. Back when hunting was legal. It was a happy memory, one from a different time.

Devlin braced his arm over the back of the booth and peered around at the other customers. Somewhere among the small crowd, he was certain he'd find someone resembling his grandfather, one of those old-timers known to frequent this type of place with their coffee-drinking buddies.

There were only a few older men and women. People these days had no incentive to work—not even with a minimum wage of nearly thirty dollars per hour. They often spent their time much like this, sitting around doing nothing, hanging out with friends because they had nowhere they needed to be.

The reason for this unfortunate change in societal behavior was a direct result of the OBA. When a country hands out all basic necessities, such as lodging, food, and clothing, the need to earn those things gradually disappears, like fog on a sunny day. At first, entitlements were only offered to folks coming in through the OBA. But when hashtags appeared at the steps of the Capitol claiming the OBA incited racism, discrimination, and anti-nationalism, Congress had little choice but to offer entitlements identified in the Act to every individual living within the boundaries of the States.

Now, those who wanted to work did so and those who didn't enjoyed living off the bountiful handouts provided.

Devlin sighed poignantly, before turning back around in his seat. All he had to do was say "give me what I'm due," and he too could collect his entitlements from the government. But he refused to stoop to that level of laziness and greed. He couldn't imagine such an unfulfilling existence.

When their waitress arrived, he deferred to Tara to place her order first.

"I'd like that big, fat cinnamon roll you have advertised on your sign there." She pointed at a whiteboard with the day's specials scribbled in block letters, her face scrunching with childlike glee. "What?" she asked innocently when Devlin cocked his head at her. "When's the next time we'll get something home cooked like this?"

She was right. He perused the day's specials again, contemplating his options with a frown. Nothing, yet everything, interested him. With a resigned sigh he gave his order. "I'll have the biscuits and gravy. And can I get two eggs over medium and two slices of real bacon with that, please?"

The waitress nodded cheerily and promised to return shortly with their meals.

"Oh, like that's any healthier than what I ordered?" Tara teased, flashing him a brilliant smile. "But I might want a bite of your bacon and eggs. To get some protein, of course."

"Why do you think I ordered so much? I knew you'd eat half my meal, so I got extra just to be safe. The government's paying for it, so why not?"

They'd only been working together a short time now, but already he was learning her quirks. Food was one of them. He liked that they'd connected so quickly. Their conversations were easy, even with difficult topics. It had been a long time since he'd experienced a friendship with anyone besides Josh, Mario, and even Conrad to a degree. He'd had no women in his life, friends or otherwise. It was a foreign feeling to experience this camaraderie with the opposite sex, but he'd already noticed her presence had done a lot to quiet the anger bottled inside him these last few years.

She slapped at his hand, the one not holding his coffee cup, her face a show of mock affront. "Well, I'm glad you're still gentlemanly enough to consider my needs."

It was rare to see any man, especially one below the age of forty offering a respectful gesture or showing gentleman-like etiquette around women. It wasn't officially banned—only because it would be impossible to manage—but thanks to the Degenderizing Act, men were no longer expected to treat women differently from them, in any way. Old habits die hard, though, and Devlin found it impossible to not hold open a door, or carry a bag, or allow a woman to order first in a restaurant.

It was the reason he still addressed Tara as Ms. Carlson. His grandfather would have whacked him upside the head if he'd caught him caving to such disrespect as society had begun to demand. It was too bad people couldn't acknowledge that scientifically and spiritually, men and women were designed as they were, each having elements of their being that complemented the other.

"Earth to Devlin." Tara snapped her long, elegant fingers in front of Devlin's face. With his attention back on her, she re-asked her question before sipping on the perfectly brewed black coffee. "Where'd you go last week?"

He lifted the little tin pitcher of cream substitute their waitress had left along with their coffee and added some to his cup. His spoon made a light tapping sound as he stirred. "I had something I needed to take care of. You know how deadlines are? Anyway, got it done and made it back in time for this." He licked the spoon clean and then waved it in a small circle. "Thanks for waiting for me." There *had* been a deadline to meet, however, it was a personal deadline, not a work one, as he knew Tara assumed. He didn't want to discuss the details with her, not yet anyway, so he steered the conversation in a new direction.

"I haven't had much luck talking to all the business owners down by Carl's place. Between me and Mario, we've only been able to contact the ones whose businesses are still open. We can't locate the owners of all those closed up or destroyed, and I do mean all," he added with a thoughtful shake of his head. "We've got names and contact information, but they're simply not responding to our inquiries."

"They lost their livelihoods. I suppose it makes sense if they left the area to start over somewhere else?"

"It's possible. Or were they run off? Or did something worse happen to them?"

Their meals arrived, and they settled into the delicious food. Devlin eyed the cinnamon roll across from him appreciatively. When Tara reached for a piece of bacon, as he knew she would, he cut a small wedge of the sticky bun off her plate and popped it into his mouth, savoring the sweet, brown, sugary goo dissolving on his tongue. He chewed slowly.

Picking up the conversation where he'd left off pre-cinnamon roll, he said, "I mean, it wouldn't seem overly suspicious if we could've talked to at least one person. But to not contact any of them? And we've found dozens more destroyed businesses in the area, too. It doesn't feel right." He swallowed, washing his bite of food down with a sip of coffee while glancing up at the television.

A reporter was standing in front of a large, ornate building with a tower shooting up from its center, the dome at the top crowned in gold. The words Nebraska State Capitol appeared in the lower left of the screen.

Devlin, unable to hear everything the reporter said, read the subtitles as they appeared, telling them about an unusually high number of deaths that occurred in Nebraska in a twenty-four-hour period. High being nearly two thousand, many of whom lived in rural communities across the State. Family members of the deceased confirmed their loved ones had not had any illness or visible symptoms of anything prior to their deaths. The dead ranged in age from the twenties to the eighties and they were a mix of genders and race. Some were here through the OBA while others were original citizens, so nothing specific to any demographic notable at present.

"That's interesting." Devlin pointed at the TV with his fork. He grabbed his phone and shot a quick text to Mario. "I need to make sure Mario's on this. He probably is, but I'll check."

On screen now was an older man, his skin slightly wrinkled with age, and his hair color a solid gray verging on silver. He told the reporter he'd found his wife in their front yard, lying on her side as if she'd curled up and gone to sleep.

"Poor thing," Tara whispered. "Probably a heart attack or stroke."

But as soon as the words left her mouth, the grieving man on camera went on to explain how he'd made the same assumption as Tara. But then he'd heard about five other locals from his own town who'd experienced a similar loss. To a small town like that, one right outside of Lincoln, whose population boasted only four thousand people, six deaths was a high number.

Tara's brow knitted, and she sat up straight, her fork hanging from her fingers. "Did Mario reply? Six people dying suddenly? It almost sounds like a Brockovich story. Like toxins in the water or something."

His phoned chimed. "Yes, he's on it. He said he's on the other side of the State. A long way from the Lincoln area."

Both Devlin and Tara had their gazes fixed on the TV now, each taking distracted bites of their food as their curiosity grew.

"It'll be interesting to find out what happened. I wonder if the State has been adding something to the water, a vitamin additive, maybe," Tara said thoughtfully, her fingers drumming against the side of her mug. "I've heard it's a thing now since we're not getting enough essential vitamins and minerals from the processed proteins we've been forced to consume. If that's what's happening in Nebraska, and only two thousand had negative reactions, I suppose those percentages aren't terrible. The State's lucky everyone didn't die."

"I'll have Mario check with the State people to find out if they recently introduced vitamin additives." He returned to his breakfast, but his mind circled around the idea of people unsuspectingly ingesting ingredients added to their water supply. If this were true, it would be yet another layer of government control forced on the people, regardless of there being good intentions behind the idea. For every action, there's a reaction. And in this case, if the assumption proved true, the reaction to fix a problem created by a government-controlled mandate, meant possible death for many.

He wrinkled his nose as he looked down at his plate. The idea of tainted food was stealing his hunger. But meals like this were becoming harder to find with each passing day. He needed to take advantage of every opportunity provided him, because someday soon, he feared it'd all be gone.

At the same time that Tara reached across and stole a bite of his biscuits and gravy, Devlin's cell phone chimed again. He flipped it face up on the table and opened the incoming email message from Mario. It was a video clip. "Mario says he's got something else for us." Before pressing play, he took another bite, then set his fork down and pushed his plate away. As Tara eyeballed the remaining half piece of bacon he'd left for her, he started the clip.

The scene that came to life on his screen was a familiar one, a section of the street opposite Carl's pizza place. The businesses in the picture hadn't yet been boarded up or burned out. This was the camera footage he'd asked his manager to find. And, if his assumption was correct, whatever was in the clip Mario had deemed it important enough to send, rather than wait to share it with him when he returned to DC.

Tara craned her neck to see. "What is it?"

Lifting the phone, he held it in a way they could both watch. "Proof, hopefully, of who's been threatening Carl and the others. Look there, this was captured before the business owners failed to comply." On screen, the sidewalks were filled with pedestrians, the streets packed with all manner of motorized and non-motorized transportation. A typical day in the nation's capital. The shops in view were open, people coming and going at each.

"What are we looking for?" Tara asked, staring hard at the images playing out before them.

Devlin shrugged. "Not sure. There's something, though, or Mario wouldn't have sent it." His eyes searched every centimeter of the screen, from the movement of people and vehicles in the foreground to the store fronts in the background all the way up to the top of the screen where nothing but windows and brick wall were visible. He scanned every window. Maybe it was someone inside looking out who'd been captured in digital memory. Seconds later the clip ended.

"Hmmm." Tara leaned back in her seat. "There's nothing there I can use that'll help Carl." Her tone was matter of fact, but Devlin was certain he heard remorse, too. Then she added, "I did find out he was telling the truth when he said he'd contacted the Agent Department for help. The call was scrapped. The department head deemed it a level zero priority as there was no violence involved, with him specifically, and no proof."

Agents weren't cops. They were merely enforcers when situations arose that were deemed level four priority. Tara typically got involved at level four. It also reached that level with murder, but only those instances where the perpetrator was immediately identified or when someone confessed. Most all other crimes went unresolved because Agents weren't detectives. Law enforcement no longer existed. The Consequence Clause was all the enforcement the people had now.

Devlin hit the play button again, certain he'd missed something. Mario got a kick out of making him search scenes like this without telling him what he was to look for, very much like finding Waldo. If he were on a time crunch or grumpy, his manager would be forthright in the telling of what was in the clip. But in this situation, Mario knew Devlin was out of town and that Tara wouldn't be addressing the Carl situation right away. Plus, Mario was busy in Nebraska. And so, the game was on.

Hundreds of people filled the screen; people going places, some hawking wares, others crossing the congested street, and more moving in and out of the shops in the background. Devlin braced his elbow on the table and pressed his palm against the side of his head while staring hard at his phone.

"Hold up." Tara shot upright in her seat. "Rewind that," she demanded as she folded both arms in front of her on the table and bent closer. Devlin did as instructed. "Look there."

Her index finger hovered near his phone, pointing below the image of a figure entering the scene near the left side of the screen. A man wearing a hat pulled low, covering his ears, entered the first establishment in the row of three in view.

Devlin knew from his visit to Carl's restaurant that the shop the man with the cap had entered was not one of the ones destroyed. The next two hadn't fared as well. Less than a minute passed when they saw Hat Guy leaving the business before continuing down the sidewalk, moving off to the right across the screen. The hat seemed out of place. Hats were casual, not business-like, which the rest of his attire was. In a break among the crowd of pedestrians, Devlin saw that he wore dark slacks and a suit jacket. As he approached the doorway to the next business, he raised his arm to push on the door but paused to glance up and down the street before slipping inside the building.

He'd only been out of view a moment before the door opened again and he reappeared. Quick on his heels was a woman, expostulating with words and abrupt arm movements and hand gestures. There was no sound to the video, but her demands that Hat Guy depart her company, leave her place of business, was evident in the way she pointed a finger, her arm bending at the elbow several times, in and out, clearly telling the interloper to go.

Hat Guy stepped close to the petite woman, bending down to say something while pointing at the building behind her and then at the opposite side of the street, Carl's side. He squared his broad shoulders, turned on a heel and strode away, leaving the shopkeeper behind, mouth still flinging what were clearly angry words. Hat Guy disappeared behind the door of the next business, only to emerge moments later, this time shaking his head as he walked off, eventually disappearing off the screen as the clip ended.

"We've got him," Devlin breathed, his forehead pressed against his open palm.

"Not quite, but it's a good start. Clearly, he's the threat. We've got to find those business owners, show them the tape, and get them to confirm our assumptions."

"I'll show it to Josh. See if he's seen the guy around the Capitol. We find him, " he dipped his head at his phone, "we find who he works for and get this bullying behavior out of our government."

He clicked a button to close out his screen, pushed his phone aside and sipped his coffee, thoughts tumbling through his brain. The way Hat Guy was dressed, the assumption could be made that he worked on the Hill, he was one of them, or at the very least associated with one of them.

Tara remained quiet, lost to her internal thoughts. She looked up at him behind long, dark lashes and offered him a wry, crooked smile. "Merry Christmas, by the way," she whispered. "I got you a little gift but left it in the car."

Devlin's breath hitched. "Oh, crap."

He'd completely forgotten it was Christmas. Not a single twinkling light, electronic dancing reindeer, or evergreen tree—fake or real—stood on display to brighten people's moods or as a reminder of the occasion. Not since holidays had been banned. Due to the influx of immigrants to the country who didn't share the same views or recognize the nation's practices and traditions, hashtags had sprouted up crying prejudice and discrimination when it came to holidays. Since there were now so many different religions and beliefs infiltrating society, Congress made the decision to erase all special days causing strife, beginning with the religious ones.

Other holidays soon came under attack, too. Not everyone believed in honoring past military members, those from the States who'd lost their lives defending this land. Many of the people living here now came from places Americans had once fought against. Honoring anything or anyone specific to this country had been deemed discriminatory, and as such, needed to be banned. Now, any celebration of holidays formerly recognized in the States or in any other country, had to remain within the confines of a person's home. There could be no outward public, visible displays. This meant no tree in the window, no lights on the house, no fireworks, or other past traditions. The rules applied to everyone, regardless of race, religion, or resident status.

Discrimination in any form was not permitted.

"Happy Winter, you mean." Devlin peered over his shoulder, like he'd been caught doing something wrong. He hadn't, but Tara certainly had when she said Merry Christmas.

There were only four holidays in the States now, each occurring on the change of the season. It was on each of those dates that people exchanged gifts or had festivals and work parties. It was neutral and, so far, unoffensive, except to everyone who'd been stripped of the rights to their country's past and traditions. Devlin wasn't optimistic the new holidays wouldn't draw ire from a group out there somewhere. Eventually, it was likely the four seasons would be found controversial somehow.

"No, I mean Merry Christmas," Tara said again, with some bravado this time. The look in her eyes dared him to make her back down, which Devlin knew he couldn't do.

"Of course," was all he said, which got him a triumphant smile in return.

She'd previously told him that Christmas had always been her favorite holiday. It was the one she missed the most after they'd all been banned. Devlin made himself a quiet promise to make the day special again for her, next year. For now, it was a day of business as usual.

After a quick glance at his watch, he sighed. "All right. We should get going." They both stood. He slipped on his jacket on the way to the register, bracing for the cold outside. After Tara ran her arm beneath the blue laser light, quickly paying for their meals, they left, wishing their waitress a Happy Winter on their way out the door.

Devlin shivered at the cold as he dropped into the passenger seat of the car. Grabbing his camera, he readied it for the upcoming situation he and Tara had traveled across the bridge to Virginia to experience.

They had little information to go on, besides an anonymous tip Tara had received about this being worth her while, calling it something of "potential epic proportion." Tips like these, the anonymous type, weren't uncommon, so it wasn't unusual they'd check into it. Back in the day, law enforcement were the ones contacted to investigate crimes, but in their absence, Tara's job, and now Devlin's, often took on an investigative role as well as compliance officer and reporter.

Today's "epic" situation had instantly piqued both their interest.

They arrived at their destination in short order as it was not by coincidence they'd dined where they had. Three city blocks away, off the main drag running through Alexandria, Virginia, across the Potomac River from Washington DC was the hotel where they were to witness whatever they were meant to see. They parked near the end of the building.

"I'll go in first and look around. It's early yet. I was told to be in the hotel bar by ten-thirty." Tara announced this as she brushed past Devlin. He snagged her wrist, forcing her to a stop.

"Ms. Carlson. Are you sure you can trust the tip? That this isn't a trap?"

They both knew their jobs were necessary and done with the greater good in mind. They also knew there were haters out there who weren't beneath trying to make either of them look bad. His was a fair question to ask.

"I don't know exactly. The person who called me said this could wind up being the biggest case I've had to date." With a small shrug, she turned her back to him and headed toward the building's entrance. "Stay ten feet behind me. And keep your camera out of sight until we're settled," she said over her shoulder.

THE CONSEQUENCE CLAUSE

Devlin's sixth sense as a reporter was on full alert. It was a sensation that had saved his ass on more than one occasion, before, during, and since the revolution. And that was saying a lot, as people had guns back in the day. The anger and regret he still harbored over his sixth sense choosing not to knock on his door the day the woman at the border had been killed burned hot and deep within.

"Damn it!" he hissed before stalking after Tara.

Pulling his ballcap low over his forehead, he walked through the lobby toward the lounge area. Inside the dark bar, made so by dimmed lighting and no windows to the outside world, he searched the room and wasn't surprised to find only a few patrons present. Locating his partner near the far end of the bar, he went to her, and perched on the stool directly beside hers. The bartender came to take their orders.

Devlin asked for a soda. The one available wasn't his first choice, but other more popular beverage companies had already escaped the States in their efforts to avoid death by taxes. So far, few companies had been willing to pay the high tariffs imposed on their products, so the people in the States continued to go without the other once-popular drinks.

Tara discreetly lifted a finger to her lips then tilted her head, indicating the people seated in the booths behind them. According to the tip she'd received, whoever and whatever they were there to witness would happen around ten-thirty. But among those occupying the booths, who were the targets? Devlin settled into his seat. He and Tara would have to eavesdrop until something of interest caught their attention.

"Anyone look familiar to you?" He bent close to her in such a way someone watching would have assumed they were a couple sharing a private conversation.

With one elbow on the bar, she leaned her chin against her closed fist and casually craned her head around. Devlin saw her eyes shift from one person to the next, moving up and down over the upper parts of their bodies, what was visible from this angle. Her lips pressed into a thin line, her brows dipping inward as her head moved in a barely noticeable side-to-side motion.

She turned forward on her seat. "Nothing. You check. I can barely see the ones over in the corner."

Tugging his hat as far down on his forehead as he could, he mimicked Tara's casual observation of the room. Two men sat in the nearest booth, the one facing Devlin's way looking bleary-eyed, his hair a blond mop that might not have been combed, or it had been styled that way. It was hard to tell.

"That was one hell of a party, man. I can't believe you stole that car," the blond guy, who looked to be in his mid-thirties, said to his companion.

The response from the other man, the dark-haired thief, as he'd been called out by his friend, started with a chuckle and a hand raking through his hair. "It was too easy. I do it all the time. I'd heard someone say they knew of a law or something, I guess, that makes theft legal or at least not a crime." His shoulders lifted and he added in a cocky tone, "They said if someone steals something it's because they needed it more than the person they stole it from did. Last night, I needed that car more than that old woman did."

His table mate's eyes rounded, lips curling into a shady grin, his expression revealing awe and reverence.

"Thieving little bastard," Devlin muttered. He hated stealing about as much as he hated lying.

Apparently, Tara had heard enough of the thief's confession to agree with Devlin's sentiment. "That can't be why we're here, but it's true what he said. Theft was ruled an 'existence hardship'"—she air quoted without lifting her arms from the bar top where she had them crossed before her.

"Because thieves were given a free pass when they claimed they were desperate, enough discrimination claims resulted, so it was the President herself who made theft a non-crime. It wasn't advertised much, but word is obviously getting out anyway."

Devlin harrumphed his disgust at the lack of integrity the two men exhibited, regardless that their actions were now considered legal. The law was a stupid one.

These were not their targets. He shifted his attention to the next booth where an elderly couple sat together on the side facing Devlin. Neither spoke, each sitting with their hands curled around their drinks, which from the looks of them might have been . . . milk? Big spenders they were if the liquid was real milk. That product was a commodity, since dairy cows were almost non-existent in the States, compliments of the nation's stance against animal proteins.

Tara was already shaking her head as Devlin came to his conclusion about the silver-haired couple.

In the farthest booth, beneath the dull hue of an overhead light, were the last of the occupants, seated opposite each other. The one facing Devlin was a man dressed completely in black. Even seated, it was easy to discern the guy was huge, the faux leather jacket he wore might've been made from the hide of one entire cow, or whatever material was used to make fake leather. His hands were covered in black leather-like material as well and atop his head, pulled low on his brow, similar to how Devlin had done with his own cap, was a black, thug-looking beanie— the best way Devlin could describe it. He had a muscled neck and a clean-shaven square jaw which emphasized his severe look, aided by the stern set of his lips. As he stared hard at the person across from him, his thick, dark brows, had drawn together so tight they were nearly one above his eyes.

Something about the man seemed familiar, yet Devlin was certain he'd never met him before. Like gliding through the

images on a microfiche screen, his brain scanned through his memories, searching for a past encounter. But nothing pinged.
He could tell the other person at the booth was a female. She was bent forward, an elbow braced on the tabletop and one hand stretched along the side of her face blocking her from view. Her hair, what wasn't hidden beneath the fluffy knitted cap on her head, was dark, like Tara's. The woman nodded her head to something the man said, the fuzzy ball atop her hat wobbling with the movement.

Devlin's shoulder brushed against Tara's as he reached for his phone. He'd have preferred his work camera, but that would have been too conspicuous, so his phone camera would have to suffice. Slipping his other arm around Tara's waist, he shifted closer, enough to give the impression they were an ordinary couple seeking the quiet of a dark space, which happened to be a bar. At ten-thirty in the morning.

"The ones on the end. Recognize anything about them?" He had to lean even closer to whisper in Tara's ear.

She peeked over her shoulder. "No," she said softly.

Devlin lifted his phone out and up for a selfie. The picture on his screen showed them in the foreground and the two in the booth in the background. When the woman in the hat lowered her arm and turned her head slightly to look across the room, Devlin sucked in a gulp of air.

"What is it?" Tara whispered as her eyes shot back to the screen.

"Holy shit."

Before the woman in the booth turned back to face her partner, there, blazing a path across the length of her cheek was revealed the very visible and very recognizable scar possessed by none other than the President of the States, Anita Grant. Devlin's gaze raced around the room's interior, searching automatically for the Secret Service who were supposed to be present. But he couldn't find any of the stiff-shouldered armed guards about.

The microfiche film still whirring away inside Devlin's brain suddenly slammed to a stop. His eyes shot back to the black-jacketed man as he recalled where he'd seen him before. It had been at the border. That day. He'd been up on the stage standing guard behind Senator Clarkson and the then-Representative-now-President Grant. It was Hulk Guy.

Devlin quickly switched his camera to video mode. Tara leaned back, forcing a gap wide enough between them so he could aim the camera at the couple without appearing he was doing so. But at this distance, they were unable to hear more than a few mumbled words between the pair.

The elderly couple in the center booth slid out from their places, him holding out a hand for her. Together, they shuffled from the room, the man lightly touching the woman's lower back. It was sweet. A protective gesture rarely seen these days.

"Excuse me." Tara lifted a hand to gain the bartender's attention. The guy strode over. "We'd like to move to a booth, if that's okay?" Her sweet Southern accent was suddenly strong, syrupy. She pointed over her shoulder to the only empty one in the room.

"Sure thing." He walked around the bar, grabbing a wet rag situated near a sink at the end, wiped down the table and removed the two empty glasses. "It's all yours." He winked as he passed Devlin and Tara.

They both got slowly to their feet, neither wanting to draw attention. Tara looped her arms around Devlin's waist, leaning into him. He slid his hand around her back, acting as if he couldn't get close enough to her. Keeping their faces turned away from the corner booth—at least Devlin hoped they were successful at it—they hurried into the cushioned seat, their backs closest to the President's back.

As he and Tara settled into their spaces, the conversation behind them halted for a moment. But soon, the man began talking again. Devlin slid his phone, still in video mode, toward the edge of the table.

"This is reckless of you." Hulk Guy spoke in a way that made Devlin wonder if he was trying to mask his voice. It seemed forced, fake, but it very well could have been his normal voice. "Why couldn't we meet in a room here?"

"I'm so sick of being followed and interviewed or locked inside an office all the time. I'm never alone," Grant whined. "Literally. I can't even use the bathroom without someone from the Secret Service lurking outside my door. I wanted to have a moment where I feel normal again."

"Having the Secret Service to protect you at all times is what you signed on for when taking office." There was no sympathy in his response, and it almost sounded as if he were irritated by her actions.

"This couldn't wait," she said, dismissing his comment.

Tara and Devlin sat silent and still. Too quiet. Tara suddenly giggled at nothing and leaned her head against the back of the booth. Devlin responded similarly. They'd certainly be caught if they sat motionless. He hoped their acting skills were good enough.

"I want to make sure all our plans are in place. The clock is ticking on this." Clothing rustled and then Devlin felt the President shift against the cushioned booth at his back.

Craning his neck slightly, as if looking around for something or someone, Devlin saw she still wore her hat and coat, neither necessary in the warmth of the room. They must not be planning to stay long.

"I've made all the arrangements. Our guy will do what you want. But he told me to tell you, after this, he's done," Hulk Guy said.

Grant didn't acknowledge his comment about this other person's plan to be done with whatever it is he'd been asked to do. Instead, she continued the conversation as if he'd not spoken at all. "I'm doing everything I can from the inside. Once this is started, there will be no turning back." The gentle slurp of liquid indicated one of them was sipping from their drink.

"You'll get him in place, right?" The man asked in his falsely deep and raspy voice. "This can't work if he's not working with the VIL."

"Oh, I'll get him in. I'll even *interview* him," she said, emphasizing the falsehood. "He'll have plenty of time to get situated."

There was a long pause, with neither saying more.

Suddenly it seemed like nobody in the room was speaking and everyone was listening. Devlin shifted in his seat and said something to Tara about nothing, just words to fill the silence.

So, Grant, with the help of another, or two others, was planning something that required someone to work with the Voter Information Log database. Was she trying to manipulate voting again, like had been done in the days before the revolution and before the new voting requirements were implemented? As Devlin began to wonder about Senator Clarkson's involvement, Grant spoke.

"My wife isn't to know any of this. Not yet anyway. The fewer people involved . . . ." Her words trailed off as a tiny sliver of conscience—maybe?—presented itself.

The man replied without hiding his irritation this time. "I won't say a word. But after this, I'm retiring, too. What you do going forward you do on your own. I'll finish this job. You'll get your desired outcome, your glory. But I won't be part of anything after that."

Grant's response was menacing, with a pinch of threat added in. "Yes. Yes. If everything goes off without a hitch, you both can go away." She breathed a loud sigh. "I'm not going to lie, there's part of me still on the fence about it. I'm not heartless. I do have my wife to consider."

Again, a hint of conscience?

"Then don't go through with it," the guy snapped. "Nothing's happened yet. I'll cancel the arrangements then me and my contact will disappear. You'll never hear from us again."

A heavy, pensive silence filled the space around Devlin and Tara, who were intensely curious. Tara gripped her fingers over Devlin's knee, squeezed hard, and quirked one eyebrow up in question.

"No." Grant's response might have been to the idea of stopping whatever it was she had planned or to the guy's promise to disappear, Devlin didn't know. "I need to go." Movement again. "You know what happens if you fail in this?" She paused a second, then threw at him, "Or if either of you betray me?" This time there was no *hint* at a threat.

Devlin barely heard a grumbled, "Yeah, I know what you're capable of."

Without daring a look, Devlin waited until he heard them sliding out of the booth and walking away. Only when he was certain they'd gone, did he meet Tara's equally confused gaze as they got out of the booth.

"She's barely in office, and she's already planning something sketchy. Otherwise, why meet in secret like this? What is it, do you think?" Devlin's reporter instinct was telling him this was bad, but they had no information that pointed to anything. Grant's covert behavior wasn't illegal; but it was irresponsible, at best.

They fast-walked back to the car like they were escaping something evil and dangerous. The hair along Devlin's neckline prickled up as he sensed eyes following them down the sidewalk. Tara glanced back over her shoulder, too, searching for an unknown something or someone. She must have felt the same thing Devlin had.

But what was it or who? Nobody besides their tipster knew they would be there. Unless the tipster was present, because he or she knew more than they'd admitted, and wanted to see how he and Tara would respond to the situation. All they'd learned was that the President of the States had an unknown plan to do something she clearly didn't want anyone to know anything about.

"Do you think it's possible President Grant is planning a protest at a hashtag event? Something that opposes Senator Clarkson, maybe? That'd be ballsy, right? Legal, but ballsy. Why else keep it a secret from her wife?"

Finally at their vehicle, Tara jumped into the passenger seat while Devlin circled around to the driver's side. He cranked the ignition, and they sat a moment, both briskly rubbing their hands to stave off the cold. Devlin rocked his head side-to side-against the headrest, his hands gripping the steering wheel, elbows locked straight.

"I honestly don't know. It sort of sounded like it might be something like that. But a President initiating a protest? We haven't seen that in years." Yes, this was definitely something he needed to inform Josh about.

Devlin drummed his fingers against the steering wheel. "It can't be that. This President supports the hashtags; she doesn't oppose them. Well," he countered, "she supports most of them." He began to nod, as if reaching an understanding only he'd been considering in his mind. "We need to start with a little digging to see what groups out there have events coming up. Anything conflicting strongly with Grant's or even Clarkson's agendas would be the most likely, enough to garner her attention."

Tara searched the terrain as if answers were out there, somewhere. "Whoever tipped us off on this had to be hoping for some claim to fame or something." Her brows furrowed and she tucked her bottom lip behind her teeth. "I hope this wasn't a complete waste of time. I have precious little of it to spare." She groaned dramatically.

Devlin, too, looked out into the parking lot, searching for pieces to an invisible puzzle. "There's nothing for me to report on. What we saw today could easily be interpreted as little more than a lover's rendezvous. It's little more than gossip at this point. And I don't report gossip. If Grant follows through with a riot, well, that would be news. I agree about the guy. From the sound of it, he's got someone set up to work with the Voter Information Log. To do what? Who knows?"

He shot off a quick message to Mario, updating him on the situation, asking him to keep a close eye on anything either President Grant or Senator Clarkson did. Those two together were a powerhouse big enough to destroy a country. He didn't know much about Grant yet, but Harriet Clarkson he certainly knew had it in her to unravel a nation. She'd tried too many times to count, until the WTP intervened.

It was only a matter of time before the likes of Clarkson, and now it also seemed the President, got something past Josh and the WTP. Knowing vipers denned together, it wouldn't shock Devlin if President Grant had only pretended her wife didn't know what she was up to. Regardless, he planned to keep a close watch on them both, waiting for the opportunity to reveal just how evil and destructive the Senator and possibly the President were to the country and to its people.

NINE

"I heard on the news last night about Bizzy Jax. Do you know that rapper? Or was he a pop singer?" Tara shot Devlin a questioning glance, but he shrugged his ignorance. "Whatever he was, he got popular back when I was in school. I can only remember one song of his I thought was decent," she said as they traversed the lane doubling as a driveway. "He's in Chicago now and has petitioned for the right to have an armed bodyguard for protection. I guess he's got folks down in Guatemala who aren't too happy with him yet claims he doesn't know why."

Devlin grunted as he hurdled the carcass of a sheep, the third one they'd seen so far since leaving the car near the bottom of the hill. Tara stepped around the dead animal, too, but when she pressed her foot onto the embankment of fresh snow outside the rutted lane, she shrieked when she sank knee deep into the drift. Her arms flailed as she fought for balance, but Devlin managed to grab her elbow and help her return to solid ground before she went down completely.

They'd arrived in Montana a few hours earlier, the countryside blanketed in heavy snow. On the drive here from the airport, Devlin had reviewed Tara's schedule of confirmed Consequence Engagements, ones she'd arranged for the upcoming weeks. Where they were headed now was the first of many. The list of those not confirmed, marked as "potential" or "watching" was significantly longer, running a close second to Santa's list of those who were naughty.

Up ahead was a ranch house and another two hundred yards past that a colony of Tiny Homes. That was their destination. Before they made it to the boundary of the ranch, Devlin pulled at Tara's wrist, forcing her to a halt. Puffs of white air escaped her lips as she panted heavily while bending at the waist and bracing her hands against her knees.

Devlin rolled his eyes. It hadn't been *that* much of a trek.

"I'll be sure to add Bizzy's request to my report tonight," he began, then asked, "If that's okay? I'm thinking for some of these on your watch list we should publicly announce the names and why they're being watched. Call them out a bit, draw attention to their requests so folks hear how people are still trying to have the rules bent for them. If we're lucky, we could circumvent violators before you have to enter the picture. Maybe, just maybe, the subtle warning to the ones on your watch list will help them rethink their actions."

He'd learned over the last several weeks that this job was a work in progress. At first, it had been strictly about filming and airing Tara's interactions at her Consequence Engagements. He preferred airing them live but quickly learned the nightly segments he ran were capturing more viewers than live feeds. So many viewers in fact, Mario had already made the decision to run two segments, one midday and one at prime time. He'd told Devlin they could slot in a morning segment, too, if things kept going in the direction they were up to that point. Today's CE would hit at prime time.

Tara had been directed to travel to Montana to check in on a situation regarding the deaths of two children.

"Should we divide and conquer?" she asked, scanning the rows of tiny structures situated in symmetrical patterns through what was once a crop field.

They stood on a slight incline, so the peaks of each of what had to be at least two hundred shingled roofs below them appeared like a hedge maze. Walkways had formed between and in front of the homes, giving it a subdivision-like appearance. Children ran about within the lines of the maze as well as on the outskirts of the village. The bleat of sheep sounded from somewhere nearby.

"I'll get a statement from the family. You talk to the rancher," Devlin said, agreeing to her suggestion.

Tara touched his hand as he reached up to slip the backpack from his shoulder. "Be careful. They're hurt and angry. It could be directed at you."

He gave her a small smile. "I know. But we're here to help them, not hurt them."

They both paused, looking out and around the vast openness, beyond the house, beyond the village, to the wide-open space of the Montana landscape. Far off in the distance, leafless deciduous trees blended in with tall evergreens edging the perimeter of acre upon acre of fields and land. He hesitated, breathing in the crisp, cool air. For the span of a few heartbeats the world was silent and still.

Tara turned and began the march up the snow-packed driveway to the house. Devlin watched her go, knowing the outcome of this day would not be a good one. He made his way carefully across the slippery path etched in the deep snow between the house and the village. Soon, he reached the edge of the field.

Sliding his phone from his pocket, he retrieved the address: TH Village Number 764, House 87, Missoula, Montana.

Drawing in a deep, steadying breath, he began to wind his way through the maze, counting the houses, until he reached number eighty-seven. Some of the people he passed greeted him, others eyed him suspiciously, but none of the adults were so bold yet as to rush up to inquire about his presence there.

Children, however, weren't as inclined to ignore his passing through their tiny community. They raced about him, like puppies playing at their mother's feet. Innocents, all of them, from a variety of backgrounds, cultures, and religions.

One child helpfully said, *"Es por aqui!"* His little fingers clutched the sleeve of Devlin's jacket before tugging him in the direction in which he was already headed.

They knew why he was there.

"Gracias." Devlin smiled down at the little boy, nodding his thanks to the other two who "helped" lead him to his destination.

At the door of a home painted a faded teal, he knocked softly and only had to wait seconds before it cracked open. A set of pained and haunted eyes as dark as obsidian peeked out.

"Yes? Who are you?" A small, fragile-looking woman inquired softly, her words coming out slow and pieced together. Her voice sounded thick and wet as if she had a cold. Or that she'd been crying.

"I'm Devlin Johnson, from *The People's News*. I'm so sorry for your loss." He swallowed around the dryness that suddenly crept into his mouth. He'd seen a lot of terrible things as a reporter, especially during the years of civil unrest, but nothing clawed at his gut more than witnessing the agony in a parent's eyes when they'd lost a child. His camera, the strap wrapped around his forearm for safe keeping, hung limp in his hand against his thigh. He lifted it to chest level. "I heard about what happened and wanted to tell your story."

Tears pooled in the woman's dark eyes. They fell over her lashes, leaving clear tracks across her cheeks. She licked away the moisture before swiping the back of her hand across her mouth to remove the rest. Still, more tears followed.

"You. Come." Pulling the door open, she stepped aside and welcomed him in. She pointed for him to sit on a small sofa lining the wall in front of a window. Devlin eased down onto the soft cushions, pushing aside a bed pillow and rumpled blanket that was in his way.

He lifted his camera again. "I'm going to turn this on and record our conversation." He nodded, encouraging her agreement. "Can you tell me what happened?"

A moment's hesitation was followed by a shake of the woman's head. Before Devlin could persuade her to talk, she shoved her feet into tall, furry boots, grabbed a heavy parka off a hook mounted on the wall and stepped to the door. Pulling it open, she said, "Follow me." Urging him with a hand gesture, she exited the small structure which had him jumping to his feet in compliance. Curiosity may have killed many a cat, but it called to a reporter like a moth to flame. He couldn't stop from following her if he'd wanted to.

They slipped between the small space dividing her home and the next. There was a path, worn down to the packed dirt beneath the snow; it led past another wide vein of similarly packed dirt and snow mixed between yet another row of houses. They repeated this, moving between Tiny Homes three more times before exiting into an open area. Beyond were unsown fields, their boundaries demarcated by berms created where ditches ran. The woman led him over a path formed in the snow, straight into the center of the nearest field. From this distance, he could see an area where the knee-deep snow had been tamped down into a misshapen circle. The woman slowed as they neared it, halting three feet from the ring.

"There." She pointed, while looking directly into the eye of Devlin's camera now aimed at her. "My babies were killed there." With a wracking sob, she sank to her knees. The hands covering her face muffled the woeful, agonized cry that comes from a grief so deep there could only be one cause. A child's death. Or, in this case, two children.

Devlin stepped into the ring, inching forward as if he were sneaking into forbidden territory. He drew up short when his feet almost, but not quite, touched on a splash of a dark, reddish-brown substance staining the snow. The flattened area was partially packed, but not as much as the pathways behind him. He zoomed his lens in on the stain, noting how the blood had sunk into the snow, creating fissures from the splatter. The lens zoomed out and he turned in a half-circle to a spot four feet away where a similar stain splayed across the white backdrop. Spatters of blood splashed against the side walls of the snowy circle, flung there with violent force.

Devlin turned the camera around, so it faced him. "I'm in Missoula, Montana, reporting on the killings of two children at Tiny Home Village Number Seven-six-four." He paused when he caught sight of a black SUV moving slowly up the driveway he and Tara had hiked across moments ago. "Earlier this week, it was reported that two young children, brothers who'd recently relocated to the States from Nigeria with their mother, were killed here in the field directly behind where they lived. As you can see, it's a gruesome scene."

Suddenly, the woman behind him began to wail, a deep, keening carried over the sharply cool air. Devlin turned the camera back on her. He saw Tara headed his way from the direction of the ranch house, struggling to keep on her feet as she trudged along the same path he'd followed. Behind her was an older man, white hair, his face revealing years of exposure to the sun and the climate this far north. He was a brawny fellow, his wide shoulders and thick arms noticeable even beneath the canvas jacket protecting him from the harsh winter climate. His name, Devlin already knew, was Stan Littleton, the owner of the ranch.

THE CONSEQUENCE CLAUSE

Two Agents, identifiable by their standard-issue apparel, had jumped in line behind Stan. The sight of their uniforms twisted the dagger permanently buried in Devlin's heart. Their presence had not surprisingly drawn the attention of others as well. Coming down the path behind the Agents were two more men, one a clean-cut blonde, the other sporting a mop of spiky brown hair. They were holding hands; both men had grim looks on their faces. They stopped beside the despairing woman and knelt on either side of her, each wrapping an arm across the top of her back and shoulders.

Tara took a long step, landing in the circle of snow with a grunt of success. "Holy shit!" she exclaimed, a horrified look on her face when she saw the aftermath of violence before her.

When Devlin frowned and pointed at the camera motioning that it was recording, she clamped her mouth shut, her face slackening into a deadpan look, not an apologetic one. The farmer also stepped into the circle with the Agents closing in at his heels.

Devlin shifted the camera to focus on Tara.

"Tara Carlson of the Consequence Compliance Oversight Committee is here to help shed light on this for us. Ms. Carlson?"

Lifting her chin and pushing the ends of her dark hair off her shoulders, she faced Devlin. "We're near the property belonging to Stan Littleton in Missoula, Montana. The rancher called in a report yesterday, indicating there'd been wolves roaming the area lately. When he heard the gut-wrenching screams from children, he claims he jumped in his truck and drove as close as he could to this spot. That's when he saw wolves feasting on the mangled bodies of two boys whom he knew lived in the village." Tara looked back over her shoulder at the Tiny Home Village behind her. "He admitted to carrying a gun inside his vehicle, which he retrieved and fired on the wolves, wounding at least one. He believes the sound scared off the pack, as they quickly ran away. Unfortunately, not before the wild hounds had already fatally wounded both children." Her gaze shifted to the bloodied areas near her feet. Grimacing, she inched slightly back before turning to the rancher.

"Stan Littleton, based on your own admission, you're in violation of the terms of the Gun Control Act by being in possession of a firearm."

The Agent standing closest to the rancher grabbed Littleton's wrist and pulled it behind his back. Gasps issued from the two men kneeling beside the distraught woman still on the ground.

"Mr. Littleton—" Tara's words were interrupted by a wet, throaty shriek.

"No!" The grieving mother got to her feet with the help of the two men at her side. "He tried to save my babies." She shook her head furiously as she reached past the Agent to clutch the rancher's arm.

One of the other men present, the one with spiky hair, took an aggressive step closer to Littleton and the Agent. "This isn't right! He did nothing wrong!"

"According to gun control laws enacted in twenty-fifteen, modified over the years to keep up with changes in our society . . . ." Tara read from her cell phone, "'no person is permitted to own or be in possession of a firearm, unless said person is a member of the military and performing duties as such; is an Agent who may only be in possession of a government-issued weapon while on duty; or is a member of the Secret Service protecting the President or the Vice President during their terms in office. All other instances where a person is in possession of a firearm is a violation of the law enacted and is to be held accountable under the rule of the associated Consequence Clause.'"

She lowered her phone. "Mr. Littleton, as unfortunate as the circumstances were and the decisions you've made, I have no choice but to have you arrested. The punishment for violating gun control laws is imprisonment for a period of two years." She held up two fingers.

"But I was trying to save those little children. They were attacked by wild animals, for god's sake. I can't even keep my livestock safe without a gun. Those wolves are killing my sheep every day, and now targeting these folks." He pointed at the grieving mother with his free hand. "My ranch provides work and food for everyone here. If I'm not around to care for things, what'll become of them and my place?"

"Well, sir, unless you have someone who can take over your ranch for you—family, perhaps?—I suspect it'll be given to the government as restitution for the expense of your incarceration. As for the families here, their subsidies should be enough to sustain them comfortably."

"This isn't right!" he bellowed as one of the Agents hooked a hand around his elbow and began steering him away. Devlin's camera continued to record as the rancher called out over his shoulder to the three village residents. "Care for my ranch until I get back. Please!"

The two men huddling close together were visibly shocked by the events that had played out. They gazed into each other's eyes, silently asking and answering questions.

Finally, the taller one, the darker-haired man, responded. "We will, Stan. We'll take care of everyone here. Don't you worry about us."

Devlin didn't feel the need to wrap up this segment with a monologue. He panned around, focusing briefly on the shocked and agonized faces of the Tiny Home Village residents present, then over to the red-spattered ground at his feet. And finally, he panned out wider to the vast openness of the beautiful landscape beyond.

TEN

The days that followed their leaving Montana blended into each other. After the Treasure State, they'd hopped over to Oklahoma and then Nebraska before shooting up to Chicago where they were now. Devlin lingered at the back of the courtroom; his trusty video camera perched on a tripod before him. He zoomed in, then out, panning over what had been determined to be a jury comprised of the defendant's peers. The camera relayed what words could not. The facial expressions of the nine women and three men were a mix of concern, disgust, and shock. A few stoic expressions screamed, "I'm only here because I can't escape my civic duty."

An attorney, a lanky woman wearing a black pencil skirt, white blouse, and a tangerine-colored jacket stood at a podium before the witness box. From this angle, it was difficult for Devlin to capture both the witness and attorney in his viewfinder. He was forced to shift the camera back and forth between them when each spoke.

The woman in the hot seat was Charlene Williams, a fifty-four-year-old attorney who'd accused one Thomas Flannigan, also an attorney, of making certain promises in exchange for sexual favors. The defendant, Flannigan, had denied the allegations, claiming their sexual encounters were consensual. From the looks on the faces of the jurors, Devlin didn't expect things to lean in his favor.

"Ms. Williams." Tawna Holloway, attorney for the defense, stepped up to the podium. "May I address you as Ms.?" Though the issue of degenderizing had appeared on the ballot only a few weeks back, the process of removing titles and pronouns that might identify one's sex or gender had been happening for years. Taking away the privileges people had based on gender had also been slowly diminishing. The recently signed Degenderizing Act simply made it the law. As Devlin had expected, there were already claims of discrimination and sexism being tossed about like candy at a parade because gender could no longer be used to gain an advantage.

The witness responded. "Yes. You may call me that."

"Thank you," Holloway said automatically. "Ms. Williams, you are one of several who've come forward claiming that Mr. Flannigan here"—she pointed behind her without turning to look at Tommy Flannigan—"propositioned you by promising a full-time position in his firm if you'd engage in a sexual act with him back when your career was starting out. Is that correct?"

Along the walls and beneath windows running the length of both sides of the room were dozens of women, each holding a poster or sign. They read: "Women Don't Lie" and "She Said It? He Did It!" and yet another "No Matter What, He's Guilty."

The hypocrisy in protests like this one always astounded Devlin. Women were no longer allowed to be identified as women, and yet, their use of pronouns specifically pointing out the opposite sex was considered acceptable. But it didn't matter what Devlin thought about the situation. His opinions weren't what news was about. The proceedings before him, whether he supported the cause or not, would air exactly as they happened—unedited.

"Yes," Ms. Williams responded.

"At the time, you were an intern at Mr. Flannigan's firm. Correct?"

"Yes."

"Did the defendant threaten to fire you or revoke your internship if you were to reject his proposition?"

Charlene Williams' eyes darted to her lawyer, a stout woman half her age. She too wore a bright-colored jacket, like her counterpart at the podium, but hers wasn't as flattering against her complexion as Holloway's. Charlene held her attorney's gaze an awkwardly long moment before glancing quickly at the jury and finally back to Holloway. "Well, no. I-I was—" she stuttered.

"So, if you said no to him, that you weren't interested in Mr. Flannigan sexually, then you would have been free to continue on with your job as you did each day prior to that point?" Holloway flipped through some papers on the podium, a tactic Devlin had seen used in other court proceedings he'd witnessed. It gave Charlene time to worry what proof the attorney might have and follow the thought through to where the questioning was headed—neither conclusion working in her favor.

"Objection." Charlene's lawyer stood up. "Speculation. There's no way to prove the witness would have been able to continue working."

"Sustained. Counsel?" the judge said. He was a somber-looking Asian man with glasses perched on the end of his nose.

Conceding the judge's decision, Holloway redirected her questioning. "Ms. Williams. Did the defendant proposition you more than once?"

Charlene's gaze tracked straight to Devlin's camera. Through the lens he made eye contact with her, until she looked down at her clasped hands tucked against her lap. "Yes."

"Then I ask again, Ms. Williams, each time you said no to Mr. Flannigan's advances, were you free to go about your work, like any other day prior to each proposition?"

There was an uncomfortable pause. "Yes."

"Did you have sexual intercourse with Mr. Flannigan, Ms. Williams?"

The woman closed her eyes and drew in a deep breath. "Yes. To my utter shame."

"And when did that happen? How old were you at the time?"

"It was during my last year of law school. I was twenty-four."

There was a shuffle of movement around the room. Observers and jurors alike shifted in their seats and there was more than one murmur of anger uttered.

"And how old are you now?"

"Fifty-two."

"So, that would be . . . ." Holloway tapped a finger against her chin, as if mentally counting the number of years that had passed since the initial incident had occurred. "Twenty-eight years, correct?"

"I think so."

"Did you have sex with Mr. Flannigan more than the one time, Ms. Williams?"

With head still bowed and eyes closed, she answered quicker this time. "Yes."

"And what happened after you passed the bar?"

The moment Charlene understood where the defense was headed with her line of questioning was immediately evident. She pulled her shoulders inward to the point she was hunched forward as if a pain had reached her gut and she curled in to ease it. "I was offered a job in the firm."

The crowd in the room bristled with an energy of anticipation like a balloon filling with too much air—it was only a matter of time before it burst.

"Where do you work now, Ms. Williams?"

There was a long pause, long enough that Holloway had to repeat the question.

"I still work at the same firm. I'm a partner there."

Audible indrawn breaths and whispers zipped about the perimeter of the courtroom. Tara, who sat in the front row aisle seat behind the prosecution's desk, cast a quick glance back at Devlin. Her brows rose, then fell, but no other emotion showed on her face.

"I see," Holloway continued. "So, over the past three decades, you've done well, and it appears you've been quite happy with your success in Mr. Flannigan's firm. I'd like to produce Exhibits B through J for the record." The exhibits were news articles and photos of Charlene Williams standing beside Thomas Flannigan at numerous charity events the firm sponsored for which she'd received recognition over the years. There were pictures of the two of them smiling for the camera as they stood alongside clients following positive outcomes of various cases. It was clear that Charlene's life was full of great successes, and not the devastation one might expect from a forced or unwanted sexual advance three decades back.

"Ms. Williams. Mr. Flannigan took advantage of your youth when you first started at his firm, even if you were of legal age. However, you consciously chose to engage in sexual acts with him to further your own career. Not once, but on several occasions, you engaged in these sexual acts, which, by your own account were not coerced. Whether you enjoyed the encounters or despised them, you chose to take a path that you knew would benefit you. Is that correct?"

"Objection. Leading the witness."

The judge pondered the objection for a split second. "Overruled. Answer the question, please."

"I didn't know that it would benefit me."

"Really?" Holloway's head jerked back, her chin dipping toward her chest. "He propositioned you, promising exactly what the outcome was, yet you say you didn't know it would benefit you?"

"I-I, it, I mean—"

"I have no more questions, Your Honor."

Holloway returned to her seat beside her client. She whispered something to him, he nodded, then she scratched her pen across the paper on the table.

The judge excused the witness from the stand.

Following Charlene, others were called to the stand and a similar process of the accuser claiming wrongdoing and sexual assault went on for another five hours. In total, six more women were questioned, all of them attorneys who either still worked for or had worked for Mr. Flannigan because of promises made in exchange for a range of private physical and sexual situations. Two accusers, both of whom no longer practiced law, spoke to how Mr. Flannigan ruined their lives after they'd engaged in sexual acts with him. One of the women, who'd left the firm after ten years, had gone on to become a political analyst for a governor somewhere. The other married a professional basketball player whom she met at a charity event sponsored by Flannigan's law firm at a time when she'd still worked there. Holloway asked each witness the same questions as she'd asked Charlene Williams, receiving similar answers and outcomes.

When the defense finally rested, the jury was released to deliberate. By five o'clock that afternoon, members of the jury were again seated in the jury box. Devlin zoomed in on each of their faces. Some looked straight into the camera, boldly daring the world to question their decision, others stared hard at the defendant, a mix of sympathy and accusation in their eyes.

Tara sat rigid in her seat, one hand gripping the back of the bench in front of her. Her body was stiff, like she was about to spring up at the slightest provocation. She turned, her gaze drifting to the four Agents standing near the edge of the room off both sides from where Devlin stood. Her head barely moved up and down, acknowledging whatever internal monologue was taking place inside her brain. Clutched in her hand was her little blue book; her thumb wedged between the pages.

The court was brought back into session and the judge read the charges against Thomas Flannigan.

"On all counts of aggravated assault, the defendant is found not guilty." Mumbles of assent and murmurs of surprise lit the room but were immediately hushed by the judge rapping his gavel several times. "On seven counts of unwanted sexual advances resulting in a sexual act, the defendant is found guilty." A roar of excitement and joyful cries of justice raised the roof. The women along the walls jumped up and down, chanting what their posters read, hugging one another, victory tears in their eyes.

The judge whacked his gavel again. "Mr. Flannigan, you have been found guilty by a jury of your peers. Sentencing will be immediate, as determined by the Consequence Clause related to matters such as this one. This court is adjourned." The gavel slammed down with a loud whack.

Devlin didn't shut off his camera. He trained the lens on Tara where she now stood in the center aisle only six feet away from him. The Agents who'd lurked in the corners of the room strode forward. Two continued past her and stopped beside Mr. Flannigan while the other two waited behind Tara, out of the way of occupants exiting the courtroom.

"Ms. Williams." Tara stepped into the aisle, blocking Charlene's exit. Her husband, a distinguished-looking man was at her side.

"I'm Tara Carlson from the Consequence Compliance Oversight Committee."

The husband's eyes widened in acknowledgment, while Charlene shrank into his side.

"Yes. I've seen you before."

She looked past Tara to Devlin. No matter that they hadn't been working together long, they'd already become a well-known pair, what with Devlin airing more and more Consequence Engagements. It didn't surprise him anymore when people did the double-take once Tara introduced herself.

She pushed open her little booklet of rules and gazed down at a page. "Ms. Williams, according to information we retrieved from the Voter Information Log, you voted in favor of a law passed several years back where an assailant accused of sexual assault, sexual intimidation, or other similar crime should automatically be guilty until proven innocent. Per the Consequence Clause associated with this law, I'm here to inform you that your culpability in this situation must also be addressed." Charlene drew in a sharp breath and the lines over her broad brow deepened. "As a result of your silence twenty-eight years ago, you are to be held accountable for the sexual assault of each and every person who came forth today in these proceedings."

Charlene's knees buckled, and she clutched her husband's arm.

"That's ridiculous," the man said. "The only person responsible for those heinous acts is that man, Flannigan."

"Facts of this trial indicate that your wife was the first victim of Mr. Flannigan's actions. Had she reported the crime years ago, immediately before or even right after it happened, anytime up to the point of the next victim, then she may potentially have prevented the incident that resulted in further victimizations. Each one that followed your wife's, as explained in the Consequence Clause, is the direct responsibility of Ms. Williams' actions, or lack thereof, to stop the perpetrator from offending again. You had all the power, according to the law, on your side, yet you failed to act. As a direct result of that negligence, several more victims, known and possibly some unknown, were the outcome."

Charlene's mouth formed an O, and she tried to speak, but it didn't look like she could get enough air into her lungs to force out words.

"Ms. Williams, you're to be charged for the crime of perpetrating an assault on a victim by way of irresponsible negligence and as such are subject to half the sentence bestowed upon Mr. Flannigan." She stepped aside so the Agents could move forward. "Affix a bracelet on Ms. Williams so she can be monitored and notified of the date of her transport to the FRP."

Charlene looked like she was about to get sick. Her fists were knotted against her mid-section and her chest rose and fell as she pulled in deep gulps of air. "Y-you said my sentence will be half his. Th-th-that," she stuttered again, barely capable of speaking. "How long is his sentence to be?"

Tara nudged open the book at the place where her thumb was wedged and skimmed the pages. "His sentence is fifteen years. Which means yours will be seven and a half."

Charlene's knees nearly buckled. She leaned more heavily into her husband, who was forcibly trying to hold her up.

"This can't be! She's the victim here!" he bellowed.

One of the Agents lifted his hand, showing off a device half the size of Tara's little blue book. He knelt before Charlene, but it was the other Agent who spoke.

"Please present your ankle so we can affix the tracking device. This tool will record your whereabouts at all times." Then, saying words he'd clearly recited more than few times, he explained how the device worked. "Should you fail to respond to our efforts to communicate with you as you await transport to the Free-Range Prison, a warning taser shock will occur through the device. Should you attempt to remove the device, a shock stronger than the first will emit, and Agents will receive the notification. Should you attempt to exit the country at any border, the device will automatically register a shock that, I have been told," he shook his head gravely, "is powerful enough to buckle your knees. Should you manage to cross the country's border, the device will set off a warning that will last approximately thirty minutes. At that time, if GPS does not register the device back on home soil, it will detonate enough of a blast specifically designed to maim you until Agents can pinpoint your whereabouts in order to collect you."

These devices were how Nevada's inmates remained within the boundary of the State, since fences were not permitted. Prisoners who'd attempted escape and who'd lost part of a limb were mended, if necessary and if possible, but returned to their own recognizance within Nevada's boundaries with the GPS tracker affixed to their other leg or other limb if an ankle was no longer available. Since there were no jail facilities, people like Charlene Williams and Thomas Flannigan were braceleted this way and tracked but otherwise were free to go about their normal life until such time as their trip to Nevada could occur. Rarely did anyone fail to show when and where they were supposed to these days, since the visual representation of what happened to escapees had been a strong enough deterrent for others considering their choices.

It had taken a solid couple of years and a more than few hundred runners during the testing phase of the project, with reports and rumors of the outcomes spreading. The mainstream media downplayed those early incidences, but now that Devlin was employed to do what he did, people would realize the government didn't hesitate to activate the bracelets when violations occurred.

Charlene's head fell to her husband's shoulder. His eyes remained round as an owl's. Mr. Williams' voice trembled when he managed to force words past his lips. "But she did the right thing by coming forward. It wasn't easy for her, but she knew she had to. She shouldn't be the one punished here!"

"I understand that Mr. Williams, but she made others a victim by her long-held silence and is accountable for her actions, too. According to the trial and in her own words, she was not threatened in any way, and went willingly to Mr. Flannigan in exchange for a promise. She should have come forward long ago to stop him if she truly felt what he was doing was wrong."

"B-but," Charlene forced out as the condemning click of the anklet latched into place. "But what if I wasn't the first?" There was rising hope in her voice. "What if there's someone else out there who was before me? Shouldn't I be freed and considered one of those secondary victims?"

Tara, who'd seen the desperate attempts of too many criminals to count search for a way out of the predicament they'd gotten themselves into, nodded. She wasn't unfeeling, Devlin knew that with certainty, but her position was one which garnered better outcomes when she didn't give hope where hope might not exist.

"If there is indeed another or others before you who it is determined failed to report, then yes, your sentence would then be reduced to a fraction of whatever that person's fate is." At Mr. and Mrs. Williams' confused glances, she elaborated. "Though for now, you appear to be the first who said nothing of the crime committed by Flannigan and failed to tell anyone who might have had the power to stop his behavior, you weren't the only one. You see, each of those women who came forward today because of your forthrightness also failed to do her duty. Once we get a clear picture of the order in which the incidences occurred, each of those women today will get a fraction of your sentence. Of course, those sentences will be determined by information pulled from the VIL. If they voted in the same way you did, then the sentence will be similar. If not," she shrugged, "well . . . I'll need to check the VIL."

By now, the courtroom had nearly emptied. Those few protesters who vowed all women were victims remained suspiciously silent when they heard the edicts issued from Tara's booklet of Consequence Clauses. This wasn't the first time Devlin had seen people hesitate to rush in and fight for their cause, whatever it may be, when things didn't end up roses and rainbows for one of their own. He'd seen more people hesitate to speak out on old crimes like the one today, uncertain as they were as to what consequence might be handed down under whatever law they violated—and what information had been collected in their own Voter Information Log. What would Tara find on the other women's VIL records? He didn't want to guess, nor did he have to. The truth would be revealed, and justice would serve each victim who failed the one who came after her.

He waited behind the lens, capturing it all until everyone left the courtroom. Until it was only him and Tara, and then he let the screen fade to black.

ELEVEN

Tara had declared the rest of January as office time, refusing to schedule any new Consequence Engagements until she'd tended to work neglected during their travels around the country. After two weeks of this imposed downtime, Devlin wasn't sure how he felt about the time off, as it had left too many hours in the day to think of the woman from the border and a cold-blooded killer who got away with the crime. No. He couldn't allow himself to get swallowed up in that obsessive searching again.

He paced the length of the old brick building butted up to the edge of the sidewalk. Near a rusty downspout, he pivoted and strolled back the opposite direction, passing a grime-covered window positioned at shoulder height, and a ruddy-colored wooden door inset slightly into a brick alcove. The oversized bricks edging the corners of the entry near his feet were crumbling and broken. He moved beyond two more windows set at ground level, the top of the panes reaching slightly higher than Devlin's head. Here, he leaned against the brick façade stained black from mold or pollution, or both. Directly in his path were concrete steps, nine to be exact—up one side and down the other. Both led to red double doors with crusade-style Anglican crosses carved in them. A black iron railing demarcated the half polygon shape of the stairs and landing.

Two pedestrians made their way up the steps on the far side of the doorway. When they got near the top, Devlin saw one was Conrad. He tilted his chin at Devlin as he pulled open the large door. Patty, the redhead beside him, offered a small smile. Devlin lifted three fingers of the hand holding his phone in response as he pushed away from the wall.

"I thought we were taking January off," he said into the phone, distracted by Conrad's appearance. If it were possible, the man looked even more haggard today than he had the last time he'd seen him.

"That's what I'd hoped for." Tara sighed. "I'm sorry I dropped this on you at the last minute, but I got the call today. I'd have gone on my own, but honestly, this is a big one. It should air live." He could hear her pecking at a keyboard in the background, which explained the way she paused in between sentences. "Especially those working in any government setting."

Devlin's curiosity spiked exponentially.

That rush associated with reporting, being on the ground right as a scene goes down overtook him. He'd once been one of those reporters who raced around the country following grand stories. But things changed after the OBA.

As he hadn't fully resigned himself to taking a month off work anyway, he jumped at Tara's offer. "Sure. I'll swing by soon. I gotta go. It's time for my meeting."

As Josh had suggested, Devlin popped into group sessions every chance he got in between trips with Tara. It kept him grounded. There were times when he'd tried to give it up, as if the meetings, the talks, the quiet camaraderie were drugs he needed to quit. However, during those times he'd stayed away, he'd experienced more panic and anxiety attacks, like an addict going through withdrawal. Deciding there were worse things to be addicted to than group therapy, he'd committed to sit in as often as his schedule allowed.

Once inside the old church, he took his seat, offering silent greetings to those around him. He even nodded at Ken who, in his typical scowling way, didn't nod back and instead rolled his eyes before looking the other way. Devlin immediately began rethinking his plan to offer the guy some friendly encouragement.

Conrad was in his regular spot on the far end of the same pew as Devlin, only he was sitting and not standing, as was his usual way. Yet another indicator of his fatigued state. Something was definitely up with him.

"Welcome." Steve, the group moderator, made eye contact with each person, stopping on Devlin. "Glad to see you here, Devlin. Things going well?" As Steve asked this, his gaze flicked to Conrad, and his lower jaw shifted as he bit the inside of his cheek. Steve, it seemed, had also noticed Conrad's declining state.

"Thanks," Devlin said. "It's been good. My new job has been great."

"Glad to hear it. You look good." Again, Steve's worried eyes darted to Conrad. "Who'd like to start off sharing today?"

Surprising everyone, including Devlin, Ken got to his feet. "I've started a new job." His voice sounded unimpressed, and certainly not excited at the prospect of his newly employed status. Because Ken was usually so distant from others, or because everyone was in a little shock by his speaking, the congratulations offered were small, mumbled with hesitation and trepidation.

"I'll be working with computers," he added with a hard and heavy sigh as if the prospect bored him. Had Devlin not heard the words, he might have believed the man was talking about his dog dying or something more tragic by the way he was acting.

"Is there a reason why you don't sound happy about this new job?" Steve asked what everyone else was likely thinking.

But with Ken and his typical bottled-up emotions, nobody really knew exactly how or what to say to him to not lead to an angry outburst. He'd never gotten aggressive with anyone, not physically. But beneath the surface, there was a very dark and damaged forty-something-year-old man nobody fully understood.

Ken shook his head as if waking from a trance. "Just because I have a job, doesn't mean I have to like it. I do what's needed to survive," he said cryptically before lowering to his seat, his expression a mask of what Devlin could only surmise as fury. "Us military guys," he glanced over to Conrad, who was staring back through narrowed eyes. "Seems we're useful for something besides killing after all."

He spoke of killing as casually as someone might talk of a football game while at a dinner table. He came across as unaffected by the idea of snuffing out a human life, yet Devlin knew that wasn't the case, otherwise he wouldn't be here. Conrad, on the other hand, even after all the time spent in therapy, still struggled with his past.

Ken was such a strange man, Devlin thought.

"But you hate the government as much as I do. So why there?" Conrad asked, a hard edge in his tone.

Staring down at his feet, Ken nodded. "Once a puppet, always a puppet, I guess."

Steve clapped his hands twice, drawing attention away from the brooding pair of ex-military men. "Okay. Who else wants to share?"

While another voice chimed in, saying something about a new relationship she'd started and was excited about, Devlin kept his focus on Conrad. He stared hard at him, perplexed and worried about what was happening to his friend. He'd always been quiet, internalizing his pain, sure. But from the time since Devlin had first met him, until now, his progress had gone backward. Years of group and any improvements Conrad had made seemed instantly gone. He was as tormented now as he'd been back on day one.

Conrad sat slouched in his seat, head hanging so low the cords of tendon along the back of his neck pulled taut. He turned his head, meeting Devlin's worried gaze. Then, he got up, and without a word to anyone left the church.

This was it. This was the moment. If Devlin didn't do something to pull Conrad back in, bring him to solid ground, he knew he'd be lost forever. Nothing good came from a lost soul, Devlin knew. He'd been at the brink of that abyss before. He had to at least try to help the man somehow. With a quiet nod to Steve, he slipped out of the congregation hall.

Outside, he stopped at the railing to look both directions. Spotting Conrad near the end of the block, he took the steps two at a time, gripping the rail for support and then moved into a jog, dodging patches of snow and ice.

"Conrad! Wait up!" When Conrad didn't stop, Devlin picked up his pace, catching up to him quickly. "Damn it, man. Stop, will you? Talk to me. What's going on?" He fell in step beside the hulking man, accepting that Conrad had no intentions of stopping. Well then, Devlin would tag along, and they'd have this conversation out in the public.

"Leave me be, Devlin," Conrad growled, determined to move along his path.

Path to where, Devlin had no idea, but it was at least leading in the same direction he needed to travel, so he felt justified in his decision to ignore the command.

"Something's changed. You're back to how you were when I first met you. What gives?"

A weighty silence met his inquiry. Conrad tugged the hat on his head low, covering his ears and the entirety of his forehead, including his brows. The ends of brown hair poked out from beneath his beanie, reaching to the edge of his squared jawline. It had always surprised Devlin to see him with longer hair and not buzzed short, considering he'd been a military man for so long.

They were nearing a busier side of town, one closer to the Capitol, where Devlin needed to be soon now that his January hiatus had ended abruptly. Conrad zigzagged past motorized vehicles and pedestrians while crossing the intersection of Independence Avenue and First Street. The latter ran along the East Front side of the Capitol Building.

Once across, Conrad abruptly stopped. "Look," he said sharply, "I'm not your friend. I'm not anyone's friend. I lost that freedom a long time ago." His chest rose as he sucked in a long, heavy breath of crisp, cool air. He shoved his fingers beneath his cap and scratched his scalp before dragging his hand down and across his face. The gesture told of his weary state, as did the dark shadows beneath his eyes.

Devlin's refusal was at the ready. "No, you didn't. You have to let the past go." He dared to place a hand on his shoulder, as they'd never been *that* close as friends. "You had no control over things. You've expressed remorse and nobody blames you for your actions from the past. Nobody but you. For things you did in your job." To press his point, he even added, "Hell, nobody blames Ken, either, but with him it would be easy to. He doesn't do anything to help his plight. Unlike you."

Conrad tilted his head to the sky and barked a derisive laugh. He yanked back, forcing Devlin's hand to fall away. "Goddamn it, Devlin!" he yelled, his emotions coming out in furious waves. "You're wrong. Everyone would blame me if they knew the things I'm capable of." There was pain and agony in Conrad's eyes. There was also sadness, anger, and something Devlin could only describe as pleading. Wearily, Conrad let his head fall. "I'm sorry," he whispered before turning his back on Devlin and walking away.

Like that, the conversation and Devlin's attempt to help was snuffed.

He stared at Conrad's retreating form as he took off down Independence Avenue, stunned by the outburst but also disappointed in himself that he couldn't ease at least some of the burden the man so clearly bore. Admittedly, and somewhat guiltily, as it was opposite of what he felt about Ken, Devlin feared the day Conrad stopped showing up to group, because deep down he knew it would mean Conrad's demons had won. With a resigned sigh, he veered down Front Street and then into the Capitol for a meeting with Tara.

Offices for WTP staff, like Tara's, were situated in the hallways near Josh's office. After first stopping by the latter, only to find it dark and the door closed, he ventured farther down the corridor. Tara's door stood open. She was on the phone but waved at him, bidding him to enter. He stepped inside and wandered quietly around the room, trying not to eavesdrop on her call, but also not overly concerned if he inadvertently did. She had invited him in, after all.

"Yes. That's right." Tara leaned an elbow on her desk and pinched the bridge of her nose, her eyes scrunched tight. "Attach the bracelet. Let him know he has until the end of the week to square things away."

Tara's position didn't rank high enough to warrant a fancy office like Senator Clarkson's, but Devlin supposed it was decent enough. She'd decorated the space exactly as he'd imagined she would. Sparse, black and white, clean and precise.

There was nothing out of place, and nothing frilly. The only splash of color in the entire room was an overly large painting of a field of wildflowers with a bright yellow sun high in a clear blue sky and an old, white farmhouse tucked in the background. Devlin cocked his head, considering the art like a collector might, which he was not.

"Uh-huh," Tara muttered behind him. "We'll reach out to him." At this, Devlin turned and found her staring straight at him. Somehow, he knew "we'll" referred to him and Tara. "He'll leave Friday for Nevada. Eight years is the sentence."

She shook her head and abruptly ended the call, slouching into her chair as if her spine had suddenly turned to jelly. It was uncharacteristic of the Tara he knew, and the hair at his neck prickled at what might have caused the defeated gesture.

"Why do I have the feeling I should sit down?" he asked as he approached her desk and eased onto the black, metal-framed chair beside it.

"I had to call it, Devlin. I'm sorry. We delayed as long as possible, but . . . ." She pulled herself upright, moved the computer mouse on her desk, bringing to life the monitor in front of her. "It's Carl." Her dark eyes were sharp, unblinking when they met his. "He broke the law. He had the right to choose, but he also has the duty to face the consequences for his choices, like everyone else on every matter in existence. Without law enforcement out on the streets to do the enforcing, the only recourse we have for all crimes, big and small, is the Consequence Clause and Nevada." Reaching into a desk drawer, she retrieved something and cupped it in her hand.

"The CC was designed specifically to make consequences swift and just. They're examples to others who might be considering breaking the law. Any law. If you know your only outcome for punishment is Nevada, it might deter bad behavior. But if we let this slide, everyone else will expect the same outcome, like the way things were before the CC." The tight-lipped smile she offered was sympathetic now, apologetic, and matter of fact, all in one. There was nothing she could do differently, and deep down, Devlin knew it, too.

He reached up to massage his trapezius muscle, which had suddenly grown tense. "I get it, but that doesn't mean I have to like it. If we can prove he'd been blackmailed or threatened, we can get his sentence reduced at least, right?"

She nodded with some enthusiasm. "Definitely. The sooner we find the real criminal in all this, we can get Carl out of there in six months' time."

No matter what, he had to own up to his role in breaking the law and would still need to serve time. Racism was racism, and under rules established by the WTP, any form of it was immediately called out and punished harshly. Carl had had a choice to make, and he chose poorly.

"Now"—Tara had her professional armor back in place—"I have come across something I think you might find useful, if you haven't already seen it." She turned her monitor toward Devlin and clicked open a file. It was video footage from a news network. Not Devlin's.

"It's raw, unedited footage from that day when the borders were opened," she said, as if the scene on the screen needed an introduction.

He recognized it, of course. He'd been there, watched it all with his own eyes. What was on screen now was different yet similar to what he'd aired on *The People's News*. The images running across Tara's monitor revealed the scene with Clarkson praising her efforts, but it was shown from the opposite side of the stage from where Devlin had been filming that day.

"It's something from one of the mainstream networks."

They both watched intently, neither of them speaking while the clip played through to the end. The blood in Devlin's veins came to a screeching halt, his breath catching in his chest, before a slow boil took over, heating the life force racing through him. He made Tara replay it a second time.

"This is something." He didn't try at all to hide his enthusiasm. "How'd you get it?"

She beamed at him. "Believe it or not, I have friends out there. Well," she countered, "they're not actually friends who I associate with, but they're connections willing to grant an occasional favor. In fact, I'm expecting one of those *friends* any minute to help with another situation I'm working on."

Devlin cocked his head at her, wondering if by the way she emphasized the word friends she meant something more than a work-related acquaintance. She wasn't in any sort of relationship that he knew of. At least, she'd not shared any personal information like that with him. He admitted to being curious now.

When he'd agreed to work with Tara, he'd done so with the intention of giving up his mad searching, which he'd known had bordered on psychotic. At first, it was with purpose and the need to know who and why the woman from the border, an Agent, of all the people there that day, had been the one and only target. But when he realized he was losing himself in the searching, he'd tried to stop. That's when the nightmares came, the scene playing on repeat in his head. His quest, it seemed, had kept his brain busy enough to hold back the visions.

But now, as he sat with Tara after having watched this incredible piece of evidence, one he himself had not been able to attain, was suddenly overwhelmed with gratitude and something more. He moved around the end of the desk, then leaned down to wrap his arms around her in an awkward hug.

"Thank you so much," he breathed against the side of her head before quickly releasing her. "I've got to find the Senator and show this to her." With a renewed sense of hope he hadn't felt during his years of searching for answers, he hurried out of Tara's office, forgetting all about his reasons for being there to begin with, intent upon beelining it straight over to the Senate wing.

Staring down at his palm, at the miraculous gift from Tara, he blindly skirted around the suits walking slower than him and the ones conversing in the middle of the wide hallway. He maneuvered past a trio of women directly in his path, and nearly face-slammed into the wide, hard chest of someone coming from the other direction.

Devlin's head shot up, his eyes wide and a quick apology on his lips. "I am so sorry!"

Bright green eyes clashed with his before raking him over, head to toe. Time slowed around Devlin. His feet moved him forward, his head craning to the side as they continued past each other. The man barely nodded before he turned face forward, silently dismissing Devlin. The guy didn't belong in government. Instead, he could have been on the cover of a men's magazine, he was that polished and attractive. Not that Devlin looked at men like that. It was just that he stood out like a daisy among a field of mushrooms here in these cool marble walls. Then, disbelievingly, he watched him disappear through the open doorway to Tara's office.

"Well, that answers that question," Devlin said to himself. But seeing the guy he assumed was the "friend" Tara had been expecting really answered no questions at all. He didn't know nor did he care if they were seeing each other romantically or merely as work friends. At least that's what he tried to convince himself, as he admitted to an unsettling feeling deep inside his chest, one he didn't understand.

Minutes later, Devlin stood waiting as patiently as he could in the corridor near Senator Clarkson's office. It was approaching noon, which meant there was a chance she would break for lunch and return here. Standing a short distance from her door, hidden slightly behind a large column, he watched in silence when she eventually appeared down the long hallway. After she'd slipped inside her office, he let another couple of minutes pass, giving her time to settle in behind her desk. Finally, he crossed the hall and stepped into her domain.

As he'd hoped, she was already seated at her desk and had begun arranging her lunch before her. When Devlin cleared his throat, her head shot up. Suspicious hazel eyes met his, the deep wrinkles around her mouth and at her temples giving her the appearance of an old crone. Registering the lack of threat in Devlin, she proceeded with her task, but the loud sigh she made relayed her irritation.

"I don't have time for this," she snapped. "I have an interview in fifteen minutes. Leave. Or I'll have you removed."

She could threaten all she wanted. But, considering the WTP were the ones roaming the halls who possessed any sort of security-type authority, and their presence only happened if Josh was on the premise, he'd take his chances. He was going to make her watch the video. It'd only take minutes of her precious time. Disregarding her threat, he strode deeper into her space, laptop pressed against his hip. Without asking, he set it on her desk and opened it.

"I've come across something you have to see." When he suspected she'd refuse on whatever grounds she could make up on the fly, which she'd gotten good at over the years, he interrupted her. "And it's your *duty*," he emphasized, "to help your people. Like it or not, I'm one of the people."

Tossing her uneaten sandwich onto the paper wrapping laid out like a plate, she thrust her arms across her chest and leaned back. "Hurry up, then. I have a massive list of things more important than this goose chase you've been on far longer than any normal person should."

Letting the jab slide, he opened the file Tara had given him. Without any introduction, he pressed play, ignoring the anxiety welling up deep inside his chest as the memories from that day unfolded before him.

The cameraperson who'd shot the film they were watching had been situated on the opposite side of the stage from where Devlin had been that day while filming the opening of the borders event. The other media had taken up their posts to the left of the stage and part way between there and the border wall, while Devlin had positioned himself to the right. The stage where Senator Clarkson stood praising the day's accomplishments, and her own, was the obstacle providing the gap of space between the two sides of media. In hindsight, Devlin recalled seeing other camera crews in the background, when he'd panned his camera around toward the stage and then back in the other direction, out toward the border fence.

From this viewing vantage point, when the camera panned back and forth like how Devlin had done to catch all the people and things going on, there was a moment when, off in the background on screen, the blonde talking with the two hashtag leaders whom he'd been filming came into view. She'd been facing away from Devlin as she talked to the pair. He remembered, because right before she'd been shot, she'd turned to look back his way and waved at him. On screen beyond her, stood Devlin, hidden behind his camera. It was a mirror image of Devlin's recording from that day.

In the wide space between the camera capturing the scene and where Devlin was off in the distance, were the separate groups of protesters demarcated by their signs or hats. Those for the cause stood closest to the Senator and those against it off in the background. What wasn't visible on screen from the angle recorded, was the huge wall and all those entering the country. Among the crowd on screen now, there were other

Agents present besides the blonde, there merely to keep the peace between the protesters, not to control the immigrants' movement.

Anxiety began to well deep inside Devlin's chest, growing at an alarming rate. He couldn't tear his eyes away from the screen as his memory replayed over and over the events about to happen.

"Watch there." He touched his finger on the screen below the image of the blonde right as she lifted a hand in a small wave, a wave he remembered she'd directed at him, to which he'd replied with a thumbs up. Devlin and the Senator watched as a man holding a pistol approached the blonde Agent, unchecked, no hesitation in his step.

"There's the shooter. You can see him here from a different angle than what I've shown you before." He pressed pause and pointed again. "Has he ever been at any of your riots—er—protests?" he corrected when Clarkson shot him a dark look. "And, here, let me zoom in."

Pressing the cursor over a button at the top of the screen, he increased the image to one hundred seventy-five percent and centered it directly on the man whose arm was already lifted. The stilled image of the gun pressed to the back of the woman's head was haunting, surreal.

If only Devlin had the power to rewind the scene and freeze the frame when the man was two feet away. If only he could pluck him from the shot, thus removing the threat to the Agent, before pressing play and allowing the rest of the day's events to happen as they should have—peaceful, welcoming, and calm. If only he could.

But he couldn't do that. He relived the moment in his head, remembering the look of shock and fear that registered in the woman's eyes the instant the gun fired. He squeezed his own eyes shut and forced the haunting memory back into the dark recesses of his brain.

"See his hand?" The screen shifted again. Part of the woman's long ponytail was visible in the frame. She'd pinned her hair up that day, as was typical for her when out on the job. "See that mark right there?" He pointed at a splotch of color on the underside of the murderer's wrist, where the cuff of the jacket he wore had shifted up when he'd extended his arm. "Does that look like a tattoo?" The shape of the mark was indistinct no matter how far in Devlin zoomed the shot. But it was something.

The man holding the gun was tall, broad-shouldered. The large hoodie he wore had no defining emblems of any sort. Notwithstanding the fact it had been July in Arizona and a hoodie like that should have stood out for that reason alone, the garment was nondescript. The hood covering his head hadn't drawn anyone's attention because many of the people marching in the background had them pulled over their heads as well. Devlin had always only seen the man from the angle he'd filmed him. This footage was taken from the other side, revealing the shooter's hand and the indistinct mark that was the most significant piece of evidence he'd come across to date.

Devlin's filming that day had recorded from behind the blonde, the shooter having entered the scene from Devlin's left. When the killer had lifted his gun hand, he'd captured the back of his hand. This new view showed the underside of the shooter's wrist.

Clarkson's thumbs pressed back and forth into her palms, in a circular motion. "There's nothing there that draws my attention or suspicion. Now, if you'll excuse me, I need to finish my lunch before my appointment." She dismissed him with a flick of her fingers and leveled an unfriendly, unempathetic gaze on him. "No more," she bit out. "I'm finished with you and your chasing theories and *evidence*." She air-quoted the word, clearly mocking Devlin's efforts.

Then, as if a switch had flipped, she added in a much kinder tone, "It's time you let this go, Devlin. I've read everything and searched through all the files you've brought to me for years now. It's over. As tragic as it was, this is a crime that clearly can't be solved. I'm sorry."

At her words, Devlin's anger warred with his sadness and frustration. There'd been so many people there that day, it was possible the blonde had simply been a random target, the first Agent the killer saw, the first authority on site. Someone from either side of the fight could have suspected the Agent of supporting one over the other. Picking sides was, after all, the type of divisive action that nearly brought on a war. Any number of possibilities existed. But as if the blonde were reaching out to him from beyond the grave, telling him to keep trying, he knew—he just knew!—she had been the target and not a random victim. And somehow, his filming the event live had been the reason.

"Sometimes, I think you enjoy the chase more than you care for any real answers." Clarkson casually lifted her sandwich and took a bite as if none of the hateful and devastating actions she'd watched had any effect on her at all, which, in truth, they probably hadn't. She remained fixed in her ivory tower, safe from all the damage she'd done to this country.

Like a red-hot dagger sliced into his heart, Devlin hissed sharply, his rage threatening to boil over. "It's sad that someone's life is what you consider a goose chase. Someone who was an Agent of this country, someone who stood at the ready to protect *your* cause! You." He thrust a finger at eye level. "Were it not for you and your wife," he spat vehemently, "that Agent wouldn't have been at the border that day. Whether you care or not, her blood is on your hands. And I'll chase that goose, as you put it, all the way to hell if it leads me there." He slammed his hand against the top of her desk, making Senator Clarkson jump.

They stared hard at each other, her chewing her food as if she hadn't a care in the world, him biting the inside of his cheek, his chest rising and falling in his fury. He hadn't played the video all the way through to the end, saving Senator Clarkson the horror of watching the gruesome finale. But the entire thing was etched in his mind, every nuance, frame by frame.

Clarkson's suggestion to let it go and move on with his life was something he knew he needed to do. Hell, he'd even recently begun to do just that. But her cruel and heartless words were like adding fuel to the fire of his hatred for her, renewing his determination—consequences be damned.

TWELVE

Devlin sat as passenger beside Tara as they headed west on Interstate-94 out of Detroit on their way to Ann Arbor, Michigan. His computer was perched on his knees. The magnified image of the man seen near Carl's restaurant filled his screen, but it was too pixilated to view the minute details. Sliding his fingers in on the control pad, he slowly shrank the image, allowing the dotted picture to gain more clarity.

"It's circular-shaped?" He tilted his head one way, then the other, like a dog might upon hearing an unusual sound. "But maybe not. It looks like there are sharp points at the edges, so it could be a square design?"

Tara leaned over for a quick glance and then shook her head. "I agree, it's probably a tattoo. If we can pinpoint exactly what it is, we'd have more to go on. You know," she said hesitantly, "it would have to be extremely specific to track someone down."

"I know." Devlin minimized the picture before opening every file he could find with the name Clarkson in the nomenclature. He selected one, and with the volume muted let it play as Tara drove them to their next Consequence Engagement. A large, black SUV followed closely behind them.

"Did you already talk to the subject and explain what was to happen?" Devlin's gaze wandered over every inch of the screen, searching for a face, a profile, a hat, anything that remotely resembled the man in the footage Tara had found for him. She took her eyes off the road for half a second to look at him. "I did. The guy seemed nice enough, I suppose, but he gives me the creeps. Considering the circumstances, he should be incredibly pleased with his situation."

Their exit approached and she steered onto the off ramp, then headed northeast on Highway 14.

Michigan may have been known as the Great Lake State, but it could easily have been tagged the Tree State. The trees were so dense in places, entire subdivisions might have existed behind them, remaining hidden from anyone traveling past, even in winter when the leaves had all fallen away. There were still enough pine trees to keep it thick and relatively green. It was a complete contradiction to everything he'd heard about the State, much of which geared more toward what Detroit was like. The little he'd seen of that area, back before the OBA changed everything, was it had been a depressed and rundown city, with abandoned factories crumbling or destroyed, like something from a war movie. Sadly, it was only one of many urban cities where politics had ravaged the place before civil unrest started.

Devlin clicked open another file, then another, cursing under his breath each time he came up empty-handed. Fifteen minutes passed before they left the highway and drove past several streets lined with old homes, no Tiny Home Villages nearby. They turned into a subdivision that was more than the next level up in terms of status and wealth. These had easily once been million-dollar homes, large and stately, but since the inception of the THV program the traditional housing market had lost nearly all value.

He'd just opened an old file, one from before the OBA, displaying Clarkson verbally and physically harassing a State

Representative from Oregon who'd opposed the idea of open borders, when the car began to slow down. They pulled into a large, circular, cement driveway at a home with a three-car garage angled perpendicular to the main part of the house. Above the garage were two windows. A curtain moved and Devlin saw the faces of two young children peeking out, one boy, and the other a girl with ponytails poking out off the sides of her head. Devlin eased the laptop lid down, tearing his gaze from the kids as he did.

"Ready?" Tara asked.

Three men got out of the SUV behind them. Two wore Agent attire, the third, who'd been seated in the back, wore jeans, black loafers, and a pale, yellow button-up cotton shirt covered up with a heavy jacket. Across the front of his neck, the tailings of a tattoo snaked upward reaching to his chin and ears. One of the government men collected a large duffel bag from the cargo area and handed it to him before gripping his arm above the elbow and directing him toward the house.

Devlin readied his camera and recorded them as they approached the front door.

Knock knock knock.

Seconds later, the door opened to reveal a lithe, shapely woman decked out in a gray wool skirt and an off-white knitted sweater. Her hair was perfectly coiffed, lips painted a rose shade of red, and pearls circling her slender throat.

"Hello? Can I help you?" she inquired. But no sooner did she say the words her smile faltered.

"Senator Stewart?" Tara's tone bore no emotional inflection.

"Yes? Why are you here?"

"Ma'am, I'm Tara Carlson from the—"

Before Tara could provide her credentials, the Senator's face blanched and she sucked in a breath. She looked beyond

THE CONSEQUENCE CLAUSE

Tara to the Agents and their charge, her eyes barely touching on the latter, whose intense brown irises focused directly on her. When her gaze drifted to Devlin, her throat convulsed in a hard swallow. Pressing her hands flat against her thighs, her perfectly manicured fingers twitched slightly, causing the sun to glint off a huge diamond floating atop her left ring finger. It sparkled like a chandelier.

"I know who you are." The hesitant tone of her voice during her initial greeting had disappeared. "What are you doing here?" Her eyes darted again to the man standing between the Agents before shifting away.

"Ma'am. Per the Consequence Clause affiliated with the Humanity Act, we have a prisoner who, according to the system's parole board, has successfully completed his sentence. As such, they have granted a probation term of eight years." Tara paused long enough to flip to a page in her trusty blue book, not that she needed it. Devlin knew she felt it sometimes gave her a greater sense of authority when referring to it, while the person she spoke to watched.

The Senator's face paled even further.

"According to the Voter Information Log, you voted to approve the Humanity Act. Ma'am, as one who supported the issue, I'm sure you'll agree that time served is fair and appropriate and that Richard Gil here"—she waved a hand in the former prisoner's direction—"should be granted the opportunity for a humane and safe transition back into society. Per the Consequence Clause, your name was randomly selected from those who voted in favor of the Humanity Act. As such, Richard is being turned over to you for housing and care so you can provide a humane environment for the duration of his probation."

The Senator wobbled slightly. She pressed one hand around the edge of the door, her knuckles turning white as her grip tightened even more. "This is ridiculous. I'm a Senator. I can't be part of this . . . this . . . ." She lifted her free hand and flicked it in the direction of the grinning Mr. Gil.

Devlin inched forward, far enough to capture Richard's reaction to the information. He had been incarcerated at the time the Humanity Act was passed. Chances were, he'd been apprised of the Act and subsequent outcomes when he'd been transferred to Nevada, following the closure of the prison where he'd been incarcerated. But, not having been a free man during all the main events that affected the country these last handful of years, the possibility existed he didn't fully comprehend how the new laws impacted ex-convicts.

Richard gave a nod to Senator Stewart. Devlin recorded it, then continued recording when the man glanced over his shoulder and quickly back, the corners of his lips lifting ever so slightly.

Angling the camera up, Devlin couldn't quell the sinking feeling that settled in his gut as he eyed through his viewfinder the faces of the two small children still perched in the open window above the garage. Their elbows rested on the sill, chins braced in their palms as they observed the scene below with a typical child's curiosity.

"As a Senator, ma'am, you must certainly be aware of the things you supported and approved related to this type of situation. I'm happy to read you the specifics of the Consequence Clause affiliated with the Act, if you'd like."

She lifted the book, her fingers holding it open to the section she'd offered to recite from. The Senator numbly shook her head, her mouth moving, but no words coming out.

"It's all right here," Tara added. "If you somehow missed it, then I'm sorry to have to be the one to inform you that you are now fully responsible for Richard's care and management as he transitions back into society." She paused, letting this information sink in before offering the final punch to the gut. "He's your charge for the next eight years. This is a second chance for him." She turned to said charge. "He knows what happens if he screws up. Don't you, Richard?"

The Humanity Act's primary goal was a result of a hashtag group that deemed prisons not only inhumane but in direct violation of an individual's civil and human rights. Written into the Act were specifics about those who got released on parole or probation. The first related to the home remanding rule, the other was about recidivism. Offenders who re-offended, regardless of the severity of the crime, during their opportunity at freedom were given no second chances. If Richard screwed up during this second opportunity granted him, the ensuing consequence for his actions would result in permanent banishment to Nevada with no possibility of release. Ever.

Richard nodded eagerly. "I sure do know. This is so much better than being locked up, even in the FRP."

"He has some things with him, but, as you can see it's very little. You'll need to help him get more until he manages to find employment, if he chooses to, and can provide for himself. Of course, keep in mind, he's to be treated fairly and humanely. If we get reports that you're not complying with the mandates of the home remanding process, then you will face consequences for that."

What Tara said was no threat. Failure to comply had consequences of their own. Those consequences could be life-altering, especially for the likes of Senator Stewart.

"Here's my card if you have questions."

Tara held out a business card. With trembling fingers, Senator Stewart took it from her. A tight frown formed a deep crease between her eyebrows, the lines so deep it was evident she wore the expression often. Devlin's camera rolled as she asked in a shaky voice, "What was his crime?"

The camera focused back on Tara, then on Richard. Tara's thumb swiped across her phone's screen until she'd located the file information. In her official voice, she read the charges. "Mr. Gil was charged with first degree sexual assault . . . ." There was a long pause.

The silence was so thick, Devlin almost imagined he could hear everyone's hearts beating, but in reality, all he captured in the video was the sound of a car's horn somewhere far away and a dog barking.

"First degree sexual assault on a child while in a position of trust."

Senator Stewart's shocked gasp wasn't hidden by the hand that rose to press against her mouth. "I can't have a sex offender here. I have children! How am I to protect them? We'll never be able to feel safe in our own home."

Tara shrugged. "I can't say, ma'am. We didn't select you specifically for this. It was random, from the pool of voters who approved the Humanity Act, those like you who believed everyone deserves humane living and second chances. Your number came up in the VIL, it seems. You'll need to figure it out. He's your responsibility now."

Richard remained standing on the porch step as Devlin, Tara, and the two Agents turned away. Devlin didn't look back, nor did he try to record any more of the interactions between the Senator and her new housemate. Only when he got into the car alongside Tara did he let out the breath he hadn't realized he'd been holding. As they backed from the drive, he stared up at the two children whose little faces were framed perfectly in the window above the garage as Richard stepped inside the house and closed the door.

"I sure hope he takes to heart this second chance at life," Tara said, her tone laced with a healthy dose of doubt.

THIRTEEN

"Him." Devlin pointed to a shadowy figure in a doorway at the back of a crowd of rioters. The image had been captured on film during one of Senator Clarkson's protests.

"Well? Is it the same person you've seen in those other clips? Either the one around Carl's business or from the border event?" Tara asked as she glanced back and forth from the computer screen to the road.

At first, he nodded, but then switched to shaking his head. "It's hard to be sure, but it could be. I mean, they both have similar physical attributes. This guy looks taller than average, compared to others in the shot. He's also wide across his shoulders. The one from the border had on a bulky hoodie but I could still see he was big. And look there." He touched on a spot below the man's outstretched arm. He leaned in closer and then lifted the laptop so he could get it even nearer to his face.

"Do you see that? It looks like he has a mark, right there, on his wrist." His head tilted slightly one way and then the other. Setting the laptop back onto his thighs, he minimized the screen and pulled up the file from the border opening, freezing it on the shot of the man approaching the blonde. He then fast-forwarded to the frame where the man's hand holding the gun was level with the woman's skull.

Sweat began to bead on Devlin's forehead and his stomach grew queasy as the real-life imagery branded in his brain tried to play through to the end. He retrieved the image of the man hiding in the shadows and displayed the two stilled screenshots side by side.

"It could definitely be the same person." His conclusion held a level of certainty. "I'd be willing to bet my next discretionary allowance on it. Look." He angled the computer toward Tara. "Both have something in the same spot on their wrists. It's too coincidental not to be the same man." He glanced at Tara who kept trying to peer over at the screen and the road at the same time. "Now all I have to do is find out who the hell he is."

"Hmm," Tara murmured. "Clarkson is married to Grant. What about the man we saw with the President over in Virginia? Hulk Guy, you called him. You said you remembered him from the border?"

Devlin's jaw drooped open. "Oh, my god," he whispered as he pressed a hand to his forehead. "Yes! The similarities are there. How could I have overlooked him?"

His eyes darted back and forth across the screen as his mind searched through his database of memories. He clicked again on the video of the border event and rewound the tape. Once it got to the part where he'd been filming images of the people coming through the hole in the border wall, he pressed play. The scene immediately began to shift away from the wall, moving left over the crowd of immigrants and protesters, slowly working its way toward the stage where he'd seen Clarkson, Grant, and Hulk Guy.

"Everything was so organized," he said softly, deciding to reveal memories he'd not shared with Tara before. "The protesters were behaving. Clarkson was doing her normal thing, patting herself on the back. Agents were wandering through the crowds. The immigrants coming over had a comfortable place set up for them where they were given all their necessities, including their Tiny Home Village assignment, their Unilateral

Socially Fundamental Control Device, and a cell phone." One hand hovered over the mouse pad of his laptop, the other clenched into a tight fist against his waist.

The video had finally reached the part focused on the platform. This, Devlin recalled, was seconds before he narrowed the angle of his lens back to the blonde and the two hashtags. If he were to let the scene play another few seconds beyond that, he'd see the moment when his real-life chaos had begun. But he didn't allow it to play that far. He paused where it showed Clarkson with both her hands held out, megaphone in one. Behind her, slightly to one side, was Grant, frozen in the motion of clapping, her smile wide and hideous. But the space on the other side of Clarkson, where he knew for certain Hulk Guy had been before Devlin had turned to watch the people coming through the wall, was empty. Hulk Guy was gone.

"He was right there." Devlin's finger touched the screen where the man had been; the same man they'd seen with Grant at the bar in Virginia. "Sometime in the span of the few minutes I'd had my camera turned to the wall, he must have left the stage." His throat tightened and he pressed a hand to his neck, massaging at the tension building there. In his peripheral view he saw Tara lean slightly to see where he was pointing.

"I didn't even think to make the connection to his not being up there. Right after this, the shooter came into the screen from my left. I was looking through the camera and didn't see him until he was in my viewfinder. Until he lifted the gun." Devlin was sweating and his hands were trembling, both signs of an impending panic attack. He gently closed the laptop, gripped it with both hands, leaned his head back, and closed his eyes.

"Are you all right?" Tara asked, compassion and concern thickening her accent.

He nodded, drawing in and exhaling in deep, steadying breaths. "Yeah, I will be." A few minutes passed before the panic subsided. "I've got to find out who he is," he repeated his earlier statement. "So, we can bring him to justice."

"It won't be as simple as that," Tara challenged gently. "Unless we have definitive proof Hulk Guy was the man with the gun"—she nodded toward Devlin's computer—"there won't be much we can do. We can't see his face, so it's going to be hard to connect the shooter to the man we saw with Grant." After a small pause, she added, a bit more hopefully, "If he's the same person who threatened Carl, we'd need to catch him in the act of issuing the threats, an illegal act big enough to warrant my intervention. If we can do that, we already know we have a direct connection to either or both Clarkson and Grant."

Carl's assumptions that the guy worked up on the Hill was likely spot on. But when Devlin got the list of staff and their security badge photos from Josh, including all the members of Congress, Hulk Guy hadn't been in any of the files.

Still, hope wriggled at Devlin's core. Somehow, he knew he was getting closer to the truth. He could almost hear the blonde's voice, clearer than he'd ever sensed her before, ushering him on this path in the right direction. He turned to look out the window. As the landscape outside blurred past, his spirits began to lift.

He'd spent years traveling the country, East Coast to West Coast, driving through small towns and big cities alike, and his least favorite places to visit were large cities. This hadn't always been the case. His entire adult life he'd lived in urban areas, enjoying the offerings found in such places. But since the OBA, big cities had become more congested than ever. Every metropolis in every State now resembled one of those places he'd seen in old entertainment shows that used to be popular. The shows in which celebrity foodies would immerse themselves into diverse cultures to sample cuisines found all over the world. In those foreign places, the streets were alive with hundreds, if not thousands, of people walking, biking, riding scooters, with a few automobiles and buses crammed into the mix. That's how the city of Dearborn, Michigan, was now—their next stop.

Dearborn used to be a very depressed city, following the collapse of the auto industry and other manufacturing plants. It had existed for years as a rundown part of the greater Detroit metropolitan area, yet another city hit hard by failed economics, prior to the Open Borders Act. Not a decade past, Dearborn's population hovered near a comfortable one hundred thousand. Since the OBA, that number had quadrupled.

All around him now was a sea of color—green, black, blue, white—a mass of fabric, moving like a river. It was exactly as he'd seen in those food shows.

The people in the market today were covered head to toe in fabric, sometimes so much, Devlin could only see eyes staring out beyond the veil of a niqab. There were other forms of dress, too: hijabs, khimars, or chadors. The long cloak and coverings of the latter hid every inch of skin of a woman's form from view except her face, in most cases.

There were men in the crowd as well, though far fewer of them than women. They stood out like lighthouses, in their floor length, white thobes, their heads adorned with a ghutra—a scarf that was either red and white or black and white. Atop each scarf, was a black circle egal perched like a crown. The men weaved through the crowd like eels through a sea of anemone. Devlin noticed that many of the city's inhabitants had turned to watch the interlopers—he, Tara, and the Agents with them—as they progressed through the market.

Dearborn was an hour's drive away from Ann Arbor. Following the visit to Senator Stewart's home, they'd zipped back toward Detroit, with plans to make a stop at another Consequence Engagement before their late flight out that night.

Devlin kept his eyes on the back of Tara's head as they worked their way through the square. He watched her shock of dark hair, pulled tight into a bouncy ponytail high on her head swish back and forth, like a metronome holding time with the pace she set.

When she'd fiercely refused to wear a hijab, he'd suggested she at least wear a hat or something to help make her less conspicuous in the crowd of covered women. She'd refused to conform to the laws that ruled in this area, as was her right in her official capacity, but she had at least agreed to pull her hair back. Fortunately, her heavy jacket and boots aided in hiding the rest of her body, for the most part.

Their intent behind being where they were, one of the largest Islamic communities in the States, wasn't to disrupt the colony that had formed. With approval through the OBA, Muslims and any other religious or special interest groups who chose to settle an area and operate under their own set of laws were permitted to do so. It was allowed as long as they let folks like Tara and Devlin, government people and news people, move about freely to do official States' business.

Today's purpose in Dearborn was to locate one person.

Talal Siddiqui.

Following Tara and Devlin were four armed Agents. Laws within the States prohibited the possession of guns of any kind, but Tara had been provided intel about men in the Dearborn community who may possibly be carrying them. The Agents were a necessary presence. Siddiqui was a powerful man, the leader of this community. It was presumed he, or men assigned to protect him, had weapons.

The throng of people filling the street parted as Tara and her entourage moved through the crowd, intent upon their destination. Devlin warily observed the expressions of those they passed. He smiled warmly at ones who made eye contact,

THE CONSEQUENCE CLAUSE

trying to reassure them with a welcoming gesture that they weren't there to interfere with their lifestyle.

Finally, they made it to the end of the street-converted-into-a-market, turned the corner and approached a home that sat back from the road. The house was an unassuming brick ranch-style with a two-car garage. Behind the house, rising high into the air were pine trees and other varieties of trees that had shed their leaves for the winter, leaving behind towering skeletons. Tara strode purposely up to the front door and knocked. The Agents waited solemnly around her, two on the small patio with her and the remaining two along the walkway in front of a large picture window. Devlin stood off to the side in the yard, positioned so he could capture the scene about to take place.

The door opened and a man wearing similar headwear to those seen in the market appeared. "May I help you?" His command of the English language was strong, but his native accent even stronger.

"Talal Siddiqui?" Tara inquired, knowing already that this was the man she was addressing. She and Devlin had reviewed his file on the drive over from Ann Arbor. They'd both seen photos of him with and without the headdress.

Siddiqui nodded, his gaze shifting from Tara's uncovered head downward over her body and then back up. His eyes darkened, his lids shrinking to thin slits and his mouth twisting up slightly.

"Mr. Siddiqui, I'm Tara Carlson of the Consequence Compliance Oversight Committee. It has come to our attention that you attempted to bribe a States Congressperson and threatened her. I believe something about Sharia law was mentioned." Tara tapped an index finger against the side of her cheek, as if she were questioning the specifics of the report. But that was merely a ruse. She knew exactly what Sharia law was and what the man had implied when he'd threatened the

Congresswoman. "Apparently, you demanded she put forth a bill that would allow for immigrants living within the country to be excluded from all federal taxation." She drew in a deep breath, replenishing the oxygen in her lungs while waiting for Siddiqui's acknowledgment or denial of the claim.

Siddiqui's head dipped sharply. "I wouldn't say it was a threat."

Tara bobbed her head in affirmation. "Mmm-hmmm. Well, threat, promise, whatever you want to call it, the actions were illegal under *our* laws. When we pulled the Congresswoman's Voter Information Log, we found that she voted in favor of the Open Borders Act, which, as I understand it, was how you came into this country. As such, the threat you made to detain her by way of your Sharia law is countered and voided due to her vote in favor of the OBA, thus supporting your rights to your beliefs."

"I'll have to thank her then, the next time I see her." There was another subtle threat in his voice, which Tara could do nothing about. At least not until he approached the Congresswoman again with another bribe.

In the background, beyond Siddiqui, three women hovered in silent abjection. Two wore the traditional hijab, their faces directed downward, but the third, who stood slightly behind the two, wore what Devlin knew was called a burqa. This form of dress made it so not one inch of the woman's body from her face to her fingers to her toes was visible. Her eyes were even hidden behind a mesh window sewn into the fabric. At least they'd been hidden until she stealthily lifted the veil, briefly revealing her face. She stayed that way barely long enough for Devlin to capture on camera her mouth moving in a silent plea for help.

He recognized her. Her picture had been splashed across the news for months last year. Wide blue eyes on a pale face pleaded wildly for an intervention from Devlin. Tara's position in front of Siddiqui prohibited her from witnessing the woman's actions. At least she'd given no indication of having seen it.

The woman was Natalie Hayes, a realtor from Michigan who'd gone missing. The mainstream media outlets had aired the search efforts on their story line of "Where's Natalie?" for months, once they'd learned she was the daughter of a Hollywood celebrity. The MSM had shown images of her every night on the evening news, until eventually her disappearance became old news. He couldn't recall the last time updates were made as to clues of her whereabouts.

He did remember his resentment at the lengths to which they'd aired her story, and their efforts to enlist the help of the public to find her. It stung quite a lot that her status as a celebrity's child ranked her life far more important than the woman from the border's had been, enough to warrant the MSM's efforts to broadcast news about the missing realtor. They'd never offered to help Devlin find the blonde's killer.

"The reason I am here, Mr. Siddiqui, is due to the violation of *our* laws in relation to bribing a political official, which occurred outside your established boundary here." She pointed at the ground.

A heavy and uncomfortable silence ensued, at which time Devlin took the opportunity to interject. "Who are the women behind you?"

Siddiqui's dark eyes shifted to Devlin before turning his head enough to look at the trio hovering demurely behind him. All three had their heads lowered. "They are my wives."

Tara leaned slightly to the side to peer past the man obstructing her view of the women.

"Mr. Siddiqui, the Consequence Clause attached to the Open Borders Act indicates that as an immigrant welcomed into this country, you are permitted to establish boundaries and apply your laws here. But outside those boundaries you are to act according to laws of the States. You, of course, did sign and swear to uphold this edict. In the situation with the Congresswoman, you violated that which you agreed to abide by when you attempted to bribe her. Bribery of a politician is one of the most serious of crimes in this country."

Siddiqui made a thick, disgusted sound from his throat. "You dare to enter my city, where the laws that apply here are what I say they are? How do you know she was not lying about where our conversation took place? I abide by the laws of this country outside the boundaries of my city. Here, I rule." He again scrutinized Tara, his expression dark, menacing.

Were it not for the Agents standing close by, Devlin might have been concerned for his and her well-being. But he was hopeful the threat of armed men hovering behind Tara would subdue whatever it was Siddiqui thought he had the power to do to them. That, and the fact that it was all being recorded.

"Are you threatening me?" Tara barked with an unfunny laugh. "For that—" She began to flip through pages of her little blue book.

"I'd like to see the face of your wife, Talal." Devlin intentionally called him by his first name. He wanted to unsettle him, catch him off guard.

There was the slightest twitch of a muscle in Siddiqui's jaw, and his eyes and mouth flattened into thin lines across his face. Behind him, the woman Devlin knew to be Natalie flinched, her head lifting in response to the request.

"My wife will not reveal herself." He crossed his arms over his chest in finality.

Tara looked back to Devlin awaiting the next play in the match she was unaware he'd initiated.

"You there, in the back," he called out to Natalie. "Come forward and reveal your face. The camera is your witness."

Siddiqui whirled around and pointed at Natalie. In a stern voice he commanded, "Don't move."

Devlin decided to appeal to Tara for assistance. "Ms. Carlson, the woman inside this house revealed herself to me seconds ago. She is Natalie Hayes, a local who disappeared from this area nearly a year back. I believe she's being held here against her will."

A shocked expletive fell from Tara's lips, a departure from her typical unemotional persona during Consequence Engagements. "What the hell, Devlin? Are you sure?"

"Ms. Hayes, show yourself. You have nothing to fear." He really hoped that was not a lie. Siddiqui wouldn't try to harm her knowing he was being recorded. Would he?

Natalie's plea for help indicated she was being held against her will. Kidnapping and rape were still felony crimes in the States, but he knew there were hashtag groups out West pushing to make all crimes legal. As far as he knew, nothing like that had been approved by the federal government, at least not yet. Here, however, in Dearborn, Michigan, and other areas around the country like it, things were a bit different. Sharia law had been given free rein, but only within the boundaries established by those claiming it their rule of law. Outside those boundaries, federal law still prevailed. But kidnapping and rape? Certainly, those were big enough crimes to warrant federal intervention, just as bribing a politician had been labeled extremely heinous.

Natalie's hands shook like leaves on a tree as she pushed the veil up over her head. Tears slipped down her face, but she didn't move past Siddiqui. Frozen in place after a year of subjected obedience gripped her in an iron fist.

"Please, help me." Her plea did not fall on deaf ears. Certainly, help would be offered.

Tara flipped open her book of rules, turning past page after page in a desperate search for something. Her eyes devoured the words before her. Every few seconds she'd give a quick shake of her head and an occasional heavy sigh would escape her lips. Finally, she closed the book and scraped a hand over her face, holding her closed fist against her nose and mouth. "Damn it."

"Ms. Carlson?" Devlin lowered his camera slightly as he inched closer to her. "Get her out of there."

The Agents stepped in front of Tara. They'd been about to enter the house to rescue a severely distraught Natalie when Tara's voice rang out.

"Stop!" She nearly shouted as she shot her hand out and gripped the bicep of the Agent closest to her. In the background, Devlin saw and heard Natalie wince, her soft cry loud enough he knew his microphone would capture it, too.

Tara lurched past Siddiqui who stood large and imposing, only half blocking the doorway to his home. Devlin was surprised he'd granted her entrance. Upon reaching Natalie, Tara gripped the woman's upper arms with both hands, like she intended to shake her. And then she did.

"Ms. Hayes." Her voice was strong and clear.

Devlin doubted anyone but him would notice the tenseness in her jaw. What triggered alarms in his head is that she hadn't immediately dragged Natalie from the home.

"Ms. Hayes. I need you to explain to me exactly how you came to be here." When Natalie's eyes flicked to Siddiqui, Tara gave her another small shake. "Look at me and tell me how you got here. I must know."

A sick feeling began to churn in Devlin's stomach, like it does in those moments leading up to a terrible vomiting bout.

Natalie's voice was barely a breath when she first spoke, like her vocal cords hadn't been used in a long time. Devlin slipped inside the doorway, ignoring Siddiqui's grunt of irritation or acquiescence he couldn't be sure.

"I had a client who wanted to see a house east of here." She gulped, then ran her tongue over dry lips. "It-it . . . w-w-was a normal scheduled showing," she stuttered.

"Was it in Dearborn's city limits?" Tara asked sternly.

She shook her head. "No. I checked the listing. It was in Dearborn Heights, which is outside the city of Dearborn's boundaries. I'd been careful about it since the laws changed and began allowing this . . . ." Her words drifted off as her eyes darted to Siddiqui and then back to Tara.

Tara yanked her cell phone from her coat pocket and pecked at the screen. Her lips moved as she read silently. A few swipes of her finger, right and then left, followed by more typing with her thumbs, resulted in a whole new set of lines Devlin had never seen appearing high on her forehead. Her brows dipped inward on a tight frown. "Son of a bitch!"

One side of her cheek sank inward as she bit down on it. She turned to stare thoughtfully at Siddiqui. Devlin's camera zoomed out to capture them both in the viewfinder. Tara's chest lifted up and down too fast as she forced air in and out of her lungs. One corner of Siddiqui's lips went up in an arrogant smirk.

Tara swiveled her head back to Natalie. Their gazes locked and then Tara's shoulders slumped, her head moving slowly side-to-side, before finally, she turned and walked past Siddiqui, exiting his home.

"Talal Siddiqui. Under the terms of the Consequence Clause of the OBA, which you violated when you bribed a political official, your punishment is that you and your family are to be stripped of all assets in reparation for the crimes committed against the States, and you're to be sent from this country, with no opportunity in which to return."

Cries of alarm fell from the lips of two of Siddiqui's wives, while Natalie's expression brimmed with hope.

"It is unfortunate," Tara added in a softer, almost sad-sounding voice as she shifted her gaze to meet Natalie's, "that under terms of *your* laws applied within boundaries you have claimed, in this case necessary paperwork had been filed sixteen months past absorbing Dearborn Heights into your boundaries . . . ." She stopped mid-sentence.

"Wh-what does that mean? Am I free to go?" Natalie moved forward, but Tara's raised palm drew her up short.

"Mr. Siddiqui, your disrespect and disregard for that which you came here to take advantage of, are not what the people of this land will tolerate. These Agents will give you time to collect those personal belongings you can carry before escorting you to the airport where you'll be put on a plane and transported back to your country."

She looked to the three women standing in wide-eyed confusion behind Siddiqui. "You, along with your *three* wives and any children you may have, are hereby directed to return to your homeland." Two of the wives shuddered, their faces going pale. They held tight to each other. "Never again will you or any of your immediate family be permitted to set foot in this country."

Devlin recorded the reactions of everyone as Tara turned on a heel and headed toward the street. Natalie rushed forward to follow her. At the doorway, Siddiqui reached out a hand, his fingers curling around her elbow. She yelped as she was pulled back against his hard chest.

"Release me," she hissed with bravado. "Ms. Carlson? Why aren't you helping me?" she called out to Tara, who'd already stepped down off the front porch.

Tara turned, regret showing in her dark eyes. "Under the agreement with the federal government, only specific federal laws supersede those laws established by foreigners who legally claim territory as permitted through the Open Borders Act." She lifted a hand in the direction of Siddiqui. "Sixteen months ago, your h-husband," she faltered as she said the word, "filed claims to Dearborn Heights and declared Sharia law rule within its boundaries."

A wet throaty moan sounded from Natalie and her body began to rock back and forth when the reality of Tara's words sunk in. "No," she cried. "You don't mean—"

"According to the laws that now govern here," Tara lifted one hand, palm up, "you were claimed within Siddiqui's rightful boundaries. There is nothing I can do to change that. As such, you belong to him and as part of the family group will be escorted from this country. I'm so sorry, but those were terms made part of the OBA to which we must abide," she whispered at the end.

Devlin rushed over to Tara, sensing she needed him by her side. Before shutting off his camera, he turned it once more toward the doorway and watched Natalie crumple to her knees.

A satisfied smile appeared on Siddiqui's face as he pushed the burqa back into place, covering the realtor's red and tear-stained face. And then he slowly closed the door.

***

"Damn it, Ms. Carlson. Stop!"

Devlin finally caught up to Tara near their parked car. After giving the Agents instructions on what to do with the Siddiqui family, she'd stormed away, leaving Devlin to chase after her. "We can't leave her there. She's got a family, a real family. Not one she's been forced into. How could you leave her there and walk away?"

Without giving a response, she opened the driver's side door and fell into the seat. Devlin scrambled around to the other side and got in, pulling the door shut with as much force as he could manage before swiveling around to face her.

She let her head fall against the headrest and scrunched her eyes tight. Her chest rose and fell as she heaved air in and out of her lungs, and then she grasped the steering wheel with both hands and pointed ahead.

"*That* is called the law which the leaders of this great nation have sanctioned." Her cheeks puffed out as she expelled a long sigh. "To not allow groups of people, like Siddiqui and his countrymen, to assemble and establish boundaries they claim as their own, as they've clearly done, was deemed discriminatory." She met his dumbfounded stare. "Like the Mexicans have done in Arizona, the Koreans in California, the Amish, the Chinese, the Scottish, the Mormons, and so many others. All they have to do is demand their rights and stake a legal claim, then cry discrimination if they don't get what they want. And *that*." She pointed again at the street in front of them. "Is the hellish answer to your question."

"But-but . . . ." Words failed him. "But what protections are in place to safeguard the rest of the people, people like us who don't choose to live in places like these?"

Tara turned the key in the ignition and shifted the car into drive. It was several contemplative minutes before she answered. "The People, people born and raised here or not, need to avoid those boundaries claimed by different representative groups, so they don't fall prey to the laws or religious claims of others. Unless they choose to. Natalie's lack of caution landed her in this situation."

More minutes of silence passed as they both mentally reexamined every aspect of what had just happened. They stared out the windows, neither fully paying attention to their surroundings, as they traveled the highway on autopilot.

Devlin rubbed his palms back and forth against his thighs, and then he reached up and scraped his hands through his hair. "What did we do to that poor girl?"

He covered his eyes with his fingers as if he were trying to scrape away the images branded on his lids. A sense of sadness and anger swamped him as he considered the life Natalie Hayes had had forced upon her. Would Siddiqui grow to care for her and treat her well? Or would the young woman's life be one filled with torment? Would she be permitted to contact her family before her exile from the States? Would her famous parents be able to negotiate her release? Or would they fail and lose her forever?

It wasn't something Devlin needed to contemplate. His job was to report the consequences handed down to people based on laws established by government leaders. In many cases, those laws were the result of what others demanded and as such fought to change in their favor.

Resigning himself to Natalie's fate, he retrieved his laptop, and directed his focus again to the project he'd been researching moments before they'd essentially destroyed a woman's life.

"*We* didn't do anything to her, Dev."

Tara's irritation was evident in her tone as well as in the stiff posture and white-knuckled grip she had on the steering wheel. "Decisions made by our government allowed this. The OBA allowed this. All *we* did was do our job and enforce laws put into place by people who, quite honestly, were greedy and power-hungry. They allowed this to happen." Her lips twisted and she made a derisive sound from her throat. "The only reason we were here today was because of a broken federal law, not because of anything related to Sharia law. People like Siddiqui haven't done anything wrong. It's our politicians who thought allowing foreigners to enter our country and establish boundaries was the right thing to do. Not doing so would have been discriminatory. Siddiqui was within his rights to do as he did with Natalie." She flung a hand in the air as she continued her tirade.

"No, the reason we were there was because the politicians who allowed all of this to happen were idiots. They made bribery a bigger offense than kidnapping. And yet many still accept bribes thinking they'll get away with it. We got lucky that the Congresswoman in this situation wasn't one of the ones lacking an ethical backbone and reported it."

When her voice broke, Devlin's head whipped around. There were actual tears brimming on the edge of her eyelids, though none had breached the lashes. She took a restorative breath, composing herself. It was the first time he'd witnessed this level of emotion from her in all the time they'd spent together.

She cleared her throat. "At least now we know about Natalie. Maybe her family can arrange a bargain with Siddiqui and get her out of there." She bobbed her head toward his computer. "Keep looking for your mystery man. You're on the right track to eliminating some of the corruption still happening in our government. We've got to find it and put a stop to the power-hungry sources of evil lurking out there."

Devlin gawked at his companion as the scenery around them blurred in the background. When he opened his mouth to say something, she shook her head.

"I'm sorry. I didn't mean to lose control like that. It's just . . . sometimes everything builds until I can't take anymore. I'm good now. It won't happen again."

So, the almighty Tara Carlson wasn't a robot after all, as many in the MSM had portrayed her. Devlin was beginning to understand her more and would watch for the next build up and be better prepared when it happened.

FOURTEEN

Josh clacked the gavel against the wood surface. Congress was back in session after a lengthy break following the mandated State home visits. Today, members of Congress would be debriefing about their experiences.

"Welcome back, everyone. I hope your travels were effective and proved helpful to what your job here in this room is. Who wants to begin?"

Like a classroom of unruly students who refused to wait for the teacher to give them permission to speak, men and women rushed in with their complaints and grievances. Others pushed to their feet and waited for a gap in the less-than-melodic symphony of voices.

"It's outrageous what we were subjected to," bellowed a man of short stature standing in the middle of the mob around him.

"There's no morality left in this country!" exclaimed a woman close to Devlin.

"What was once open space and federal lands are being overrun with Tiny Home Villages. They're metastasizing like cancer!"

"Kids don't go to school."

Then, above all the complaints and shouts of the atrocities members of Congress experienced in their journeys, one deep, booming voice rang out louder than all the rest. It came from one of the newer members of Congress, a Representative from

New Jersey. Devlin knew from his bio that he'd come to the States from the Middle East following the OBA. "We must close the borders."

The impact of his words silenced the melee in the room like a wet blanket on a fire. With hands clasped before him, House Representative Sayyid Ashraf addressed Josh while the media watched, cameras recording.

"I am thankful to have been offered the opportunity to sit on this Congress, and I appreciate the chance to have engaged with families around my State. What I found shed light on issues that are both endearing and heartbreaking. The situation in my State is no better than what it was in the country I left behind, before matters there improved to what they are now. Things here are worse than it is over there. So many immigrants like myself are not living the American dream, the one we'd heard about." Ashraf paused, carefully choosing what he was going to say next. "We need to stop giving into the demands of everyone. We need to bring back much of what has been lost over the last two decades. And to do so, we must close the borders until we clean up the mess in the country that this body of people helped create."

An older woman seated on the opposite side of the room from Ashraf stood up. "We tried to tell those who pushed the OBA this is what would happen, but they wouldn't listen."

As Devlin panned the camera around the room in search of the speaker, his movements stumbled when Senator Harriet Clarkson appeared in the crosshairs. She wasn't one of those who'd risen to their feet. Instead, she remained seated, a haughty scowl on a face already heavy with jowls. When another person chimed in with his complaints, her scowl shifted into a smirk.

If ever there was a poster child for corrupt, evil, selfish, greedy politicians, Clarkson was it. Her motivations, her actions, with the support of many groups and people, including past presidents, and of course the current one, had nearly brought one of the greatest countries in the world to its knees. She'd been integral in turning the country from a place of prosperity and freedom to one that was two years away, three at best, from ranking in the top three among third world countries.

"It's impossible to change what's been passed. Try taking back the entitlements. See what happens. There'd be a full-on civil war this time." This came from a man somewhere in the room who had to yell to be heard over the other voices.

Still focused on Clarkson, Devlin watched as a young man dressed in khakis and a white button-up, long-sleeved shirt with a red tie scurried down the aisle closest to Clarkson. He crouched low when he got to her row and hurried past all the other Senators until he reached her. Kneeling, he handed over a slip of paper, and while she read it, he looked up, peering around the room.

The man would be Clarkson's page, there to run her errands, bring her messages, do her bidding. If he were one of the luckier ones, he'd get to be involved in the finer details of her work, see firsthand how a Senator's job was done, or should be done. But Devlin highly doubted she'd treat the kid with much regard beyond errand boy, considering he was Caucasian and likely an original citizen, too. The hateful woman didn't treat those subsets of people with respect.

The kid's head swiveled around and suddenly Devlin found him looking his way. His eyes darted down to Clarkson and back up again. And then his chin dipped down in a slight nod, as if he were communicating a message. Yet Devlin had no idea what it meant. He'd never met the page before.

The young man bent closer to Clarkson when she spoke to him. And without a backward glance at Devlin, he exited the row in the same way he'd come in, hunched and in a hurry, before leaving the room altogether.

The curious event had lasted but a few minutes, all while Josh allowed more arguments and loud discussions to fill the room. Finally, he whacked the gavel against the podium. "Representative Ashraf, would you care to elaborate on your findings, share your experiences from New Jersey?"

Ashraf nodded majestically. "The Open Borders Act is not solely to blame for the problems out there. Most issues existed before the OBA came about; however, opening the borders the way we did has added an unsustainable level of challenges to what already existed. I am an immigrant to this country, allowed here through the OBA. My family has prospered in New Jersey—"

"Of course, you have," someone muttered.

Ashraf ignored the rude outburst. "But after my assigned visits, I saw that people like me, like my family and friends, only prosper within the confines of our communities we lay claim to, where *we* teach our children, care for one another, work our lands to provide food for ourselves. We have little exposure to the America we believed we would find when we arrived here. I'm certain all people, immigrants and original citizens, who live in other States, are doing the same. If we wanted isolation and to live among our own, we could have stayed in our home country, which ironically, in my case has thrived heartily these last few years. Again, because of rules implemented by this body of people." He held his arms out wide. "But I wanted the American dream for my children. This is supposed to be the Land of Opportunity, yet it's become nothing more than the Land of Anything Goes. It has become a country of handouts and people who are lazy, unethical, and immoral. That is not what I want my children to learn."

Senator Hamilton from New Mexico got to his feet. "We

should have considered all that years ago when the OBA was pushed through without a full review and more discussion between us."

Representative Ashraf's head swiveled in his direction.

Hamilton asked, "Do you propose we cancel the OBA now? Like that's going to happen," he scoffed. "What are we to do, send all the immigrants we let in back to their home countries? Come now, don't be obtuse." He huffed and sank down into his seat.

Voices of approval and denial raced around the room. Josh held up a hand and whacked the gavel again, demanding silence. He turned toward the media pit.

"As Representative Ashraf stated, the OBA only added to the massive list of problems this country faced prior to its passing. Introducing hundreds of thousands of people to join in on issues already in play has created the bigger challenge. This country belongs to the People. *You* have the power to fix what needs fixing. Talk to your Senators and Representatives, these folks here." He pointed out to the audience of Congresspeople. "They are who can decide to close the borders or change the process of immigration to something that works better, something sustainable."

To Congress, he said, "Right now, we have no border patrol, no law enforcement, and no protection because many of you all, or your predecessors, said it wasn't needed. You said it was inhumane and cruel to stop immigrants from coming into our country. Therefore, those obstacles were removed, but then you made it so nobody had to work toward anything, and everything became a handout. These are only a few of the issues Representative Ashraf is referring to when he said the problems existed before the OBA, not simply because of it. Your logic on what's inhumane and discriminatory got so blown out of proportion, you caved to every demand made by every hashtag out there. You did it then and you're still doing it now, yet I do think with less frequency."

His tone was the one Devlin guessed was how he'd spoken to his high school students, back when he was a teacher, like they were children being instructed and reprimanded both.

"The magnitude of reversing the OBA is far too great," a long-time Senator from Arkansas drawled. "Even if we tried, it could take years to undo. Still, we must change something. I'll agree, the OBA wasn't the catalyst to the problems we face now. But it added an element of population that compounded the issues created by everything else we here have pushed through before and since the OBA was passed. This land, the Land of Anything Goes, as Representative Ashraf called it, can't sustain what's happening to it. All the entitlements are being paid for off the backs of the rich. Because that's what so many out there demanded. As if that class of people weren't already paying the majority of all taxes, before we took more from them. And look where that's got us." He swiped a hand through the air and huffed, as if he'd only then realized his argument would fall on deaf ears.

An Illinois Representative got to her feet. She was a tall brunette with short-cropped hair and a boxy frame, shoulders as wide as her hips, and dressed in a suit and tie. "Our upper echelon tax base and our businesses pay for this country, yet we're losing both of those as fast as a leaky faucet letting water down the drain. Hollywood's not putting out movies because without the freedom of speech they once had, they might offend someone no matter what they put in their films. Celebrities are losing money here, so they're leaving, going to the Middle East, Europe, or Canada, and taking their wealth with them. We've lost several of our big grocers and automobile plants and I'm hearing our largest retail warehouse is leaving for India or Italy or somewhere. If we offset that by raising taxes on those who remain behind and those in our drastically shrinking workforce, how long before they too leave or quit working altogether and decide to live off the system of handouts we've created?" She raised her hands and then let them fall against her sides in a sign of defeat.

Senator Clarkson lifted her round body up out of her chair, visibly breathing hard at the effort. She brushed the gray plait of hair off her shoulder and thrust her chin out, exposing the waddle at her neck which had gotten notably fleshier since the last time Devlin had viewed her through the lens of a camera. "The Consequence Clause is to blame for all of this."

Josh laughed. "Oh, come on now, Harriet. When you were a child, did your momma let you run into the neighbor's house without permission? Did she allow you to steal candy from a store without punishing you when she found out? You must have forgotten all your momma taught you, as did most of the country, and this government. For every action, there's a reaction, or, more specifically, for every crime, there's a consequence. Because of what's happened to the country, the Consequence Clause is the only thing keeping it a remotely tolerable place in which to live. The CC is fair and has led to a vast decline in bad behaviors over the past few years. I think our friends from *The People's News* can attest to that."

Devlin hid slightly behind his camera, embarrassed at being called out so specifically. "Uh, yeah, thanks."

Josh chuckled, fully aware he'd caught him off guard.

"The problem is not the CC. And it's not the immigrants, either. You need to come up with solutions to everything that's been mentioned here today without blaming the innocent people who came into this country seeking a better way of life. The one Representative Ashraf hoped for. You need to fix the mess you created. Giving in to every lobbyist, special interest, and hashtag group should have ended long ago. Yet even now, many of you"—he looked directly at Senator Clarkson—"are still actively trying to destroy the little that's left of our foundation by championing the likes of all those who complain and want more. Those old ways of thinking carried into the new government and has certainly landed us in quite a pickle. Now you all need to fix this."

He lifted the gavel and smacked it down, announcing his talking time was over. The real discussions were about to begin.

FIFTEEN

Pine needles crunched beneath Devlin's feet as he stepped as lightly as possible. He and Tara had returned to Michigan, to the northern portion of the mitt, and were presently standing in a heavily treed area. Directly across the water was the border to Canada.

In a loud whisper, he said, "Can you tell me where we're going, at least?" No sooner were the words out of his mouth when his foot caught on a tree root that lurched him forward, his hands grappling for anything to break his fall.

"Shhh," Tara shushed him over her shoulder, unaware of his plight.

Flickers of moonlight trickled through branches overhead like a strobe light spinning slowly. Tara was only a couple of feet ahead of him, but he could barely make out her form in the dark, beneath the canopy of trees. He trotted a couple steps to catch up to her but slowed again for fear of twisting an ankle, or worse. Stepping over a felled tree, he let out a hushed "eek" when he bumped into Tara's back.

She whirled around, clapping a hand over his mouth before forcing him to his knees beside her. She pressed her lips close to his ear. "Will you be quiet?"

Her skin was soft where it brushed his cheek; she was warm, and her hair smelled like roses. They'd spent a lot of time in close confines together, be it a car, a restaurant, and sometimes even the occasional hotel room. But rarely had they ever gotten this close. Her proximity unsettled him, and he instinctively leaned away.

"They're there, over the top of the hill," she whispered, pointing east.

The hill she referred to was barely a small berm edging the area of a city park. Behind and around them were trees and little else. Ahead, beyond the park was Lake Huron. Together, they Army-crawled up the embankment and lay on their bellies beside a massively large oak tree. Dressed all in black, including stocking caps to cover their heads, he could barely make out Tara's face. The moisture in her eyes glistened in the sliver of moonlight peeking through the trees. He reached one hand out and pressed it against her cheek, needing to somehow ground her face to her body. She directed him with hand gestures to turn his attention out in front of them.

There were two cars in a parking lot near the edge of the park. Devlin and Tara had left their vehicle along a narrow street, a quarter mile up the road. A lighthouse burning hot and bright towered high up into the sky, a beacon to ships journeying through the narrow waterways. The lighthouse was painted a bright white while the cap on top was black as night. Two people stood in front of the tower, appearing like silhouettes against the backdrop. One was easily identified as a man, tall and broad across the shoulders, this being accentuated by a bulky jacket of some indistinct color. Devlin could tell the other person was a woman. She was much shorter, and her shadowy shape was distinctly feminine.

As quietly as possible, Devlin shifted the pack off his shoulder and pulled something out that resembled a big feather duster. With his camera set to record, he and Tara pushed earbuds into their ears as he switched on the microphone.

Immediately, the hushed conversation in progress yards away filled their ears. "How do I know this isn't a setup?" the man asked.

The woman turned her head in both directions, looking to make certain nobody was around. "You know who I am, where I work. It should be obvious I can be trusted." Again, her head swiveled in both directions, her unease evident.

Silhouette Man crossed his arms over his chest and braced his legs in a wide stance. "I need you to confirm the name of the person who gave you my number. Better yet, I want to know who *he* works for. I gotta verify my sources, too, you know. What you're wanting me to do could get me life in Nevada."

"I am *not* going to give you the name of my contact. The person is a member of Congress, for god's sake; that should be enough of an assurance," the woman said matter-of-factly.

Tara growled softly, evidence of her disappointment at Silhouette Woman's refusal to speak the name of her acquaintance in Congress. She obviously knew only some of the details about this situation here, but clearly not everything. An interesting development for sure; one Devlin would be digging into. But what he really wanted to know, what Tara had refused to share with him for reasons yet unknown, was how she'd heard about the event playing out in front of them now. Who'd tipped her off? Why was this worthy of her intervention?

"You'll have to trust my source is powerful and influential enough to know how to deal with matters like this without getting caught," the woman said.

"In my line of work, I trust no one. Give me a name or we're done here." His arms lowered and he moved as if he were about to walk away.

The woman's hand shot out. "Wait! Stop." She ran her palms down over her thighs, like she was pressing away wrinkles in the fabric of her slacks. "I can't give you her name, but her guy's name is . . . ." Devlin and Tara both craned their necks forward. "Her guy's name is . . . ." She pulled in a deep breath, hesitating, like she already knew revealing her source was the wrong thing to do. Eventually, she did it anyway.

It was barely audible, but Devlin thought he'd heard the name Jenkins. And from the shaking of her head, Tara had struggled to hear it, too, either that or she was surprised by the name; he wasn't sure.

"You won't find much on him but proving his connection to my friend shouldn't be too difficult for someone like you. Is that enough?"

Silhouette Man didn't immediately answer, as if he were contemplating his decision even after she'd given him a name he could research. But his contemplation was short-lived. "If I get caught, I'll be mentioning you and this Jenkins person."

The ramifications of using this Jenkins person as bait to get to the bigger connection in this scenario, went unsaid. This did nothing to deter Silhouette Woman from continuing down the path she had set out on.

"Don't screw it up and you won't get caught," she said derisively. "Will you do it?"

They could hear the couple's feet shuffling in the pea gravel. Why was it they could hear this insignificant noise loud and clear, but the most important name they'd needed to hear, wasn't? Devlin planned to run this feed through the fancier and more expensive equipment at the studio to try to flesh out this one elusive little piece of the puzzle. The other parts of the puzzle, like how Tara found out about what was happening now, and more importantly, why she'd not brought him into the loop on it, he'd have to get from her later.

The male silhouette moved, one arm reaching up, a hand crossing over the hat covering his head. "I can do it, but I gotta have some reassurances you won't turn on me."

"Oh, for god's sake," she snapped. "I told you, you have my word. You said your motto is 'eye for an eye' right? I want you to do to him what he tried to do to my-my . . . ." Her voice suddenly went thick with held-back emotion. She cleared her throat and sniffed a thick mucus-y sound. "Will you do that?"

"I don't know. What you're asking is pretty sick." There was a strange emotion in the man's deep voice that might be mistaken for excitement but might also have been revulsion.

"Then find someone who is or find some*thing* that can do the job. Nobody will believe what he says. What he did is a second offense and he'll be sent to Nevada for life, based on the new laws." The hatred in her tone was clear. "I want him to pay before he's set free to roam Nevada forever."

It was at that moment Devlin recognized the woman's voice. He was surprised he'd not caught on before now. Tara had told him what they were there to witness was top secret and she couldn't risk even a hint of it leaking, thus keeping him in the dark. Literally and figuratively as it turned out. It was only when Silhouette Woman spoke more freely and talked in less of a whisper, he'd recognized her: Senator Lisa Stewart. And the way the conversation across the park was going, he'd be willing to bet that this situation had to do with Stewart's home-remanded guest, Mr. Richard Gil.

"Is he into boys or girls?" It was a strange question, and again there was a weird huskiness in Silhouette Man's voice that made Devlin's skin crawl.

A strained silence sat heavy on the air, broken by the hushed rhythmic sound of waves brushing against the shoreline off in the background.

"Girls." The admission from Stewart came out on a growl. "I want him to pay, and I want to be there to watch as he's violated in the worst way possible."

"So, let's make this clear. You expect me to do what you want, with you there watching? I might be willing to," he said, contradicting Devlin's initial assumptions that the guy would be repulsed by what she wanted, "but I ain't going to be able to get things going with you hanging around."

"Tell me where then, and you won't know I'm there. I have to see him suffer. I want to hear him scream."

"Gawd." The softly drawled sound coming from Tara had been said so quietly, Devlin might not have heard it, but the microphone had, and the word rushed straight into his ear.

"Fine. Tomorrow. Six p.m. Bandemer Park. In Ann Arbor. That'll give me time to make sure you're not setting me up." There was more shuffling of feet. "There's a bridge there that crosses the creek. I'll do it beneath the bridge. How will you get him there?"

"I'll use bait. I'll tell him that I'm running late, and Molly is with friends at the park and needs to be picked up. He'll jump at the chance to go collect her." There could not be any more hatred and disgust in the Senator's voice than what was captured in the words. She wanted this man to suffer beyond anything reasonable, beyond what was considered humane.

The Voter Information Log had proved the Senator's belief that criminals, such as Richard, deserved a second chance, deserved to walk free among society outside the confines of a prison's walls. This, Devlin knew, because it was the reason Richard ended up being remanded to the Senator's home to begin with. She'd championed a more humane treatment of criminals. She'd publicly applauded closing jails and prisons and treating *all* human beings, criminal or otherwise, with compassion and kindness. She believed a caring spirit would stop people from doing terrible things. That was all they needed to be better people. Keeping them locked in cages like animals was only doing more harm than good.

Those had been her words in an interview Devlin had watched after he'd first met her. He'd been curious about her political views, so he'd dug up past articles on her. Apparently, the kindness and compassion she expected the rest of the population to offer a fellow human being didn't apply to her.

All Tara and Devlin had to do now was wait twenty-four hours to capture the Senator's hypocrisy on a live feed. And while they waited, Devlin would get this clip over to Mario so he could search for the missing name hidden within the whispers. Once he confirmed what he'd heard, he'd track down the connection to Stewart's friend at the Capitol.

***

The appointed hour had arrived. Tara and Devlin sat on a park bench in Ann Arbor, with the specified bridge in view. They only had to wait now for Silhouette Man to do a very dirty deed. Anyone passing by them wouldn't think twice about the "couple" they appeared to be, ones who were taking advantage of the small amount of privacy offered beneath the tendrils of a large weeping willow.

A man wearing blue jeans and a dark bomber jacket walked across the park and approached the bridge. Tara tapped Devlin on the thigh and pointed. He flicked on his camera. Beyond the bridge, a woman wearing a blue tracksuit and ball cap stopped on the walking path and began to stretch. Devlin glanced over and caught Tara rolling her eyes at Senator Stewart's ridiculous attempt at nonchalance as she scoped out the area. Her gaze skipped over to the tree where he and Tara sat, mostly hidden from view. Sensing no threat at their presence, she disregarded the unsuspecting couple they appeared to be and lowered into an awkward lunge.

Devlin zoomed his camera in on Stewart's accomplice, and instantly tensed when he recognized the man. "What the hell?" He cranked his neck around to look at Tara. "What's going on here?" The person he'd referred to as Silhouette Man was the same person he'd seen at the Capitol, the one he'd watched enter Tara's office. Her *friend.*

"He's your friend?" At her nod, he said, "He's a criminal and you're using him to frame Stewart?"

Everything about this situation suddenly screamed unethical and probably illegal. Tara using her position to seek out a criminal was one thing. Bringing Devlin into the plan was another and it went against all his beliefs. His jaw hung open and puffs of white air raced into the ozone with each hard breath he took.

Her perfectly shaped brows drew inward above obsidian eyes. She'd been caught off guard by his recognition of her friend, someone she hadn't introduced to Devlin.

"Devlin, I . . . ." she hesitated. But when he shifted on his seat, ready to get up to leave, she pressed her hand to his thigh. "No. It's not what you think. His name is Harper. He's an Agent and the person who reached out to him is the one who works for Stewart's contact in Congress."

Devlin quirked a brow, asking without words for her to explain further.

"We had to act on the Stewart situation, of course, because what she's doing is illegal. But we're hoping she'll confess everything to avoid her own consequences." Her pleading gaze met his as she offered up a rushed, truncated explanation. "I'm sorry I didn't tell you. Harper thought it best. The man who contacted him wouldn't meet in person, only over the phone. He didn't give his name, adamant he remains anonymous. He told Harper he couldn't refuse the Congressperson's command, but with Harper's help, they could make it appear the plan went through as ordered. If Stewart gets the outcome she wants, the guy guessed she'd have no reason to discuss his not being the one doing the deed. He could say he'd contracted the engagement out to someone he trusted, or something along those lines. And this way, with Harper here, we'd get a shot at finding out who Stewart asked for the favor in first place."

Devlin considered this admission. Finally, because she'd never given him reason to distrust her, he conceded. "I want the whole story later." At her nod and visible relaxing of her shoulders, he let it go, for the moment at least, and turned his attention back to the scene playing out in front of them.

Another man appeared on camera, strolling past the willow tree where Devlin and Tara sat. He had his hands thrust deep into his pockets. It was Richard Gil.

"Hey, Molly-girl, where are you?" Richard called out before whistling some obscure tune. He strolled along with unsuspecting ease, repeating Molly's name. The man near the bridge, Agent Harper, had stepped down the small embankment and appeared to be looking at something of interest.

"Hey, have you seen a scrawny little girl, about yay high?" Richard asked as he approached the bridge.

The "assailant" turned toward Richard. With wide eyes and an urgent gesture using his arm, Harper said, "Come quick. You gotta see this."

Richard trotted the remaining steps and scurried down the embankment to investigate, his curiosity winning out over any sense of precaution. Devlin and Tara pushed to their feet and edged closer to the umbrella of their leafless cover.

Senator Stewart had already begun to move toward the bridge, too, so she could watch the things about to happen. Her nostrils flared and her eyes lit up with a look of sick satisfaction, marring her well-put-together, cosmetically enhanced face. The two men stepped deeper beneath the bridge, out of view. The

Senator jogged the last bit until she was at the edge of the bridge, about to step onto it. When she leaned over to peer beneath the curved structure, Harper was already making his way back up the embankment.

Tara pushed through the veil of tree fronds and trotted toward them. Devlin followed, the view through the camera bouncing with his gait.

"Senator Stewart," Tara called out right as Harper reached the center of the bridge.

Richard, unaware that he'd been set up to be raped, slowly hiked up the embankment, confusion evident in his expression. "What's going on?"

"Senator Stewart. I'd ask if you remember me, but the look on your face tells me that you do." Tara was already reaching for her blue book of rules.

The Senator froze; the knuckles of both hands turning white from the grip she had on the railing of the bridge. She tried to mask her shock at seeing Tara by playing dumb. "Is everything all right here? I was passing by and thought someone might need help."

"Mrs. Stewart, it has come to my attention that you hired a hitman to perpetrate a crime on a person on home remanding, someone assigned to your care. An ex-convict on home remanding is under your protection and guidance for the length of their probation. You asking this man"—she nodded at Agent Harper—"to inflict harm on Richard is a direct violation of the Consequence Clause by which Richard here came to be in your home. Fortunately for him, the person your Congressional contact reached out to, arranging for him to perpetrate this act, valued his freedom and reported your request. That report was logged into the Control Database, as all crimes are, and landed on my desk because of my previous involvement with Richard, and with you."

THE CONSEQUENCE CLAUSE

The Senator, whom Tara intentionally relegated back to Mrs. when she addressed her because her days as a Senator were over effective as of that moment, reproached Tara. "You don't know what he's done. You put him in my home and basically offered up my innocent babies to him on a platter. *You* did this. *You* made me do this. I had to protect them."

"Ma'am, as tragic as your situation is, it was your vote in favor of humane treatment of criminals which brought about your current circumstances. Richard served his time and was granted probation. According to laws you helped put into place, tossing criminals immediately back out into the world without any form of support structure . . . ." She paused and tapped her finger against her lips. "Without the kindness and compassion they'd need to avoid being criminals, especially after they've been isolated from normal society, was considered inhumane. Home remanding was the Consequence Clause added to balance the decisions some of y'all in Congress pushed through."

"But I only voted in favor of it because, well, because the likelihood that someone like *me*, a Senator, would ever be randomly selected through the VIL was impossible. There are millions of people in this country, I don't understand how *I* could have been picked. Why wasn't I granted exemption considering this man's crime and the fact that I have children to protect? I was targeted. This was intentional. I'm certain it's fraudulent!"

"The random selection process from the VIL is just that. Random. It's computer-generated. The truth of the matter is you voted in favor of this outcome and your name was drawn. And now you have committed an egregious crime, for which Agent Harper here will take you into custody."

"But—but *he's* the criminal. He's the molester. Arrest him!" She thrust her arm out at Richard, who by now had stepped onto the bridge and had come to a stop near Agent Harper.

"Ma'am, I haven't received any reports from you indicating Richard has re-offended. If you had made even one call, there would be a much different outcome here. As you're aware or should be in your capacity as a government leader, he'd be on his way to Nevada for life, if you'd reported him and not tried to exact your own revenge."

Senator Stewart's eyes darted in all directions, clearly considering her chances at escaping. "I'm reporting him now. He's been trying to molest my daughter. He's touched her."

"There's no report to indicate this is true. This is nothing more than a desperate attempt to avoid punishment for your crime, ma'am." Tara remained calm, unflustered, as was her typical way. She flipped the pages of her little blue book, stopping midway through. "Your claim is unfounded. Agent, she's all yours."

Agent Harper clasped his hand around Stewart's wrist and twisted it behind her back.

"You can't do this! What about him? What happens to him?" Stewart cried out as she was led off toward the nearby parking lot.

Devlin angled the camera at Richard as Tara answered. "He'll be sent back to your house. Your husband will be informed of his continued responsibility for his care and of your subsequent arrest." The camera panned back to Stewart. All the color drained from her face.

"No! My kids will be unprotected! My husband travels. Don't do this!" Real tears fell down her cheeks as she was pulled kicking and screaming across the park.

Tara turned to address Richard. "You're free to go. I hope you'll remember the CC if you re-offend. All it takes is one phone call from the husband or even the children," she reminded him.

"I certainly do. You won't catch me repeating, no, ma'am." His eyes glittered darkly, and he licked his lips like he was about to eat a tasty meal.

As Devlin lowered his camera, Richard's last statement ran on repeat in his mind, and how one word had been emphasized more than the others: 'You won't *catch* me repeating.'

SIXTEEN

Following Senator Stewart's capture in Michigan, Tara had come through on her promise to provide answers about Agent Harper. Those answers only led to more questions, but at least Devlin had been reassured what he and Tara had done couldn't be construed as unethical.

She'd confirmed Agent Harper was a friend. To what degree their friendship was, Devlin didn't know and chose not to ponder. It didn't matter. For reasons he still found suspicious, he wondered why, one: Jenkins had contacted Harper specifically. Out of all the Agents out there, why him? Why *Tara's* friend? And two: Why hadn't he simply told Harper who he worked for, in exchange for protection? He'd gone so far as to report Stewart's request to perpetrate a violent crime. So, why not tattle on the other key player involved in the whole thing? That being Stewart's contact in Congress, who apparently kept a hitman on retainer.

Better yet, why hadn't Jenkins reached out to Devlin or Tara directly? Anyone with a pulse knew who they were and what they did for a living. Clearly the man hadn't wanted to get involved with the Stewart situation, thus refusing his directive, and contacting Harper. Why not take down the other, more relevant criminal in this equation? None of it made sense.

Tara hadn't seemed overly concerned about the curious connection between Jenkins, Harper, and her, but Devlin was. Until he learned more about Harper and proved he wasn't a threat to Tara, he'd need to keep a close watch on any future dealings where he became involved. It all seemed too coincidental.

Devlin had shared with Mario what he knew of Senator Stewart's case. There were a lot of people who worked on Capitol Hill, which made the task of finding one worm among the many snakes in the grass known as Congress a seemingly impossible one. It was, however, a task Devlin, with Mario and Tara's help, had been determined to accomplish. The hypocrisy and double standards coming from the people making laws had to stop.

In the weeks since their trip to Michigan, their traveling had become endless. No sooner did Tara wrap up one Consequence Engagement when more piled into her inbox. Airports, planes, hotels, and rental cars had become a daily pattern for them.

Exhausted from the trot back and forth, from State to State and then home, only to depart the next day on a new assignment, Tara had come up with a new and improved strategy to address her CEs. She'd mapped out the next several engagements located between Alabama and Colorado, the latter being where they were headed now. Once completed with this last stop on her itinerary, they'd take a two-week break before starting all over with a new schedule of CEs. This would hopefully give them time in the office to catch up on work or have a life, not that they had much of the second.

They passed the Welcome to Colorful Colorado sign, about two hundred miles south of Denver. After completing a CE back in the much warmer state of Texas, Colorado was their next stop. It was a sunny but chilly day in March, the trees and ground sparkling with frost the sun hadn't yet had the chance to melt. Fields that were once crops of corn or beets had been converted into community gardens. They dotted the land like pox on skin, one on either side of every Tiny Home Village they passed. It was the same everywhere. Except for the largest, wealthier farmers around the country, all the little farmers had been forced out of operation by hefty taxes on resources, like water and fuel. Many had also had their lands commandeered by the government to create space for Tiny Home Villages as the country's population continued to bulge.

A self-serve fueling station was up ahead. They needed to stop. Devlin cringed at an exorbitant cost of twelve dollars and fifty cents per gallon. Fortunately, he wasn't paying this bill. They could have opted for an electric car, but as their travels had them going to so many remote locations, they'd gone with a traditional vehicle that would travel more miles on a tank of gas than the greener electric option could travel in a single charge. Gas-powered vehicles weren't the most common these days, but still necessary. Nearly all personal transportation in the country had been replaced by electric vehicles. There were now more charging stations than gas stations. People either drove one of the small electric cars or, in larger communities, like Denver and its suburbs; many rode bikes, scooters, walked, or traveled by way of public transit. Ironically, most of the latter still ran on diesel fuel, for the same reason he and Tara had opted to travel in a traditional gas-powered automobile.

Landfills had been created to dispose of the unrecyclable batteries of all the electric vehicles as well as parts from the gigantic windmills that covered the land like a forest. The government, always in search of more land for Tiny Home Villages, had begun utilizing the burial grounds where those unrecyclable parts were laid to rest as space for up-and-coming Tiny Home Villages. Not doing so would have been an outrageous waste of acreage, and the genius idea had been born. The decay of those buried products would be future generations away from today's population to have to deal with. Therefore, government leaders had deemed the land safe enough to build on. They'd claimed there was no evidence proving the unrecyclable products fermenting beneath the soil had any detrimental side effects to humans. When problems presented, they'd deal with it then. Woe to those humans who were unknowingly test subjects housed atop unbiodegradable waste.

They parked in front of the fuel pumps, and both exited the vehicle. "I want to swing through the food kiosk next door before heading on. I'm starving," Tara said as she wandered off toward the roadside bathrooms situated several yards away.

Devlin filled the tank and washed the windows, scraping away the dead bugs they'd collected on the drive through Texas and New Mexico.

They'd both finished their tasks and were soon in the drive-up lane of the fast-food kiosk. Tara ordered a number 6A, the real meat version of the burger. It cost nine dollars more than the fake meat option but was a hell of a lot tastier and, Devlin believed, was probably healthier than whatever ingredients were used to make the fake meat. He copied Tara's order, adding two water bottle refills to the list. Tara awkwardly leaned across Devlin to extend her arm out the window. When the little blue light of the scanner flashed over her forearm accepting payment for their food, she shifted back to her seat. Two minutes later a door on the wall slid open to reveal a paper bag with their meals. Directly next to the opening where they'd retrieved their food was a water dispenser. Devlin topped off both their bottles.

She handed Devlin's burger to him after she unfolded the paper wrapper around it. He chewed on the greasy deliciousness a few seconds.

"Do either of these people we're going to see have any idea you're coming?" he asked around a bite of food. Maneuvering the car onto the Interstate, they continued north.

Tara shook her head, in contradiction to her words. "They should. My office sent them notifications. But, according to the neighbor who reported them, they're still at it." She stared out the window watching the scenery fly past. In one small town they drove through, the towering structures of lights circling an old high school football field stood tall and dark, silenced a couple of years back with the onslaught of education reform.

The call to bridge gaps of socioeconomic status and language barriers inundated the free education system. The melting pot of people in the country combined with the aggressive stance against discrimination and racism of any kind meant every imaginable language had to be given equal and fair consideration. This situation was exacerbated by the demands of many newly formed hashtags and families wanting their students to be taught in their home language. As more cries for fair access to education in a person's first language were made, the government threw up its hands when it realized the impossibility of teaching effectively to all. Therefore, public education transitioned to a mandatory home-schooling system.

Enrollment in the system was required for all children between the ages of four and sixteen. Student attendance was monitored through the USFCD. Regardless of the language spoken in the home, it had become the families' responsibility to fulfill the students' curriculum requirements issued by the Home School Education Department. At first, it seemed outrageous and overly burdensome on parents or family members to take on such a task. But once leaders realized most of the adult members in a household didn't want to work outside the home, or at all, compliments of the overly generous entitlement programs implemented in the States, the arguments against home-schooling were quickly quashed.

Unfortunately for children, football, baseball, and other school sport pastimes were no more; this, of course, aided in the downfall of professional sports. Gymnasiums, baseball diamonds, football fields, and bleachers were ghosts of the past; structures abandoned, standing only as reminders of a time long ago. Eventually, they'd all be demolished to create space for new Tiny Home Villages or converted to public housing.

"It's sad that there are no more homecomings or proms," Tara said forlornly. "That should be part of every kid's upbringing. Their rights of passage." She pressed a palm against the window, her fingers splayed over the towers of lights in the background. "I'm glad I got to be part of the good old days, at least."

"Me, too. I don't see how it can ever go back to the way things were. Once change is implemented, good or bad, it's impossible to undo. We're the country of anything goes. I don't think it'll ever recover. Look around us. The statistics being reported now show birth rates are at an all-time low. It's not a good trend. It's bad enough that unemployment is at the highest it's been since the inception of tracking those stats. What it means is there soon won't be any young people to work and contribute into a very expensive tax-reliant system full of free handouts."

Tara angled her body toward Devlin, her back against the door. "What should we do then, when all this collapses?"

He glanced at her, their gazes meeting for a moment before he looked west, toward the Rocky Mountains with their snow-capped peaks standing tall and proud. It was a beautiful sight. But even that beauty was quickly being erased by change.

Instead of being thankful for the excess of "free" benefits the country offered, more and more had begun demanding what they were familiar with, what they'd left behind—like Senator Ashraf had claimed that day in the Congressional chambers.

New York now resembled Singapore; Seattle had become another Bangladesh; Scottsdale, once a lovely, eclectic community, looked like Tehran, though not a bombed skeleton of a town. The land was transforming into someplace else, and it was a place Devlin wasn't certain he wanted to be in any longer. It's not that he disliked or blamed people, either those here through the OBA or the original citizens for wanting creature comforts. Most were good and kind, simply trying to survive under conditions past leaders and some present ones, had allowed to get out of control.

No, his feelings on the matter weren't because the country opened its borders to people hoping for something better. Hell, even Tara was one of those who'd made her home here following the passage of the OBA. What Devlin didn't like was exactly those things Senator Ashraf spoke about. The country encouraged and supported laziness, immorality, and unethical behavior.

He sighed heavily. "I don't know for sure yet, but I've been looking into options."

"Options? What do you mean? Does it include me? I mean, we're a team. Right?" There was a hint of worry in Tara's eyes.

He put his hand out to pat her knee. "Of course, we're a team. I'd never leave you behind." He had been devising a plan, one that definitely included Tara. But he'd also planned to invite Josh, Mario, and possibly Conrad into his plan. These were his friends, his family, in a way. The only people he trusted in this world of chaos. He considered asking Tara if Agent Harper would become part of their team and if she'd want Devlin to invite him along, but didn't, for reasons he hadn't fully wrapped his mind around yet.

When Tara breathed a sigh of relief, all worry, or most all, left her eyes. "Whew. For a minute, I was getting worried you'd gotten tired of doing this job with me."

He enjoyed working with Tara, but he wasn't sure how much longer he'd be able to tolerate everything else going on around him.

"We're almost there," he said, changing the subject. "Which do you want to start with?" They turned into a subdivision, one with traditional ranch and multi-level homes, homes like the one he'd grown up in.

She grabbed her phone and little blue book from the console as Devlin maneuvered a corner onto another house-lined street. He didn't need to inquire as to which homes they'd be visiting, that had become immediately apparent. He braked to a stop along the curb between two houses. Tara waited in her seat as he reached behind him to collect his video camera.

"Let's start with this one." She pointed to the house proudly boasting a flag on display that, from his conversation with Tara, he knew represented France. "Know any French, by chance?" When Devlin shook his head, she rolled her eyes. "Well, you're no help, then. I'll have to use an Internet language translator."

Devlin followed behind her as she marched up the paved sidewalk leading to the porch of a single-story, wood-siding-covered home. It was unpretentious, a typical tract home, built in the early two-thousands, well before construction of new homes halted when civil unrest brewed across the land.

An overweight woman with silver hair tucked neatly into a bun answered the door, following Tara's push on the doorbell.

"Hello, Mrs. Moreau? I'm Tara Carlson from the Consequence Compliance Oversight Committee."

It was a typical response now, one Devlin had observed on any number of occasions.

"Oui? Que voulez-vous?"

From Tara's report, the woman and her family had lived in the house since coming to the States immediately following the OBA. To claim she didn't understand at least a bit of English was laughable, but that was the approach she was going with now.

"Mrs. Moreau, I've received a report that you have been displaying a flag in public." Tara turned to look at the object of their discussion, the red, white, and white vertical-striped flag hanging proudly from a wooden dowel on one of the porch's pillars. "According to the Flag Banning Act imposed in two thousand-nine, no country's flags are to be displayed in public. Per the Consequence Clause—"

"*C'est ma maison!*" Mrs. Moreau pointed hard at the ground. Her face began to turn a bright shade of pink, the lines around her pursed lips drawing into deep rivets. "*Ma propriété!*"

The recorder translated for Tara. "I understand that, but the law's the law, and you're in violation of it."

"*Vous parlez à cette écume d'à côté!*" she squawked, pointing again, this time not at her house but at her neighbor's.

Tara listened to the translator and with a sigh, flipped open her little blue book and nodded with presumed understanding. "Yes, yes. I'll get to 'the scum next door' next. Now, per the Consequence Clause, displaying a flag carries a penalty of a two-thousand-dollar fine. But, according to the VIL, you voted in favor of the ban. Because of that, the Clause indicates the fine is to be doubled and we are to confiscate your flag."

The woman shook her head and held out both hands, palms up. Tara spoke again into her phone, the words translating into French, and then she held out the device for Mrs. Moreau to read.

"The fine is payable immediately. If you can't pay now, there's a mandatory six-month jail sentence."

Rounds of expostulating, stomping of feet, and shrieks of outrage preceded the French woman's storming out her front door, past Tara and Devlin, around the front of her house until she came to a stop on the sidewalk in front of the neighbor's. Devlin panned the camera in the direction she pointed; her distressed cry clearly understood, even in a different language.

Tara closed her eyes briefly, then shrugged her shoulders. "Follow me," she said to Devlin.

They approached the porch of the next-door neighbor's house, walking slowly past the American flag on display for all to see. Tara's knuckles rapped hard against the wooden door. A short, elderly man, gray hair, hunched shoulders, and leaning on a cane eased the door open. His eyes widened at sight of Tara, but his shoulders shifted up when he saw his neighbor on the sidewalk behind her.

He pointed his cane at Mrs. Moreau. "What is she doing on my property? A shrew she is, screeching all the time about anything and everything." The cane thumped hard against the floor. The sound of someone adding further insult to the French woman outside trickled up from behind the frail man. He turned halfway around, revealing the brimless cap of the Jewish kippah. "Hush, woman. This is my property!" All this was said before Tara had an opportunity to speak a word of welcome or otherwise.

"Excuse me, Mr. Eichenbaum," she managed, interrupting his mumblings about the "blasted shrew living next to upstanding"—something, something—"people like himself"—at least that was the part Devlin caught. "Mr. Eichenbaum!" Tara raised her voice.

"Who are you? Did you bring her here?" The cane pointed again, shaking with intensity this time.

"I'm Tara Carlson, from the Consequence Compliance Oversight Committee. No, I didn't bring her here, but she and you are both the reasons I am here."

"Don't presume to lump me into any sort of category with that heathen!"

"I'm not the one who lumped anyone into anything. You, sir, have done that yourself." At that, loud squawking and insults from the woman inside the house, presumably Mrs. Eichenbaum, filtered past the mister, words that were no kinder than her husband's.

Tara talked over her. "You're flying an American flag, which is a violation of the Flag Banning Act. The Consequence Clause states that for this violation a two-thousand-dollar fine is to be imposed, payable immediately. If you can't pay now, you will be remanded to Nevada for six months, not one day more nor less." Her tone had become lilting, saying the words in a mix of monotone and musical dance.

"I did not vote to approve such a ridiculous law. It's her and people like her who are supporting stupid laws. She should be punished. And sent back to where she came from! This used to be my United States. Now, it's a mockery. We're not 'united' at all, not in name or in action."

Tara nodded. "According to the VIL, I'm aware you did not vote in favor of this law, which is why your fine is only two thousand. Hers will be doubled. Either way, the law is the law, and you pay now, or I send you off to Nevada."

"I can't leave my wife. She's old and frail." The "frail" woman in question, whom Devlin suddenly likened to an annoying blackbird perched in the neighbor's tree, gave off a loud and incessant screech.

"Then you'll need to pay the fine."

Mr. Eichenbaum glared at the French woman who stood in her robe and slippers, toe tapping, and arms crossed tight over her ample bosom. With a grumble of angry, yet not profane words, he shoved back the sleeve of his white button-down shirt and thrust his arm at Tara.

"Here. Take it and remove yourself and that woman from my porch step."

Tara tapped a button on her phone before waving the end of it over Eichenbaum's forearm. A scanner built into the

THE CONSEQUENCE CLAUSE

cellular device cast a blue light across his arm, instantly transferring the imposed fine. "Thank you. I'll also need you to remove your flag. If there's ever another report of this incident, there will be a mandatory one-year prison sentence applied. Consider your frail wife before breaking the law, will you?"

Mr. Eichenbaum shuffled out to the porch's edge, propped his cane against the railing and reached up to remove the flag. He struggled getting it far enough out of the slot to take it down, so Tara helped. Finally free from its perch, he carefully rolled it around the pole, then wordlessly, and without a thank you to Tara, went back inside, slamming the door shut.

Tara issued a satisfied breath and turned to Mrs. Moreau and said into the language translator on her phone, "Can you pay your fine or do I need to call for an Agent to take you away?" She handed the phone to the now trembling woman.

Mrs. Moreau shook her head violently, a worried look etched on her face. She marched back to her house, less blustery and now seemingly more accommodating. Grabbing the pole of her homeland's flag, she slipped it from its mooring and rolled it tidily up.

"There. Happy now?" she asked in accented English. Her face contorted into a grimace meant to be a smile, and she nodded encouragingly while pointing at the flag, proving her compliance to Tara's directive.

"Thank you. And I'll need payment of the fine." She waved her phone side-to-side and then tucked it beneath her arm. Holding up four fingers, she pointed at Mrs. Moreau. "Four thousand. You pay me."

In French, Mrs. Moreau claimed she didn't have enough money. This was emphasized with head shaking and the word "*Non*" repeated several times.

Tara's response was to show the woman that she was calling for someone to take her away and deliver her into the custody of the Free-Range Prison in Nevada.

As she dialed, Mrs. Moreau began to sob hysterically, crying foul in her home language as the three of them went inside the house to await the Agent's arrival. Dropping heavily into a worn, cloth-covered recliner, the flag offender pressed her hands against the sides of her face, sobbing with sincere regret now that she'd been caught.

Their wait was short, less than ten minutes, and Mrs. Moreau was taken away after first being allowed to change into a pair of pants and a blouse, with a heavy coat over the top for warmth. Those would be the clothes she returned home in, provided, that was, if there was someone, family or a friend who'd keep up the house for her in her absence. If not, it would fall under the control of the government and sold or turned into a home for another family needing placement.

Sometimes the consequences seemed harsh, but the Consequence Clauses decided on by Congress had been deemed necessary to maintaining balance in all things.

Though it didn't always appear so on the surface, the Clauses were having a positive effect. Overall, crime had slowed down, but what was slowing at an even faster rate were new laws from the government and new demands from hashtags. Even so, he doubted things would ever go back to what was once considered as normal, which was why he had his exit plan almost ready.

SEVENTEEN

Devlin stood on a large makeshift stage erected twenty yards away from the steps leading up to the Capitol on the East Front side. So far, he was the only one on the platform. Tara had been delayed with an assignment but said she'd get there when she could. He shifted his camera lens up and around, so it was pointed at the pillared landing near the Capitol's entrance. There, directly in front of the Columbus Doors was President Anita Grant, her wife Senator Clarkson, and a handful of other men and women, presumably staffers. Behind them were shadows of others who remained out of sight of the camera's eye.

Josh had scheduled today's event, demanding everyone be present, including the President. Because she was there, it was a safe assumption those lurking behind her were Secret Service.

Devlin's cell phone chimed with an incoming message. It was a text from Mario. *Call me. ASAP.* He'd temporarily redirected his manager away from new assignments, like today's event, hence the reason Devlin was up here running the camera. He needed Mario to finish his research on pending issues before taking on anything new. There were too many loose ends hanging about, like who'd been threatening Carl and the other business owners. Poor Carl was stuck in Nevada until they found the person who coerced him into displaying a First Rights Rule sign.

And then there was Senator Lisa Stewart's situation. They'd not found anything on Jenkins yet. Devlin wasn't so much concerned about him as he was his connection to Stewart's co-worker, another member of Congress.

Through the camera's viewfinder, he observed the scene from right to left, past all the suits standing near the President. Any one of them could be Stewart's person. He tracked lower, down along the steps. When he saw a face he recognized, he jerked the lens back, searching through the group of people.

About halfway down the steps, he saw Tara's friend, Agent Harper. He was dressed in standard-issue attire, a rifle gripped in both hands and pulled tight against his chest. Because he carried the weapon, meant that he was on duty; he couldn't be legally in possession of it otherwise. It didn't surprise Devlin to see him there. He was an Agent, after all. Agents were peacekeepers, often called to events like the one today where large crowds gathered.

Harper was working in the same capacity the blonde had been working that day at the border.

So why, then, was he not intervening with the squabble taking place between four individuals a few feet away from him? That's exactly the role intended for Agents. Instead, his attention was focused elsewhere, and not up on the President, nor out toward the stage where Devlin was or the crowd beyond him; he was looking past the Capitol's steps, off in the direction of the House of Representatives. It was as if he was watching for someone.

Devlin shrugged away his curiosity. Tara trusted the guy, and he'd given Devlin no real cause not to, either.

Mario's other research included the person Devlin and Tara had surveilled meeting secretly with President Grant, the person he'd nicknamed Hulk Guy.

THE CONSEQUENCE CLAUSE

Nothing had come of their rendezvous at the bar, at least not yet. But what he'd heard there remained on Devlin's list to be on the lookout for, considering their tipster had called it a story of possible "epic proportions." There'd been no situations at any protests he and Tara had heard about since their private surveillance in the bar. And today's event was one Josh had arranged, one he'd only announced to the public a few weeks ago. Tucking his cell phone into his pocket, he made a mental note to call Mario back as soon as he was done here.

Short notice advertising or not, an extremely large crowd had gathered today. The cacophony around him was enough to make it difficult to hear himself talk let alone converse on the phone.

Suddenly, the volume from the crowd ratcheted up even higher when several people marched up the staircase on the opposite side of the same stage as Devlin. There were six WTP members, each boasting impressively intimidating weapons. With them were four individuals who were being steered across the platform. They were made to stand shoulder-to-shoulder in a row about a dozen feet away from Devlin. The armed guards, consisting of three women and three men dressed in all black, from cargo pants to tee shirts to boots, were incredibly fierce looking.

Devlin panned his camera away from those on the stage, out and around to take in the enormity of the assemblage. It might have been the largest gathering of people to hold audience in front of the Capitol since the revolution. As he shifted the angle of the lens in a different direction, he found Ken in the crowd. Beside him was Patty and a few others from group. Devlin was more than a bit shocked to see Ken with the others at an event like this. Being here, in support of his fellow groupmates was a huge step for him. Devlin couldn't help the smile that spread over his face. Maybe there was hope for the man after all.

Automatically, he searched for Conrad, his smile quickly turning into a frown when he didn't find him with the others. He shifted his camera again, scanning the faces, looking for one boasting black-framed glasses. But still no Conrad. That didn't mean he wasn't in attendance; there were simply too many faces among which anyone could hide.

Thousands of people were present today. And more were still arriving. On the ground surrounding the stage, were groups of people, clustered together in an organized and intentional way. The scene was reminiscent of that day at the border, with Clarkson boasting and the hashtags grouped together, chanting their rally cries. It sent a chill down Devlin's spine.

It was segregated groups like these that had been, in part, the reason for his break from the mainstream media. When the politicians and the media rallied around the hashtags' causes, encouraging devastating and oftentimes illegal behaviors, he knew he had to help people see all the truths the MSM hid from the public. Day in and day out, reporters and politicians looked into the lens of cameras and shielded the truth about the violence everywhere as it grew at alarming rates. People, systems, religions, businesses, principles, and morals became targets from every imaginable hashtag's cry to correct injustices they claimed had been done to them or to ancestors from a far distant past.

As a result of all these claims, after decades of fighting for exactly the opposite, segregation had made a comeback. People of nearly every race or cause took a stand against something or someone that wasn't part of their own group. Devlin had interviewed many such groups, in the hopes of finding a way to communicate what, why, or against whom they were fighting. In one interview, a gentleman whose apology for something his ancestors might have done—he was of German descent—went unaccepted by the other hashtag leader present. Before Devlin could even acknowledge what was happening, the hashtag leader leaped over the table separating the two parties and began beating the man with his fists.

That was the last joint interview Devlin had attempted with any hashtag Party. He realized his efforts would be in vain. They only wanted what they wanted and were unwilling to be reasonable. It didn't take long for other hashtags to go after a specific population of people in the country, making them targets for every upcoming hashtag imaginable. But even that single-minded racist behavior lasted only a short while. The hashtags, angry about anything and everything, began to turn on each other. The lack of law enforcement had many of those confrontations turning into riotous bloodbaths. The more the politicians condoned their behaviors, the more violence ruled the streets, driving the country into divided unrest.

It wasn't until the WTP took a stance and began the march toward Washington DC that some semblance of unity and respect returned to society. People from all walks of life, including individuals breaking away from their specific hashtag groups, joined the WTP's cause. They were among those desperate to heal the political, religious, or any other type of divide and the Us versus Them mentality ravaging the land.

The crowd in the courtyard today, beyond the holdout segregated groups up front, was a sight Devlin believed he'd never see again. People from all levels of society, once again, standing shoulder-to-shoulder in public cheering, chanting, and peacefully gathering to hear what the WTP had to say. Picket signs bobbed up and down like Whac-A-Mole heads. Sheets made into banners waved through the air. At first glance, it might have been a typical protest event. But the reason for this presentation put on by the WTP wasn't *for* a cause. The WTP didn't take sides or stand for any specific causes. Their presence in government was merely to make parties work together and intervene when the scales of justice became unbalanced. Today's event was an indication that something had happened to tip that scale off-kilter.

Josh walked onto the opposite side of the stage from where Devlin stood. He lifted a microphone from its base. When he spoke, a techno-screeching sound rent the air, so he pulled the mic slightly away from his mouth and tried again.

"Welcome everyone!" He looked upon the massive crowd, smiling with pride at the accomplishments of the WTP. So many people coming together, working together, to do good things for the country. Then, when his gaze shifted to the front, to the segregated groups closest to him, his lips pulled into a tight line.

Only as the crowd began to settle did he speak again. "Most of you know me. I'm Josh Stevens, the Government Overseer."

Raucous cheering from the back of the huge gathering split the air, rippling over the crowd like a wave performed by spectators at any major ball game. These were his people, ones who'd joined the WTP's cause and marched alongside Josh as he spread his message of hope for the country.

"All right, all right. Settle down."

Those clustered near the stage didn't cheer, the majority glowered even, arms folded tight across their chests.

Devlin's phone buzzed again. Mario was being very persistent.

"Tell us why we're here!" one pink-haired hashtag demanded.

Josh eyed her, a level of irritation evident in his facial expression and his body language. He gestured with his hands for the crowd to settle. Getting this many people to hush was daunting, but an impressively accomplished feat.

"I have prepared this presentation because, well," he shook his head, a sigh of irritation heard loud and clear through the speakers, "well, because it appears we have some among you"—he swung his left arm from right to left in an arc around the front and end of the stage—"there are some who have begun to cry out once again for reparations due 'your people,'" he said using air quotes.

What is he up to? Devlin wondered as his adrenaline inched up a notch. Several members of the group of hashtags nearest to Josh shifted nervously, looking down and away from the WTP leader's not-so subtle accusation. Obviously, they were the ones who'd been the cause behind today's events, and who'd brought about Josh's ire, and they knew it.

"I want you, all of you along the front here, to know that what's about to happen, is because of your actions."

The threat in his tone sent a shiver up Devlin's spine. Josh pointed the microphone at the hashtags huddled together in groups on the ground surrounding the stage.

"You want to regurgitate the pasts of man's ancestry, livelihoods, or crimes, whatever they might have been?"

He moved lightly, his sneakers making no sound on the wood beneath his feet as he approached the group of four lined up on the front of the stage. Stopping, he put his hand on the shoulder of one. The girl turned wary eyes up to meet his. She was of Asian descent and couldn't have been more than fifteen years old.

To those on the ground directly below Josh, he said, "All of these folks up here are one of yours. One of your hashtags." His mouth moved around the words in an exaggerated manner, saying each syllable slowly, succinctly. "This girl is a hashtag-JLM." Shouts of acknowledgement came from a small group standing several feet away from Josh.

He turned their way, speaking directly to the girl's kinship group. "You all jumped on the bandwagon claiming that this government owes you something for what you may have found in an old encyclopedia somewhere."

Encyclopedias published, printed, and sold door-to-door decades ago, were about the only reference source of history nowadays where one might learn of this country's past. Nearly every war, skirmish, or cause had elements which offended someone somewhere. So, in a short period of time, details of the past had been erased from the Internet, from parks, and public buildings. Additionally, history was no longer taught in schools, both before they'd all been closed and in the home-schooling curriculum of today. Since everything about history caused offense to someone, a Party, a hashtag or other, most all topics of the past related to the United States had been canceled out, leaving outdated printed materials the only accessible source of historical events.

"Well, I'm here to tell you your argument works both ways. I believe reparations are due *us*. And by *us* I mean you, We The People." He pointed, sweeping his arm wide in a high arc. "As such, in like manner, this girl's life should be sacrificed because of what her great-grandfather did to our countrymen at Pearl Harbor." He pivoted around and strode to the edge of the stage, stopping before the largest hashtag group among them. "Isn't that right? Isn't that how this works?" He nodded his head aggressively, the lines across his forehead deepening as his brows shot inward. "You want money, land, retribution for things done to your great-great-grandparents?"

Devlin flinched when one of the guards poked the end of his gun at the teenaged girl. The sound of her crying out cut through him, turning his stomach. What was happening here? He refused to believe Josh had plans to kill these people on the stage as part of his demonstration to prove a point. He wouldn't.

Or would he? When the leader of the WTP circled back around and side-stepped behind the girl, giving her a little shove, Devlin instinctively took a small step back, too.

But then Josh moved on to the next person in the row.

"And this man? What shall we do with him? Shoot him? Bury him along the Arizona border for the sins of his father's father, who ran the biggest drug cartel in South America? The same man who contributed to the drug overdose of more than one from every single one of your hashtag groups here?"

As Josh touched the man's shoulder, scoffs of disbelief and incredulity, along with a few head nods and suggestive shrugs were being aired live across the country.

He moved on to the next. "Who here thinks I should execute this young man from Missouri, or Mississippi, or somewhere thereabouts for his ancestor's involvement in a well-known cult?" Surprisingly, or not, nobody cheered. Without delay he moved on, stopping before the last of the four, a woman wearing a police uniform.

Devlin stared on in fascination and disbelief, watching as she forced her shoulders back, head held high. Her body language indicated confidence, but nothing could mask the fear lurking in her eyes as she lowered her gaze to the hashtag group directly below her. Her people. The largest group of all.

Once more, Devlin's phone chimed, announcing an incoming message. "Jeez, Mario," he said in a low breath as he shot back a text letting his manager know he'd have to call back later. Before he could re-pocket his phone another response pinged.

"I brought this person up because I'm really confused by some of your loyalties to your own people and causes." Josh braced both hands against his waist, his head moving side-to-side in bewilderment.

Devlin assumed the woman's past occupation had been a police officer, considering the uniform she wore fit her perfectly. But there were no longer any police, nor any law enforcement in the country. Not since the hashtags began killing officers in the streets as easily as they might kill a rodent in their house, and they had done so without any recrimination.

Many believed it had been the government's defunding of law enforcement nationwide that caused those agencies to close their doors. In truth, they were doomed to close even before that had happened. Seasoned officers began walking off the job, no longer willing to work with targets on their backs. Simultaneously, academies stopped getting new recruits to sign up, for the same reason those others were leaving their jobs. Defunding had merely been the final straw to end protection in the streets of America. Sadly, the increased crime rate and bloodbaths in the streets were the devastating results. Much of that had ceased, but only after the Consequence Clause went into effect and the people realized crimes now carried swift and harsh judgments.

Devlin's phone began to buzz again. This time, the pause between calls and hang-ups became non-existent. The persistence of Mario's calls drove Devlin to nudge Josh to get to the point of his demonstration.

"What's all this about, Josh?"

The leader of the WTP looked his way and gave a brief nod. With a hand still on the woman's shoulder, he said, "This former police officer was one of your own." He pointed the microphone down at the cluster of the largest hashtag group, before adding, "And even though she risked her life every day on the streets of Philadelphia, protecting all people, including yourselves, you still went after her and others like her strictly because of the uniform."

Suddenly, he shot his hand up into the air. At the same time, the armed WTP on the stage behind him lifted their weapons, aiming them at the backs of the subjects lined in a row, each a representative of but only a few of the hashtag groups present today.

Devlin looked out again at the miles-long blend of humanity beyond the clusters of hashtags. He saw Patty and the others, only barely noting that Ken was no longer among them. The crowd today was an array of all races and social classes from around the world. They were here, in unity, on purpose. He suddenly saw this for what it was and would bet his second fanciest camera that Josh's demonstration was all for show, in the hopes of teaching a lesson. He was a former teacher, after all.

Screams of surprise, shock, worry, and fear filled the air as the hashtags clamored together in their groups. They hugged each other and held each other's hands as they waited in disbelief for gunshots to ring out.

"No!" shouted a large man sporting a bandana on his head and sunglasses covering his eyes. "Stop! This isn't what we want." He stepped forward, as close to the stage as possible and looked up at Josh. "You've made your point."

Josh braced a hand on the microphone stand, leaning on it. "Well, now, that's the thing. I was certain we'd moved past this too, back when one of our previous presidents went ahead and paid reparations to some of you already. I assumed the issue had been resolved then. But to my surprise, it resurfaced," he scoffed. "And lo and behold, I find it wasn't any of these other groups who'd started up the war cry again." He pointed down at the hashtag clusters filling the space along the front and end of the stage.

"No, it wasn't any of them who started it, they'd merely followed along. Who was it, I asked?" The reflective pause was intentional and meant to shame the perpetrators who all knew who they were. "It was none other than the one group who'd already been paid for the things done to their father's . . . father's . . . father." He said the last three words slowly, emphasizing the long-reaching ancestral timeline. Then, he added, "Shame on you for being so greedy. Shame on you for bringing about the events taking place here today. It's obvious by your actions, nothing will ever be enough."

He strode to the end of the platform, stopping beside Devlin. "We The People?" he called out. "Ready?" The guards, with weapons held across their chests, shifted their stance. "Aim." They raised their guns to their shoulders, barrels pointed out, toward the backs of those on the stage in front of them.

The cries for mercy had grown to a deafening level, and then Josh let his arm fall. He winked at Devlin right before he shouted, "Fire!"

The crack of guns firing was lost among the screams and pleas as people ducked to the ground or turned their heads, unable to watch "reparations" being collected.

It took several long minutes for those in the crowd to notice that none of the victims on stage had crumpled to the ground. All who'd been subjects of Josh's demonstration were now milling about conversing with one another as well as with the armed WTP.

Devlin's phone began to ring, yet again. He huffed his irritation, but knowing the production was over, he pressed the answer button and shoved his phone to his ear.

"What is it?" he demanded as he attempted to shake off his frustration at the incessant Mario. It was at that same moment, from the far end of the courtyard, off in the direction of the House of Representatives, he saw his manager, Tara, and a young man behind them all racing toward the stage.

"Get away!" Mario yelled into the phone. "Get out of there!"

Panic gripped Devlin even though he had no knowledge yet as to why. "Mario! What's going on?" His friend and Tara, who was wearing those damned unsensible heels again, along with the kid, were running headlong toward the stage. The same one Mario was telling Devlin to vacate. Instinctively, his eyes searched the stage for Josh.

For reasons he couldn't explain, instinct had him wrenching his head around to look up to where he'd last seen Harper. He immediately located him, because the man was running up the steps of the Capitol, cutting a path toward President Grant, gun held ready and pointed out.

"The President . . . and Clarkson," Mario huffed, out of breath and still a hundred yards away. "And . . . Jenkins," he got out between gulps of air.

Devlin quickly angled his camera toward the President. She was positioned in a way she wouldn't see Harper running in her direction. And she didn't appear concerned about the crazy man yelling into his phone or the long-legged, high-heel-wearing woman chasing behind him as they blazed a path across the courtyard. Both were frantically waving their arms and pointing up at Grant, or at Harper, and then at Devlin.

Senator Clarkson stepped closer to President Grant and said something to her. A wide smile spread across her face. Grant turned her head and spoke to someone over her shoulder, her arm lifting as she pointed. It was when Devlin's gaze followed the path of her extended finger, he saw Ken running up the steps, a few feet behind Harper.

What the hell was going on?

President Grant still didn't look worried or panicked. In fact, to something Clarkson said, they both tilted their heads back in hearty laughter.

What had Mario so worked up?

"Jenkins is . . . drones." Mario began to slow, his energy waning. Tara and the kid with them slowed, too. "Nebraska," he breathed through the line.

Josh came to Devlin in long strides, the microphone still clutched tight in his hand. "What's wrong?"

Devlin's eyes widened. "I don't know. It's Mario," he pointed.

The trio were now barely jogging, slowly closing the distance between them. They reached a spot near the base of the steps of the Capitol, directly below President Grant and Senator Clarkson. "He said something about a guy named Jenkins and drones and Nebraska." Shaking his head, he added, "I have no idea what it means. He's not making any sense." His adrenaline had him suddenly breathing hard, yet he hadn't moved. "But look," he extended his arm in Ken's direction.

Ken had breached the top step and stopped beside Harper. They both looked out at the crowd, then over to where the President and the others were. And finally, their heads angled in a direction that turned the blood in Devlin's veins to ice: They were looking at where Tara and Mario had stopped. Harper lifted his gun to his shoulder.

Josh whirled around to look up at the President, confusion and another expression twisting his features. It was fear, Devlin realized as his gaze shifted back to his friends. Tara suddenly stumbled, her long arms flailing as her legs buckled beneath her. Mario and the young man with them ducked their heads as they reached to help Tara.

Devlin thought he heard gunshot, but it was so subtle, he wondered if he'd only imagined it. Wide-eyed, he swiveled around in search of Harper again, but he was gone, as was Ken. There was another, louder, crack of what sounded distinctly more like a gunshot. Josh flinched and he instinctively covered his head with his hands. Devlin hadn't imagined the sound. His heart began to hammer in his chest. When he looked again to Tara and Mario, the breath left his lungs when he saw Tara sprawled on the ground.

Josh raised the microphone to his mouth. "WTP!" he cried out. All the WTP members, those on stage as well as those in the massive crowd of people who'd been with Josh since before the revolution, conditioned to his command and voice, looked to him.

Like Devlin had done so many years ago, he shoved away from his camera, leaping off the stage. He had to reach her; he had to get to Tara. He ran, a desperate plea falling from his lips on repeat, "Not again! Not again!"

Behind him, he heard Josh command, "Get to the President!"

EIGHTEEN

The crowd surged forward like the wave of a tsunami, moving across the courtyard in a unified, determined wall, sweeping around and through anything in its wake. The hashtags scurried about, scrambling atop the stage that Devlin, Josh, and other members of the WTP had vacated in their rush to run toward the Capitol. With no room left on top of the stage, many hashtags sought purchase at its perimeter, banding together, arm-in-arm with others piling on behind them. They were like a swarm of ants bridging a divide. Those unable to stay connected to one of their own were swept up in the wall of We The People advancing forward.

Devlin ran near the front of the tsunami, desperate to get to Tara and Mario. By the time he reached the conscious but dazed Tara, he was breathing hard with exertion and adrenaline. He knelt by her side, protecting her from the crowd around them. Hooking both hands beneath her armpits, he hoisted her to her feet and draped one of her arms across his shoulders. Mario was at her other side.

"We've got to get out of the way!" Devlin yelled loud enough to be heard over the shouting and stomping of thousands of feet racing by. They hobbled to the steps so Tara could hold onto the railing. "Where are you hurt?"

There was a small pool of blood forming near her right foot, but it didn't appear to be an excessive amount. Holding a hand against her shoulder, he bent down to look closer and

THE CONSEQUENCE CLAUSE

noticed a tear in her slacks near her upper thigh. A dark stain in the fabric had formed, creeping down past her knee.

Gunshots fired again, coming from above or below he couldn't tell. They all ducked.

"You've been shot!" Devlin instinctively searched the area above for Harper. His gut told him he was the one who'd done this. He knew there was something not right about the guy from the moment he'd met him. He didn't believe in coincidences.

"I'm fine!" Tara said loudly, appearing not to be in agonizing pain. Yet. The surge of her adrenaline was holding the pain at bay for the time being. But the wild look in her eyes told Devlin shock could be a greater concern.

The tsunami was gaining momentum, moving up the steps and disappearing inside the Capitol. Screams and shouting and more gunfire sounded. If Devlin didn't know any better, he'd think he'd been caught up in a time warp and had gone back to the day the WTP had first stormed this very building. Many of the people here were the same who'd fought alongside Josh back then, though in the years since, their numbers had grown exponentially.

A humming sound suddenly filled the air; it seemed far away and close at the same time. It buzzed loudly, like the sound made by the monster-like electric towers with transformers carrying electricity to or from a power plant. It was a palpable noise, vibrating beneath Devlin's skin.

Mario yelled, his voice sounding demonic. "Run! We've got to get inside!" He looped Tara's arm over his shoulder again and directed her to use the railing with her other hand to pull herself up the steps while Devlin and the kid scrambled behind. He'd only now realized the kid was still with them but didn't know why.

Glancing over his shoulder, he watched as a dark cloud, maybe twenty feet wide and equally as tall, swooped up and over the trees along the street at the far end of the courtyard. The space farther out was now mostly vacant since all the WTP had rushed the building. Like a waterfall cascading over a cliff, the cloud overhead swooped gracefully down. Devlin kept moving, stumbling up the steps as he continued looking back. The swarm settled like a blanket over the crowd, disappearing against the backdrop of people, before reappearing seconds later. It rose and fell, shooting high into the air, only to rain downward in a synchronous buzzing whoosh.

Devlin and his friends reached the topmost step. He turned and lifted the camera looped around his neck. Mario snagged his elbow as Devlin focused the lens above the crowd. "Come on! We have to get inside!"

Devlin walked backward as he recorded the swarm. The sweeping motion of the cloud was odd, mesmerizing. Were it not for the strange circumstances and Josh running up the steps ahead of him like a bat out of hell, he might have believed what was happening was nothing more than an art display the WTP leader had arranged. But that idea quickly fled when he noticed people sprawled on the ground in the area where the crowd of WTP had been seconds ago.

The cloud lifted and fell again and again. The people continued their advance forward but in their wake were even more bodies littering the pavement; they looked lifeless. The buzzing cloud breached the sky and hovered as if it were searching for something, or someone, specific among the crowd, and then it descended in another rush.

The back of the mass of people had finally reached the stage where Devlin and Josh had been standing only moments ago. There were upwards of a hundred people on and around the platform who'd stayed behind on Josh's call for the WTP to advance. The swarm moved over and around them, performing its strange dance. But nobody fell. No screams of alarm sounded from those clustered together as the cloud lifted and drifted away. The people in their path remained untouched, alive, while WTP members littered the courtyard mere steps away from them. Not one hashtag on the stage had fallen.

The anomaly moving through the air began to swirl up the steps of the Capitol. Devlin, Tara, Mario, and the kid bolted into the building and raced across the rotunda, amid the echo of loud voices and hard shoes clapping against the marble surface at their feet. They reached a side door, the one leading to the hallway where Josh and Tara's offices were located. Tara began to slow, her face twisting into a grimace as pain had finally begun to override the adrenaline rush. There was a trail of blood marking the path she'd traveled.

"This way," Devlin urged, now hobbling alongside her, the kid keeping close at their backs as they moved down the hallway until they finally reached Josh's office. They stumbled headlong into the room. But when Devlin found himself staring down the barrels of guns, he drew up short, pulling Tara closer against his side. They were both panting for air. Sweat trickled down across his partner's temple. Josh was in the middle of the room, hands braced against his hips. He too was breathing hard, nostrils flaring, and his face the color of a radish.

"Stand down! It's Devlin," Josh boomed, the moment he realized who had burst into his office. He rushed forward while Devlin and Mario steered Tara to the large chair behind Josh's desk. She slumped into it; all her energy spent. Mario knelt beside her, talking to her in a faint voice, reassuring her and hopefully preventing her from going into shock.

Devlin whirled on his heel. "What the actual fuck just happened?" He raked both hands through his hair as he looked around the room. Nearly a dozen armed WTP were there, wide-eyed with the same confusion Devlin felt. But there was also fury, menace, and something even stronger burning in their eyes. Heads turned toward the far corner of the room. He stalked past Josh to see what held their attention.

Seated on a wooden chair in the corner was President Grant. Her arms were primly crossed at the wrists and pressed to her lap. One leg rested over the other and her foot bobbed up and down. The sleeve of her jacket was torn, and her hair looked like she'd scrambled it with her fingers, black strands poking out in all directions. A baseball-sized red splotch covered her scarred cheek, adding an element of macabre to her appearance. The wetness of tears glistened on her skin, but she wasn't actively crying.

Near her feet was a cell phone and a handgun.

The kid who'd been running alongside Tara and Mario, who wasn't so much a kid after all, but still couldn't have been more than twenty, stepped hesitantly closer to Devlin and Josh. He thrust his hands into his pockets and looked down at his feet.

"Who are you?" Devlin barked. And then, as an afterthought, he said, "Hold on. Before you answer . . . ." He let the sentence hang as he slipped the camera from around his neck and thrust it at Mario who knew what was being asked of him without having to hear the words.

Tara was upright now, leaning over her leg, inspecting the area where a bullet had pierced her body. Devlin's gaze gravitated over to the handgun near the President's feet, a weapon categorized as illegal to possess by anyone in this room who weren't Josh or the WTP guards.

"He's Senator Clarkson's page." Tara hissed when she tore the hole in her slacks wider. Now Devlin realized where he'd seen the young man before. It was that day in the Congressional Chamber. "I need something to tie around my leg," Tara stated calmly. A puddle of blood had formed near her foot. Devlin worried it was too much blood. Yet she was still upright and conscious, so perhaps he was wrong. He hoped he was wrong.

He pointed at her. "It was your friend Harper who did that to you."

Tara met his eyes, her head listing slightly in confusion. "What?"

"I saw him. I saw him pointing his gun right at the same time you went down. He betrayed you. Us," he bit out, as he again raked his hands through his hair.

Josh whipped his tie from his neck and lowered to a knee at Tara's feet, cinching the fabric tight above the wound. She groaned and drooped back into the chair. The room was thick with nervous energy, the smell of it ripe in the air. It was sweat and pheromones mixed with the odor of deodorant, cologne, and even the hint of someone's lunch that day, wafting about on a belch of air.

"The kid sent us the tip to go to Virginia. Where we saw her in that bar." Tara tipped her chin in the President's direction. Tara's face had suddenly grown pale and was now covered in a sheen of moisture. She needed medical attention, but Devlin didn't know if it was safe to leave the building.

The kid, who they finally learned was Alan Webber, glanced with trepidation at the President before turning his back on her. "She hired a guy named Jenkins."

Jenkins. That name again. Devlin's fury burned deep inside him.

"To do what? Who is he?" Josh asked, casting a glance between Alan and the President. Grant attempted to tidy up her torn sleeve, but to no avail. She leveled her dark gaze on Alan.

"Jenkins is her hired thug."

And there it was. One of the many missing pieces of a most incredible and elaborate puzzle clicked into place. Devlin's head whipped around, his wide-eyed gaze colliding with Tara's.

"Oh, my god," Tara said on a low breath.

Alan swallowed hard, now brazenly staring down the leader of the States. "Jenkins is also a genius. About fifteen years ago he invented something that supposedly prevented cancer," he said evenly, then shook his head in part wonder and part confusion. "It was brilliant, really. An arm band type of device that detected cancer in a person's body before science could even detect it. The band somehow eradicated the cancer before it mutated beyond a single cell." He shrugged, clearly having done only enough research to know what Jenkins had done in his past but lacking understanding of how the miracle band worked. "It's like he'd literally found the cure for cancer or the prevention from it. Or . . . or something like that." His voice held a hint of uncertainty. Pulling his hands from his pockets, he clasped them together at his waist, then crossed his arms over his chest, unsure what to do with his appendages. Finally, he let them hang limp at his sides. "But for reasons unknown, it never got FDA approval."

The President had stopped bobbing her foot. But the satisfied smirk on her face suggested she hadn't a concern in the world.

"This guy, Jenkins," Devlin added, "was also involved in a hired hit in Michigan. But I don't understand . . . ." His words trailed off as pieces of the grandest puzzle of all continued to rumble about inside his brain.

Stewart's contact was a member of Congress. Jenkins connected with Harper by way of said member of Congress. Clarkson was in Congress. Clarkson was linked to Grant. And all, not coincidentally, had a connection to the same person: Jenkins.

Devlin lifted an arm and pointed at the President. "We better have solid information linking her to Jenkins, enough to justify our airing to the people why we have the POTS cornered in a room, seemingly a captive."

He turned to Tara. "I know you don't believe me, but Harper is involved with this. I think a guy I know from my group, his name is Ken, is part of it, too. They were together at the top of the steps, running toward Grant. To help her escape, I'm going to guess." He pointed to the President but stayed focused on Tara. "That was right when you were shot."

"When those things in the air first appeared," Josh said, interrupting Devlin, "our intent was to protect the President. But when we were racing up the steps to get to her, she lifted that gun." He pointed to it on the floor at Grant's feet. "She shot at us."

"She did what?" Tara guffawed from across the room.

Josh nodded. "That's when we changed our mission from protecting her to capturing her. Possession of a firearm and attempted murder are at the top of her list of offenses so far. But we have to figure out the mess outside first."

Devlin glanced at Tara, then back at Grant, and then down to the gun at her feet, confusion etched on his face. Had he been mistaken about Harper shooting Tara?

"Did you shoot Ms. Carlson? Are you working with Harper?" Fury bubbled up inside him at the idea of someone snuffing out his partner's life. The breath he'd only recently gotten under control began to grow heavy again. Did she—could she—the leader of the country, there to protect the people she swore to serve—attempt to kill Tara? Questions piled on top of each other in his head, one after the other, and yet there were still so many more he needed to ask.

Suddenly, everyone began to talk at once, telling what they knew or didn't know but it was impossible to follow all the conversations going on at the same time.

"Stop!" Josh's voice boomed as Devlin began to pace back and forth. "One at a time. We'll deal with her later. Right now, we need to figure out what is happening outside."

"As I said, Jenkins is her man." All eyes focused on Alan again like he was the Pope himself. "She's had him doing some really bad things."

"Bad as in how bad?" Tara asked, tugging her little blue book from her pocket.

The pulse in Alan's throat hammered wildly. "I know she's used him to make people . . . ." He faltered before finishing his sentence. "Disappear."

The President leaned forward in her chair. It was such a nondescript movement but threatening all the same.

Alan instinctively took two small steps back, putting more distance between them, as if he thought she would jump up and attack him.

Devlin's head bobbed in a confused gesture of part nod, part head shake. "She uses him to kill people?"

Alan shrugged. "I can't say for sure, but I've heard her talking to her wife and know they've directed Jenkins to 'take care of' situations."

"I'm not following the connection of a hired hitman and what's going on outside." Josh had his hand pressed against the top of his forehead, his fingers squeezing hard enough to wrinkle his brow.

Alan's throat bobbed on a hard swallow. "Jenkins made those drones out there and equipped them with the capability to take out most everyone in the crowd today."

If that wasn't confusing and shocking enough, the bomb he dropped next sucked all the air from the room. "The intent is to take out everyone registered as WTP in the Voter Information Log. Those insect drones use facial recognition and have information and photos pulled from the VIL database uploaded so they can identify their targets. They scan our USFCDs." He lifted his hand, forearm facing out.

THE CONSEQUENCE CLAUSE

The moment the air returned to the room was palpable. The sound of heavy breathing and feet shifting broke the silence. There were nervous coughs and several WTP began running a hand across their arms where their own Unilateral Socially Fundamental Control Device had been inserted.

"How do you know this?" Josh barked, his outrage growing more evident.

"I'm Clarkson's page," he said matter-of-factly, as if that were explanation enough. But then he added, "I overheard the President telling Clarkson her plans to have Jenkins placed in the VIL, so he could access records and do whatever he needed to complete his assignment."

"Why didn't you come right out and tell us what you knew when you called in the tip? We could have stopped whatever this is," Tara said accusingly.

Alan nodded. "Because, besides sensing something bad might be in the works when I'd first tipped you off, I didn't have any specifics to tell. Not really, anyway. Not until I called you today. It's illegal to make false accusations, you know?" His shoulders slumped inward, and his head drooped down as his confidence failed him. "I hoped what you'd learn at the bar that day was going to shed light on some scandalous behavior of the leader of our country. I mean, if the freaking President of the States can't exhibit some level of ethics and morality in her high position, how can we expect the people to respect her and respect the government? I had no idea it'd be this bad."

"You should have said something!" Tara thumped a closed fist against the desk for emphasis.

Webber's face flushed and he lowered his head.

From behind the camera, Mario asked, "That thing that happened out in Nebraska?"

Devlin looked past Mario to Tara. He knew she, too, was recalling the interview they'd watched together that day at the diner.

Her face scrunched tight in confusion. "We guessed it might have been supplements added to the water supply," she said, her voice laced with wonder as understanding dawned. It had been everyone's assumption; a reasonable and safe one, too. Because what other reason could there have been for two thousand people dying at about the exact same time?

Alan was shaking his head. "It wasn't that. I just learned this," he repeated, his attempt to make all those present understand he hadn't been holding onto the information for long. "They were testing the poison drones on the residents of Nebraska. There's a lot of WTP in that part of the country."

"Wait," Josh blurted. "You're saying their plan was to eliminate everyone in the country who isn't on their side? As in, anyone who is part of We The People?" The answer to this question had already been provided by Alan, but it was as if Josh needed to say the words again, to confirm the truth of it.

"My god," he murmured, "Those people outside now. They're being killed?" All eyes shifted toward the woman perched in the corner.

This had been what Devlin and Tara had overheard during the conversation in the bar with Hulk Guy. This was their grand scheme. Josh must have shared his plan for today's event with President Grant, long before he'd aired it to the public. And, knowing how loyal the WTP were, Grant would have known there'd be thousands present. It was the perfect opportunity to implement her devious plan.

Right then, the door flew open, slamming against the wall with a bang. Four people surged into the room, stumbling into each other as they came. They were followed by someone holding a gun; it was the man Devlin had nicknamed Hulk Guy.

"Stop right there!" commanded one of the WTP, the one closest to Devlin.

All five newcomers stilled. Agent Harper stood at the front of the group, his hands in the air. Behind him were Ken and Senator Clarkson. There was one other person among them, standing at the back behind Ken, but Devlin couldn't see who it was.

Agent Harper took a small step but instantly halted when more of the WTP's guns shifted his direction. "Damn it!" he growled. "You're making a mistake. I told you I'm not part of this."

He must have been arguing this with Hulk Guy prior to their entry.

Agent Harper's gaze went to Tara, his expression filled with concern. "What happened? Are you okay?"

Tara frowned, distrust narrowing her eyes—distrust put there by Devlin.

Hulk Guy's chin tipped up. "I found these four running down the corridor." Rather than direct this information to President Grant, his employer, his attention was focused on Josh, which Devlin found odd. But Hulk Guy's accusations were exactly in line with Devlin's, corroborating his belief about Agent Harper, and Ken, too.

"They're working together," Devlin accused, swirling a finger to encompass the small group. "Outside, I saw Ken and Harper running toward the President. After he shot at Tara," he added with a growl. Both his fists were clenched tight at his sides, holding himself back mentally and physically from lashing out at the traitors. An attack against Tara was an attack against the country and the People. And Devlin had every intention of making sure both wrongs were righted.

Josh lifted his hands in front of him, palms out. "Hold on a minute. Why would our Agent here shoot at Tara?"

Senator Clarkson took the moment of silence that followed the question as an opportunity to move. The entire situation in the room was so surreal, nobody tried to stop her. She had a scarf draped over her head, as if she'd been trying to hide beneath it. She shoved the wispy fabric back while bolting to the corner, falling on her knees at Grant's feet.

"Anita, we've failed." Her typically stern expression broke as she began to sob loudly, pressing her face into her wife's lap. "What are we to do? I can't face the FRP. I'll never survive there."

"*He* claims he has information for you," Agent Harper said. Everyone's attention shifted back to him. He tipped his head in a sharp gesture, indicating somewhere behind him. He wasn't talking to Josh, though, the man in charge, nor was he addressing the President for that matter. He was looking directly at Devlin. "He said he knows you and wants to talk."

The connections in Devlin's brain struggled to fire in sync. He stood there, mouth hanging open as if he wanted to speak but he couldn't make the command. The man who'd been hidden from view behind Ken stepped forward. He had both arms latched around a laptop pressed to his torso. On his face were chunky, black-framed glasses sitting too far down the bridge of his nose.

Devlin's head cocked to the side. "Conrad?"

NINETEEN

Conrad nudged a finger against the bridge of his glasses. The stark emotion Devlin saw in his eyes, ones slightly magnified by thick lenses, drew him up short.

His friend lowered his head, as if greeting a foreign dignitary. "Devlin," Conrad said in a hoarse whisper.

"Don't say anything, Conrad," Ken warned.

All four men standing in the doorway were large and intimidating. Devlin knew Ken and Conrad had been ex-military, and it was a safe assumption that Harper and Hulk Guy had been, too. Who was the more intimidating among them? Devlin would have to say Hulk Guy as he was the one presently holding the gun, and he did so like he'd been born to it. Of course, Agent Harper certainly wasn't someone Devlin ever cared to encounter in a dark alley, either.

Even without a weapon, Ken quickly claimed second place in Devlin's assessment of who ranked higher on the intimidation scale. This was simply because he knew him to be mentally unstable, not to mention he was an ass. But Devlin knew much of his personality was a result of his past, which gained him a tiny amount of sympathy, thus dropping him a slight notch in the ranking.

Of all of them, Conrad was the least frightening; the stereotypical glasses aided in placing him lowest on the intimidation-factor ranking scale, as did Devlin's long acquaintance with the man. He knew deep down Conrad was a gentle soul. However, his background as a sharpshooter would certainly tell a different story to his character. Devlin was grateful he'd never been caught in Conrad's crosshairs. Nor had he ever had to witness his handiwork while in his role as a reporter.

President Grant began to laugh; it was a dark, wicked-sounding noise that matched the evil caricature of her scarred appearance.

Everyone's attention shifted again. Grant's presence in the room had been nearly forgotten since the door had opened and the group in front of them had rushed in.

"You need to stop this. Now!" Josh demanded of the country's less-than-esteemed leader.

The armed men lifted their weapons, not pointing them at her, but readying for the action should the directive be given. But they couldn't take her out yet. She reigned supreme in this situation because she was the only one holding power over the person controlling the terrifying beasts buzzing about and killing people.

"Call Jenkins. Tell him to stop the drones." Josh bent to retrieve her cell phone, thrusting it at her. "You're murdering innocent people out there. And for what? Because you can't win their trust in your own right? Tell your guy to shut them down."

"I was trying to get to you," Agent Harper said to Josh. "To warn you about them." He nodded toward President Grant and Senator Clarkson.

"And I was trying to help him," Ken added. "We were chasing after Clarkson. She and Grant were planning to escape. He's the bad guy here," he added, pointing a finger at Hulk Guy. "He works for them."

Even as guns shifted his way, Hulk Guy didn't back down or lower his own weapon. "I wasn't following Clarkson to

THE CONSEQUENCE CLAUSE

protect her. All of you just happened to be going in the same direction I was headed."

"Exactly," Agent Harper scoffed. "We were trying to get to her. To put a stop to this. You're the one who works for them."

As if a lightbulb had flicked on over his head, Devlin grabbed Conrad's elbow. "You! You can stop this. The drones outside. They're computers, so you could do it. Right? Is there a way to shut them down?" On the heels of this question, he swung around toward Ken. "And you, you said you got a new job with the government working with computers. Doesn't that automatically get you some high level of security clearance?"

Surprisingly, Ken didn't immediately respond. Devlin had never known him to be without words, and most of those were usually biting and derogatory, meant to inflict pain. His wide-eyed gaze flitted over each of the key players in the room before returning to settle on Ken.

"If you gain access to a mainframe or server or whatever it is that holds all the voter information from the VIL database . . . ." He paused and turned to Conrad with the other part of his suggestion. "Then you could get in and stop the drones."

A bloated silence filled the room as everyone waited for Conrad or Ken to confirm their ability to help.

"Can you do it? Will you?" Devlin pleaded into the quiet of the space filled only with the sounds of heavy breathing.

The silence was harshly broken when the President began to cackle again. Not a chuckle or smirking sound, but a full-on belly laugh, as if someone had shared the grandest of jokes. Senator Clarkson joined in on the situation that was anything but funny.

"Oh, my god." Grant howled like Ursula the Demonic Sea Witch. "You think he's your friend?" Her head fell back as she laughed even harder. She stroked her wife's hair, as if the woman were a small child needing comforting. Senator Clarkson, Devlin's nemesis for so many years, mewled like a simpering cat.

"Yes," Devlin hissed, glaring daggers at Grant. "He's a friend and he's going to help us stop the treasonous atrocities you've inflicted upon this country and your own people."

He grabbed Conrad's arm again, quickly explaining about Nebraska and the drones, giving him the barest of details, but it was all he had. He didn't know if he was making any sort of sense, but only because he didn't fully understand things himself. Hopefully, Conrad could figure out the rest.

Beneath Devlin's fingers, Conrad's arm stiffened. The muscles in his jaw clenched and released, his brows furrowed so harshly, deep lines appeared above the bridge of his glasses. The color left his skin.

"This is priceless." The President—could she really be called that any longer?—cackled. "He doesn't know. Does he?" she asked, directing the question, not at Devlin or Josh or anyone else in the room. She'd asked Conrad the question.

If it were possible, the color in Conrad's skin faded even lighter, turning to a sickly ashen hue. His head moved side-to-side in short bursts and his eyes bulged, like a trapped animal's might.

Devlin had filmed many people in tense situations like this one. He'd experienced his own moments when inner feelings of terror could push a person into a fit of panic. Before Conrad tipped over that edge, Devlin stepped into his line of sight. The man's haunted gaze shifted away from the corner of the room where they'd been aimed with laser focus.

"Conrad." Devlin reached out a hand to touch his shoulder but stopped shy of making contact. "It's okay. You're safe here with us," he crooned softly, like he would to a startled horse. "It's okay," he repeated. "If you can't help us, we'll figure something else out." He shot a worried glance to his three other friends, hoping to relay the meaning that they'd need a new plan.

But Conrad kept shaking his head as if he were trying to dislodge a buzzing insect caught in his ears. His free hand, the one not clutching his laptop, crawled through his hair, and stayed there, latching onto the brown waves in tight fists. His face scrunched tight, and his shoulders drew up to his ears. Tears seeped past his squeezed-tight eyelids. The internal storm was crashing unrelentingly against the shored-up walls he'd built inside his mind.

"Tell him! Tell him now!" Grant yelled in a voice that had Devlin seriously questioning her sanity. Clearly, she'd lost it. Clarkson remained with her head in her wife's lap. Everything about her actions made Devlin think she was a controlled, abused little child. They were both mad! Had their people and the MSM they shared a bed with hidden this craziness from the public? How did Josh miss it?

"Devlin, I—" Conrad started, still locked in the position of self-preservation, eyes squeezed tightly shut.

"Tell him! Tell him!" Grant chanted, confirming the woman really had lost it.

Clarkson lifted her head while Grant continued stroking her hair. "Yes, Conrad. Tell poor Devlin what he wants to know." Dark smudges of mascara spread out toward her temple on the side of her face where she'd been pressed against her wife's lap.

"Tell me what, Conrad? What do you know about what's happening out there?"

Conrad angled his head toward Ken, communicating something to him without words being spoken.

In Devlin's periphery, he saw Josh approach, caution in his movements.

"Did you have anything to do with those drones killing people outside?" Josh asked. The serious note in his voice was enough to make all the fine hairs on Devlin's body prickle to attention with worry. Worry over the reaction that might follow the answer given. But his words weren't directed at Conrad. They were spoken to Ken.

Devlin reflected back to the last group meeting where Ken had mentioned his new job. They'd congratulated him. But now, he recalled the anger and resentment in Ken's attitude and tone when he'd said something about doing what he'd had to do to survive. Devlin had assumed the strong, negative emotions he'd exhibited stemmed from the need to take a job in government. Nobody liked the government. His recollection of Ken's announcement suggested he'd even resented his new role. Because he'd been forced into it?

Ken began to nod his head, as if he'd heard Devlin's thoughts. "She made him do it," he blurted. "That's why I went after Agent Harper. Conrad wanted me to get to him, to tell him about Grant's plan."

"She took everything from me!" Conrad suddenly bellowed. His eyes were wide and filled with a range of emotions; the primary one being hatred. "She'd learned about my skills, my military ones, and my computer ones, and targeted me to be her minion. I lost my family, my dignity, my life, because of her." He growled the last words through clenched teeth.

Tara, who'd managed to get to her feet and hobble up beside Devlin with the help of the chair on casters, asked, "Conrad. What did you do? What did she make you do?"

The wildness in his eyes eased at the sound of her voice, but the painful emotions Devlin had seen there when he'd arrived returned at the soothing drawl of Tara's usually stern tone. "I got a new job, too," he said with a glance at Ken, who nodded, encouraging him without words. "It's in the Voter Information Department. I manage the VIL."

Devlin's jaw dropped open. "That's great! You *can* help us then! Help us put a stop to all this madness." He nodded enthusiastically, knowing the solution to one of their current challenges was standing before them.

"No. It's not great," snapped Hulk Guy. In a move that had everyone gasping, he aimed his gun at President Grant. "She orchestrated all of it. All of this." He waved the weapon in a grand circle before pointing it at Conrad. "And she made him to it."

Conrad was breathing hard, and beads of sweat had formed on his brow. "I was put in place to gain access to the database. To manipulate it and upload specific information into the drones. Information that puts certain people in the crosshairs of those killing machines." He paused, and everyone leaned closer, desperate to hear what else the man had to say. "Machines I was forced to create," he said slowly, emphasizing each word.

"Oh, my god," Mario said from behind the camera with its blinking red light. "You did it? You turned the people into targets?"

The imperceptible nod of Conrad's head had everyone pulling in a sharp breath. "People not registered the same as them." His arm lifted and he pointed at Grant and Clarkson.

"I can vouch for him on that. Grant used him. He was part of their grand scheme," Hulk Guy offered.

"The event," Tara whispered. "It's today's event you were talking about. You and her that day in the bar. This is what you were planning."

Hulk Guy looked a little surprised at this.

"But we heard you helping Grant arrange what's happening now." Her voice rose in volume, and she began to talk faster.

"You said you and your contact both wanted out after it was done. You were talking about him." She pointed at Conrad and, again, Hulk Guy nodded. "You did this!" she accused. "We were there, listening to the two of you plan all those murders going on outside." Before she was even aware she'd done it, her little blue book was in hand, and she began searching. "Murder. Conspiracy. Treason." Looking up, she glared at Conrad. "You designed those things. How could you?"

"We didn't know this was her plan." Hulk Guy moved closer to Tara and Devlin. In a protective gesture, Devlin's arm slid around her back. He was ready to pull her away or insert himself between her and a self-proclaimed murderer.

"We didn't know she was planning this," Hulk Guy said again. "Well, *I*," he emphasized his own lack of full knowledge on the matter, "didn't know the extent of it at least. What you heard at the bar was my agreement to help her situate Conrad in the VIL. I thought she was planning to change people's voting response or maybe add a question about cancelling the Consequence Clause to the last ballot and have all the votes made in favor of, or something like that."

Tara's expression was still accusing as was Devlin's, but everyone else in the room looked confused and scared. And rightly so.

"Once I learned the truth of what was about to go down, which I only found out today, when Conrad made Ken come and tell me, I went after them. That's when all hell broke loose outside." His eyes glazed over as the imagery from the craziness going on in front of the Capitol played through his mind. "I swear, I didn't know." He paused, shifting his attention to Conrad. "But he did. He had to since he created the things and programmed them. At least he did the right thing by telling Ken what he'd done."

"But the people are targets?" Josh asked, although the answer to his question had been stated a couple times already. Disbelief forced his need for further confirmation. Conrad supplied the definitive and deadly final answer.

"It's We The People. The WTP."

Why it hadn't happened the first one or two times it was announced, Devlin didn't know. But at Conrad's admission, the room exploded into immediate chaos. Drawn guns were being redirected so all were aimed at Conrad. Realizing there were still other threats in the room, some turned and pointed their weapons back on the scarred and smudged ghoulish pair that was the President of the States and Senator Clarkson. Tara shuffled sideways, causing Devlin to instinctively tighten his grip on her.

Josh grabbed Conrad's shirtfront while Mario stood mouth agape, capturing the entire scene on video as the leader of the WTP commanded, "Shut them off! Can you stop them? You have to stop them now!" When Conrad looked to President Grant, Josh snapped, "She is no longer the President. You do not take orders from her any longer."

But the now-former President wasn't finished with her puppet. Devlin finally saw the truth behind what both Ken and Conrad had said in group. 'Once a puppet, always a puppet.' Conrad had obviously been made to do things, terrible things; things that went beyond the scope of his military sniper role, if that hadn't been difficult enough.

"It doesn't matter now. The command was set and all you foolish WTP will soon be eradicated," Grant hissed, victory lacing her words. "It may not be me in control, but someone will replace me and without any of you, we'll finally get everything we want. The first thing we'll do is get rid of those ridiculous Consequence Clauses." Those of the WTP growled at her, but she looked them dead in the eyes, not caring one iota for the souls of any around her, beyond herself. And possibly the cowering, simpering Senator Clarkson.

The reality of today's nightmare became even more real when they heard the buzz of drones in the hallway, getting closer to the door. Everyone stilled. An occasional loud exhale was heard when those holding their breath were forced to suck in another gulp of air.

Devlin raked a hand across his scalp, desperately thinking of a way out of this room, this situation. But was that far enough? If the drones were programmed with names and faces of all WTP, how far could a person run to get away from them? More than half the country had become targets in the grandest, most treasonous act ever coordinated.

"Since all your despicable souls are about to be set free," Grant said, interrupting the balloon of anticipation filling the room, "I think *your friend* Conrad here should share with you one more of his little secrets." At this, her hand stroked over Senator Clarkson's head, like she was petting her favorite dog. When she emphasized *your friend*, she was looking at Devlin. But when Conrad didn't immediately spill the beans, Grant frowned. "Tsk, tsk. A friendship formed in group therapy. How touching. Did he ever share why he went to those meetings? Hm?"

Devlin wasn't the only one confused by Grant's rambling. It could have been the knowledge that people, some friends, others mere acquaintances, but good and innocent people, nonetheless, were being exterminated outside that caused goosebumps to rise all over his body. However, Grant's mention of Conrad and Devlin and their group sessions, forced a furious rush of adrenaline to his heart, which began to thump heavy and hard behind his ribs.

"What is she talking about?" he asked, looking first at Conrad, then his gaze shifted back to Hulk Guy, and finally over to Grant and back again, his arms lifting, pleadingly.

Tears fell in earnest down Conrad's cheeks, his sniffling barely holding back the snot racing over his lips. He shook his head non-stop. "I'm so sorry. I'm so sorry." The mantra was an agonized whisper. "I started going to group so I could get close to you. I'd planned to tell you everything. But when I saw your pain, I couldn't bring myself to do it. I'm so sorry," he whispered.

"Oh, no." Tara gripped Devlin's arm. Fear, pain, and even pity vivid in the look she gave him.

He drew back, yanking away from her touch. "What? What's wrong?"

"Get him out of here," Tara commanded, pointing at Devlin. "Harper, Josh, anyone, take Devlin to my office," she directed with an authority Devlin had never seen her exhibit before. She rounded on Josh. "Make Conrad stop the drones." When nobody jumped into action to do what she'd commanded, she pleaded to anyone else who might be listening, her words coming out in a choked sob. "Please, get Devlin out of here!"

But that was not to be the way the next few minutes played out for those sheltering in place inside Josh's office.

"Oh, yes. Hurry him away." Grant's hideous face twisted in her lunacy.

Hulk Guy had lowered his weapon, or at least no longer had it trained on Ken or Agent Harper. He wasn't directly aiming at Conrad, either, but he remained at the ready. His actions seemed to indicate that he'd been telling the truth, that he truly hadn't known what Conrad had been up to. But Devlin struggled to believe he could be as oblivious as he'd claimed to be.

Rather than do as Tara had asked and take Devlin from the room, Josh grabbed the still-shuddering Conrad by the elbow and began tugging him toward the door, instead.

"Before you go, Conrad." The former President drawled his name, long and slow. "Let's take a short trip down memory lane. To say, the Arizona border. Four years ago."

Whatever air had been inside Devlin's lungs left in an explosive gasp. Any reference to the border in that timeframe stirred panic in his chest. Grant's mention of it had him seeing black dots in his vision. He suddenly couldn't breathe.

"Josh, please," Tara begged, her Southern drawl strong, her voice wet with her tears.

Josh had one hand on the door, the other gripping tight to Conrad's arm as he tried to tug him out of the room.

Conrad yanked free and shoved the lid of his laptop up. He tapped a few keys, glancing up at Devlin and then back down at the keyboard as he did. The buzzing of drones grew closer with each keystroke.

Devlin hoped everyone who'd sought shelter indoors and those still outdoors had found a place to hide from the killers buzzing about. He sighed with relief, certain Conrad had entered the command to end the chaos of the drones.

Slowly, Conrad partially closed the lid of the laptop. "I had no choice. My family was the target if I didn't do as they directed. She took my wife out of the country and promised her safety, so long as I did what she said."

"Why?" Josh raged. "Why stop now? What has you defying her demands?" His anger had reached its boiling point, something Devlin rarely ever saw. "If you think your actions now will exonerate you, you are mistaken." Taking advantage of the only Agent in the room, Josh turned to Harper. "Hold this man in custody until we can get the rest of what's going on here resolved."

Tara was still crying, repeating the word, "No. No. No. No." Both her hands were pressed over the lower half of her face, covering nearly all but her tear-filled eyes.

Devlin's brain, however, remained one full step behind his reality. It kept trying to reach for the truth, things deep inside he knew were about to be spoken, but his psyche was pulling him back, protecting him.

"He stopped doing her bidding when he found records in the VIL. Records belonging to his wife." Ken inched closer to Conrad but with the threatening glare given to him by Agent Harper, he stopped an arm's distance away. "They'd ensured her safety, so long as he did their bidding. He told me today that he'd learned his wife was dead. And she has been since right *before* the OBA." He shook his head, the usual harsh set to his jaw and sharp stare turned soft with sympathy as he met Conrad's watery gaze.

As Josh tugged Conrad's arm, intent to usher him out of the room, Conrad blurted out on a sob, "It was me."

The pain, the anguish in his voice was so deep, only people like Devlin, and maybe Ken, would understand the types of events that could bring it about. Devlin recognized it because he'd lived with a similar agony these last four years.

Four years. That day. Conrad. Grant's words tumbled around inside his head.

Every muscle in his body tensed, his fists clenching at his sides. He looked closely at the man he'd called friend, seeing what he'd not noticed before: The square cut of a jaw and the brown hair. The shape of a nose, seen only in profile in the video he'd watched hundreds of times. The video paused on the image of a man holding a gun to a woman's head. Melissa's head. His gaze dropped to Conrad's wrist, a wrist he was now gripping with one hand while the other rocked back and forth over the bones there.

"Roll up your sleeve!" Devlin commanded.

A sense of panic squeezed his chest to the point of pain. All the pieces of information he should have seen, should have noticed, were falling into place like Tetris blocks, but he'd overlooked them all. A low groan bubbled up from his throat even before Conrad pulled the sleeve of his other arm high enough to reveal a tattoo. A symbol. An emblem. His badge of honor as a military sharpshooter.

Devlin's legs gave out and he sank to his knees. "It was you? You killed her?" There was a heartbeat of a pause before Conrad's chin dipped down. And then, like a ninja, Devlin launched back to his feet and threw his two-hundred-pound frame against Conrad's much larger one. Together they toppled to the floor, Devlin above Conrad, his fingers clutched around the enemy's neck. A man he'd claimed as a friend. A friend who'd betrayed him.

Conrad didn't struggle.

"Why?" Devlin roared. "Why? How could you?" Tears ran unchecked down his cheeks, landing on Conrad's face.

"I felt I had no choice," Conrad countered, still not fighting back as Devlin slammed his skull against the hard floor.

"There's always a choice!" he screamed, his finger's clutched tight around Conrad's ears now, lifting, slamming. Lifting, slamming. "You had a choice," he sobbed. "You. Had. A. Choice." Each word was emphasized with a thud of Conrad's head against the floor.

"I'm so sorry. They told me I had to do it if I wanted to keep my wife safe. I did what I believed was the only thing I could do. Until . . . until," he stumbled over his words, "I found the proof that she'd been dead since even before they directed me to take out the target."

"The target?" Devlin could barely say the word, lacking the oxygen in his lungs necessary to speak.

Grant's venomous voice interrupted the haze clouding his mind. "You were a thorn."

He looked up, still holding tight to Conrad's head. Senator Clarkson was no longer draped across Grant's lap. She was still seated on the floor in front of her wife, who was mindlessly running her fingers through the wiry gray strands of her hair.

"You and your stupid news channel," she scoffed. "Everything my Harriet did, you hounded her. You trampled all her brilliant ideas, airing your disgusting versions of what she was doing."

"I aired nothing more than the truth!" Devlin fired back.

Grant's hand stilled. "Perhaps. But it made her look bad."

"And the OBA was my idea!" Senator Clarkson said in a voice resembling a five-year-old who'd been told she'd have to go to her room without dessert. "I figured if you could attack me as you always do at every turn, at anything and everything I sponsored, then it seemed only fair to level the playing field. I asked Anita to help me out. We did what was needed to shut you up. And it worked for a little while." She rolled her head back and looked adoringly into her wife's eyes. "It did, didn't it, my love?"

"Yes, dear. We did well."

The impossibility of the situation was overwhelming. The President was praising someone for arranging an innocent woman's murder? To silence a reporter who aired the truth?

"You ruined my life!" Devlin shouted to the two women, his voice loud and accusing. They were leaders of the country, people sworn to protect others at all costs. His attention returned to Conrad, who remained beneath him on the hard floor. "*You* ruined my life, my everything! You had a choice," he said again, his tone less intense, shock taking the steam out of him. And then Josh was there, grabbing him by both shoulders and pulling him off Conrad.

"She was my wife!" Devlin wailed. "Damn you, she was my wife. You sacrificed mine to save yours?" His words turned into a heartbreaking sob as Josh dragged him back toward the desk closer to Tara. She sat propped against the furniture, quietly crying her own sad tears. Tears for Devlin.

"Tara?" Her name crossed his lips in an agonized plea as the last four years of loss and pain slammed into him. It was as fresh and deep as it had been the day he'd watched Melissa's life fade from her eyes. He fell into Tara's opened arms and clung tight as if his own life depended on her.

There was a smear of blood on the floor where Conrad's head had made contact, but the man didn't seem dazed as he got to his feet. The buzz of drones grew louder and now sounded right outside the door. There were no longer any sounds of people screaming.

Conrad took a big step toward the door. Ken, Agent Harper, the WTP, and even Hulk Guy, dumbfounded by the events unfolding, allowed him to move unchecked. He gripped the handle and propped his booted foot against the corner, preventing anyone from forcing it closed.

Grant laughed, a demented sound. "All along you suspected Harriet here, which I'd become concerned about, as you kept getting closer to the truth. It's laughable really, how your wife's murderer was right beneath your nose all along. Almost from day one."

As one of the WTP stepped close to Grant, gun raised to hit her with the butt, Conrad's voice stopped the action.

"I can't change what I've done. I know now I did have a choice. I should have sacrificed myself, and probably my wife, by turning myself in long before that day at the border, rather than do their bidding." He pointed at the woman who was supposed to have worn the badge of Presidency with honor and integrity. "If I had, both our wives might still be alive."

THE CONSEQUENCE CLAUSE

She and Clarkson had been the puppet masters of Conrad's life for years but at that moment, Devlin couldn't find sympathy for him anywhere in his heart.

"I've fixed it all now," Conrad said to Devlin, shame clear in his voice.

Six drones hovered outside the door, red lights blinking, scanning, searching for their prey.

Tara cried out. Devlin twisted around and positioned himself before her, his back to her front. Mario stepped deeper into the room, but his reporter sense kept him filming, regardless the dire, and soon to be deadly, situation. Ken lunged to the far side of the room, taking cover behind the desk. The WTP and Hulk Guy all turned and aimed their guns at the electronic intruders, awaiting Josh's command.

"And finally, this," Grant cried in a joyful voice, "all the WTP, including you, their so-called leader," she said to Josh, "will finally meet their end. Now, we can make this country what we want it to be without your interference." Grant shifted aggressively in her seat, causing Clarkson's position to jostle forward as the chair's legs scraped the floor. While some had turned to look at them, most kept their gazes on the threatening drones.

Devlin focused on the sound of Tara's voice as she murmured comforting words against his ear. He squeezed her tighter but turned his head slightly and locked eyes with Conrad.

"The drones were programmed to target WTP based on the upload from the VIL," said Conrad. "But I changed it. I changed the target data. I hope this will fix the wrongs I've committed. And I hope someday you'll find it in your heart to understand and forgive me."

He shifted his foot, so the door swung all the way open. Lifting the lid of his laptop again, he tapped one key. On command, six drones, situated two by two, filled the entire doorway like one rectangular body.

Conrad squared his shoulders, thrust his chin high, eyes forward, facing Devlin.

"The new targets are President Anita Grant, Senator Harriet Clarkson . . ." and then he paused, drawing in a deep breath through his nose, and breathed the last name. "And Conrad Jenkins."

The whirring of the drones ramped up, buzzing louder as they descended through the doorway. They zipped this way and that, invisible eyes scanning Unilateral Socially Fundamental Control Devices buried beneath the skin of every person present. Upon finding their targets, two fell on Grant, while another pair pummeled a shrieking Senator Clarkson. Grant screamed as whatever poison they carried was injected into her neck, face, and any other part of her body the drones connected with. Clarkson cried out to her wife for help, but to no avail as the drones completed their objectives. In seconds, both leaders of one of the greatest countries in the world slumped over, Grant tipping from the chair and landing on the floor with a thunk when her head hit the solid surface.

There were still two drones in the room, both directly above Conrad. His laptop remained open, his hand hovering over the keyboard. "Find peace, Devlin. My consequence is long overdue." He pressed a key on the keyboard and let his laptop slip from his fingers, crashing to the ground.

The drones zipped down quickly, like supernatural mosquitos, there at his face, neck, arms, head. Conrad's eyes widened as his knees buckled and he slumped to the ground, the light in his irises quickly dulling into the stare of death.

The drones stilled, hovering above the bodies of their victims. Nowhere left to go.

Mission accomplished.

TWENTY

Devlin found the video of the press conference that had aired a year and a half ago and hit play. The podium on screen was still empty, but when the camera panned the audience, he saw a mosh pit of reporters present. Something happening off screen had all of them suddenly waving their hands and yelling out questions. When the camera switched back to front and center, there were three people stepping forward. Two lingered a couple of feet back from the one who'd positioned himself at the podium.

It was still a little difficult for Devlin to watch footage like this one, staged on the steps of the Capitol. Memories of all the unbelievable events that took place there flooded him. Never in a million years would he have imagined a sitting President would try to gain control over the people by killing those who didn't agree with their ideologies. But that's exactly what she'd attempted to do. She and her wife had nearly succeeded, too.

Agent Harper and Ken had been exonerated of any wrongdoing. Contrary to what Devlin had believed, Harper's involvement with Conrad and his friendship with Tara *had*, in fact, been completely coincidental. And Ken only learned of Conrad's involvement with Grant, her evil plan, and other things he'd done at her bidding, moments before he'd directed him to get to Agent Harper with information that would take down the reigning couple. Harper hadn't at first believed Ken, not until the rest of the events unfolded there in Josh's office.

Hulk Guy, whom Devlin later learned was named Shane Eggelston, had been scrutinized the most, considering he'd been Clarkson's bodyguard since before the OBA and Grant's accomplice in the conspiracy. He hadn't been cleared of all charges as he'd admitted to plotting with Grant, and he'd been witnessed doing so. However, his claims of ignorance as to the true extent of what he'd been helping her arrange combined with his interference and assistance there at the end, garnered him a lighter sentence than he probably deserved. There were many violations and a few CC's that came into play because of his crimes. But upon Josh's intervention, Tara was able to apply the Consequence Clause that held the lightest punishment.

Eggelston tried to argue for full exoneration, but regardless of his change of heart that day, he'd made a choice to get in bed, so to speak, with criminal politicians. It was his right to choose, but the consequences that followed were his duty to accept. He'd be in the FRP long enough to reevaluate his past decisions and plan a different future for himself after his release.

Devlin was still on the fence about him, disbelieving the man's complete ignorance to what his employers had done over the years. But, in the end, he *had* been on his way to find Josh that day, to tell him about Grant's plan for the drones. He'd encountered Agent Harper, Ken, Conrad, and Clarkson in the hallway. Fortunately for everyone else inside and outside the Capitol who were registered WTP, Conrad's confession and actions stopped the devastation that had been initiated. But with Grant and Clarkson both gone now, no proof for or against Eggelston had been found, beyond the vague plotting scheme Devlin and Tara had witnessed.

The whole situation had been surreal. Even today, Devlin struggled to wrap his brain around it all. He'd watched this press conference over and over to see if he'd missed anything.

Josh stood at the podium amid a barrage of comments and questions coming at him from dozens of reporters.

"Are you going to run for President?" someone off-camera called out.

"Mr. Stevens," asked another, "will you designate a new President?"

"Have you found any others who were part of the conspiracy against the People?"

"Will you reverse everything Grant did during her presidency?"

One after another, the questions came. Questions about the economy and an individual's dependency on government. Will the military be restored to what it once was? Will the OBA be canceled? Will taxes go down or continue to rise? Josh raised both hands, encouraging silence. The camera lens switched so the mosh pit was again the focus. Mario was being jostled around as he jockeyed to hold his ground in the front row.

"Josh," Mario yelled out, loud enough to draw Josh's eyes down to meet his. "Do you plan to bring back the fundamental principles of this country's Constitution?" He nearly dropped his camera when someone shoved at his back, but with so many reporters behind him, it was impossible to tell if it was intentional or not. Most present didn't like Mario simply because of the network he worked for was even more popular after the events of that day in Josh's office.

The camera switched back to Josh. He leaned slightly closer to the microphone. "Quiet everyone." One might have thought the command came from God as the reporters, shockingly, did what they were told. "This country," he paused with a slow shake of his head, and then changed up what he'd been about to say. "First off, no, I am not running for nor am I assigning anyone to the presidency. The Vice President has been vetted and we've all determined and are sure he knew nothing of Grant's plan. Therefore, he will take his place in the Oval Office until the next election as that is the way our system works."

"What about others in Congress? Were any found to be working with Grant and Clarkson?"

Given the egregious offense against the country by the former and now dead President and Senator, Josh had made it implicitly clear to all reporters and everyone in Congress that Grant and Clarkson were never to be referred to again with their esteemed titles, former or otherwise. They were a disgrace to the nation and were to carry the dishonorable badge for eternity.

He braced his forearms on the edges of the podium as if in need of the support. Which, after the hellacious process of restoring order to the government in the months following the incident, he probably had needed something to lean on. "It is with a deep sense of sadness that I must report . . . ." He paused and turned his head away from the cameras, struggling to compose himself.

A woman standing behind him inched close and put a hand on his back. She said something to which Josh shook his head. He patted her arm as if to say thanks before swiping his hand over his face. She offered him a kind smile and returned to her place in the background.

The woman was the new head of the Consequence Compliance Oversight Committee; well, technically she was the co-chair of the department. She and the man at her side shared the leadership role over the CCOC as everyone had come to the decision it was too big a job for one person. She was from Maine while he hailed from Texas. They were an excellent fit for their new roles.

Josh cleared his throat, once again under control. The look in his eyes told of his deep sadness. Devlin had seen him in many stages of emotion, from irritation to confusion to fury, but never had he seen him like this.

"As it relates to the treason committed by Grant and her wife, we have discovered the depths of this heinous act against the People ran deep. Deeper than we could have imagined." The sound of cameras clicking in rapid fire could be heard as could gasps of surprise. Devlin wondered how many of these reporters, except Mario of course, were truly shocked by this revelation of treachery.

The idea of Josh's fellow citizens, people elected to the highest positions of government betraying their own in this way, pained him greatly. This is what had made him sad. Devlin knew, even to this day, Josh still struggled with the betrayal perpetrated against the People. He was extremely passionate about his country and his role in the WTP.

"We have discovered the motherlode of communications between Grant, Clarkson, and several members of our Congress as well as the media, who we've learned were working together to a degree we never, ever could have imagined, on the events that took place here. As we already knew from the person who'd engineered the drones that attacked the People, the WTP were the primary targets. What we only recently discovered was the real reason We The People were targeted."

"Can you tell us why? The People still live in fear that something like this will happen again. How can we be assured it won't?"

This came from Mario, who'd been hearing from viewers about their worries of repeat attacks coming in the dead of night. It had been a horrific enough event in the daytime, but to be attacked by something unseen would be even worse.

"The reason behind the drones and the attacks," Josh began to explain in greater detail, "was because Grant and some our Congress realized the free-for-all they'd turned this country into was quickly becoming unsustainable. The extravagance of a 'free' society, they finally realized, would implode, which meant their lifestyles would be affected as the country collapsed." He didn't unclasp his hands where he'd held them folded on the podium. It seemed he was holding his anger at bay in his white-knuckled grip.

"Rather than put forth ideas to undo many of the entitlements they'd given to the People over the past few years, Grant and others decided instead to reduce the need for an excessively high budget by reducing the number of people taking advantage of the system's offerings. And they started with the WTP. But since then, we've learned, they had a schedule, written out in someone's hand even, with other targets. Those who are costly to the system: people with health issues, mental, chronic, or otherwise. People with too many children, though what constitutes too many was not defined in our trail of paperwork."

"How did they plan to locate these people?" Some other reporter, not Mario, called out.

"Well, that's easy. The government already has access to monitor every aspect of a person's life. The Control Database holds all health inquiries any of us make, every grocery store visit, every trip we take, and even each time we enter or leave our own house. All they had to do was pull our records by way of our USFCD chips."

He raised his arm and turned his wrist, reminding everyone of the one simple device that gained them access to every doctor's office, hospital, airplane, hotel, rental car, and whatever else one might need in their lives to function.

"We know now they set this plan in motion long ago, by first finding the way to make us get the USFCD. Without it, we can't survive. We can't enter buildings, buy *any*thing, or access our own money. But that, we learned, was only the surface of the information they wanted to attain. The WTP, sick people, old people; if they got rid of those categories, which makes up roughly seventy-five percent of the population, and just like that, costs go down," he said with a snap of his fingers.

Thank God, Conrad had stopped it and they found all this information, Devlin thought, with both gratitude and sadness.

"The CCOC has a lot on their hands right now, but we will make certain every consequence issued will be aired live on *The People's News* for the world to see." This drew grumbles from reporters, because they'd all lost the opportunity to get exclusive front seats to Consequence Engagements back when Tara had first teamed up with Devlin.

He missed working with her.

"And what about bringing back the Constitution?" Mario asked again.

"Over the last several years, it is true that nearly every amendment in our Constitution has been decimated or erased. Certainly not what our Founding Fathers had intended when they set out to protect the citizens of this country from an overreaching government."

He paused to take a sip of water, but the reporters knew he wasn't finished and curiously hadn't bombarded him with questions during the mini break. Everyone wanted this press conference on their channels. How they would air the events, what spin they'd put on it, was anyone's guess. *The People's News* was one that wouldn't spin or interpret anything. What Josh said today was exactly what the People would hear.

"As leader of We The People, I have no power to make changes or demand them. My role is to establish boundaries in which those who do have authority must work. It's their job." He lifted both arms straight out and pointed his index fingers to the House of Representatives and Senate buildings on either side of the Capitol. "It is their job to work together to fix the messes they've made. Take that into account when you go to vote on their replacements. As the investigations are completed and the CCOC begins issuing their consequences, we know there will be many open seats that will need to be filled."

Devlin ended the clip; he didn't need to see more. He'd watched the press conference live when it had first aired. And he'd seen the outcome of one annual election since and the dozens of seats in Congress that had turned. Now it was time to wait and see what, if any, changes the new Congress would make. As Devlin had stated aloud on numerous occasions, once something was in motion, it would be nearly impossible to reverse. That body of people in Congress certainly had a tough job ahead of them.

The direction the States was headed had yet to take the fork in the road leading it to a better place. One where kids returned to school buildings, where people worked to provide for their families. One where the government didn't dictate who could or could not achieve wealth, regardless of their job or talent or creation of the next genius idea that could save the planet. No, sadly, what had been set in motion obliterated all rights granted to the People, there to protect them. So many had spent years bathing in the "free" entitlements and had come to rely on them. They were the ones who still hadn't learned the true cost of free. Nothing is ever free.

Devlin pointed the lens of his camera toward the sky as a Gulfstream lowered ever closer to the runway. A puff of white smoke appeared the second the wheels touched the tarmac. The aircraft soon began to taxi toward the gate. The jet neared, creeping closer to a pit crew standing in its path, guiding it to the spot where it was to stop. When the flagger crossed his wrists, the bright orange batons an extension of his arms forming into an X, the plane eased to a halt. The crew scrambled about, some dropping chock blocks against the tires, others rolling out a purple carpeted mat, the length of it reaching halfway to where Devlin stood. It took another few minutes before the hatch on the Gulfstream popped open and from the top side of the door, it moved down, revealing stairs that unfolded and settled against the edge of the carpeted walkway.

Josh appeared in the doorway first and Mario followed directly behind him. Devlin lifted a hand and waved at the two, as if they hadn't seen him standing right there at the end of their carpeted pathway. Both men lifted their hands in a return gesture before clambering down the narrow stairs.

It had been more than a year since he'd seen either one in person. But he had spoken on the phone a few times with Josh and had regular virtual meetings with Mario. Following the events that day at the Capitol, Devlin had mentally, physically, and emotionally checked out.

He'd had an exit strategy planned for quite some time, but never had he expected it to come about in the nearly catastrophic way that it had. Grant's plan was one thing, but Conrad's revelations about having been the killer Devlin had spent years searching for, the person who'd murdered Melissa, his wife, well, that had been his undoing. So here he was, living the quiet life in San Francisco.

Like celebrities walking the red carpet, Josh and Mario came closer. They embraced in brotherly hugs, clapping each other on their backs before quickly pulling away.

"It's about damn time you got down here." Devlin grinned from ear to ear. These were his friends, his family, and he admitted he'd missed them terribly.

"I had things to clear up before I retired. You know that." Josh braced a hand on Devlin's shoulder again, giving it a squeeze and a little shake. He was hardly old enough to retire, only in his mid-fifties, but his work was something that could only be done in small bouts. "But I've managed to get the new person brought up to speed and turned the Government Overseer's hat over to her. She'll do an excellent job."

"And I had to wrap up that last CE before turning the reins over to the new manager, Gabriel. But it's done!" Mario clapped his hands and rubbed them briskly together. "I want to go see your property."

It was hot today; humid, too. The molecules that made up humidity seemed to hold onto the briny and fishy odor of the ocean. But it was clean air. They climbed into Devlin's vehicle, a Jeep with the top and doors off. Except for times when it rained and during the winter months, he rarely covered it up. The open air was soothing and exhilarating, if not a bit sticky.

They traveled down the paved highway headed toward his property. His hand lifted from the steering wheel in a small wave to each vehicle he passed.

"Give me the cliff notes of what's going on back home," Devlin said.

Josh stared out at the landscape. Both he and Mario were quiet, as if finally letting go and relaxing into a state of calm. The road was lined with miles of wood fence posts, tall green weeds and grass as well as trees shaped like slightly flat mushrooms. Devlin hadn't lived in the area long enough yet to learn all the various types nearby, but in time he knew he would. There were fruit trees and a few palm trees, though these were shorter palms, not the tall kinds he'd seen in Florida and Hawaii.

"Let's see, Congress is finally starting discussions about modifying the OBA, getting rid of USFCDs, and returning to a more normal and less controlling lifestyle for the people. We might even bring back that wonderful thing called Capitalism. I know, I know, it's a stretch," he said when Devlin's head shot around, his jaw falling open. "But it's a start."

"Whatever happened with reopening law enforcement agencies around the country? Did that get through?" He saw Mario shaking his head in his rearview mirror.

"No. They decided the cost wasn't worth the effort." Mario shrugged. "As a collective, they're still saying their uphill battle to fight crime with law enforcement would be too discriminatory and inhumane. They'll let the People go after each other and let the Consequence Clause go after those who break the law. If they're caught, that is. The Free-Range Prison will continue to be the answer for all criminals."

There was a gravel road up ahead. It was more a gravel entrance leading to multiple roadways. He blinkered left and then veered left again down another dirt road running alongside a cattle feedlot that was, surprisingly, operating and thriving by the looks of it. The landscape down this way began to change, opening into large acres of crop fields abandoned and left in whatever state of planting they'd been when the owners had walked away from them in search of greener pastures, otherwise known as free entitlements. Devlin turned left again and then right into what he called "The Subdivision."

"This is it," he announced proudly. Josh and Mario stared out across the vast land around them. "All this, one thousand acres is mine." He pointed off to the right, past Josh. "And a quick ten-minute drive that way is the Gulf." The fields were not surrounded by a fence, but every so often a stake painted white stuck up from the ground. "Those are boundary lines. Mario, that could be yours."

Mario's eyes rounded and his mouth split wide into a Cheshire cat grin. He ran a hand through his hair. "I can't believe it. How far does it go?"

"See those trees way at the back there?" Devlin indicated where he referred to by pointing. "That's the border for each one-hundred-acre section I've divided out. This one is yours."

And then when they'd passed another stake in the ground, he added, "And this one could be yours, Josh, if you want it. There are ten in total. If there's one you'd rather claim as yours, instead, let me know. All you need to do is fence the boundaries and post it as private property."

Josh and Mario remained quiet as Devlin drove deeper into The Subdivision. "There's my place." Atop a small knoll stood a house, beautifully crafted in a style common to the area. Clay tiles adorned the top, covering the three peaks, each angled a different direction over the four-bedroom home. From this view, the brightly painted yellow door and red shutters were like a rainbow of happiness against the green of trees in the background. This was Devlin's sanctuary. His home. This had been the plan he'd worked on during those months he and Tara had traveled about the country.

He continued to drive at a slow speed, giving his passengers the grand tour of The Subdivision. Eventually, there'd be ten residents, maybe more, depending on how each one-hundred-acre lot got subdivided by their owners. Any new tenants would be vetted by Devlin and the owner of each section of property. None of them wanted or needed controversy in their lives any longer.

Devlin slowed when another white stake appeared. He pulled to the side of the road and cut the engine then lifted his camera and aimed it out across the lot.

The lens zoomed in on the woman standing fifty yards away. Her back was to him. She wore a bright pink tank top that exposed her shoulders and lean arms, the hint of a tan line showing when she moved. Her lower half was covered with a pair of denim shorts that reached high on her thighs. From her knees down, her legs were swallowed up by tall, green rubber boots. It was an interesting uniform to say the least; one she wore often, sans the boots. It had rained the night before, so she'd traded her normal every day high-heeled, very unsensible, sandals for the more protective footwear to avoid mud squishing between her toes.

She held a fence-post driver in her hands. Lifting it to face level, she forced it down on top of a metal pole sticking up from the ground. To her left, positioned nearly eight feet away, was another post lying flat on the ground. More followed in a row of equal intervals, extending far beyond to the edge of the property line in the distance.

She was ambitious, Devlin would give her that. He climbed from the Jeep, both Josh and Mario following him. They walked toward her. Devlin grinned at the messy knot of black, silky hair at the base of her neck. Everything about her today was messy, disheveled, and yet she fit into the scenery perfectly.

When Mario laughed, she stilled before whirling around.

"Excuse me, ma'am?" Devlin called out with an exaggerated Southern twang. "We have visitors."

"Ma'am?" Tara repeated, propping one hand on her hip. The address sounded much more natural coming from her than it had from Devlin. "I haven't called anyone ma'am in well over a year and you know it, Dev." She swiped a gloved hand across her cheek, leaving a trail of dirt behind in the sweat glistening there. She began to move toward them, faster and faster the closer she got, until finally, she broke into a run, precariously maneuvering through the muddy tracks made from a plow, slipping but managing to avoid face-planting in the mud.

When she got to within a foot of the three men, she launched herself against Josh and Mario, pulling them both into a huge hug, her voice sounding watery when she said in her best attempt at a Spanish accent, "¡*Bienvenidos a Mexico!* Welcome home!"

ABOUT THE AUTHOR

RJ Flynn lives in the western part of the United States. They've spent much of their career working in public education. When not working, they like to travel and plan to visit all 50 states in the nation. They're halfway to their goal. RJ is a member of Rocky Mountain Fiction Writers and the National Association of Independent Writers and Editors.

Find RJ on Facebook @RJFlynnAuthor.

Made in the USA
Columbia, SC
30 October 2022